"You think she was the old man's mistress?"

Rafe considered Morgan's question. "He didn't seem the sort, but when there's a pretty face involved... You did notice Christine's right easy on the eyes?"

Morgan kept a poker face. "I suppose," he said casually. Too casually?

Rafe raised an eyebrow. "Then again, a man would have to be dead not to notice."

"You'd better not let your fiancée hear you say that. Or else—"

"I said notice."

"Or else you could find yourself standing at the altar alone."

"I wouldn't be alone," Rafe told him. "You'd be standin' right up there with me."

Morgan grinned. "You know, Rafe, as your best friend, not to mention havin' the honor of bein' your best man, there's a lot of things I'd do for you. But marryin' you ain't one of 'em!"

ABOUT THE AUTHOR

Ginger Chambers claims that from her earliest childhood she's always loved cowboys—the way they look, the job they do and the way they feel about the land. In fact, this book (like *A Match Made in Texas*) is dedicated to them—past and present—especially those in the Lone Star state.

Ginger's family roots run deep in Texas. Her great-grandfather raised cattle and drove them on the Chisholm Trail!

Books by Ginger Chambers

HARLEQUIN SUPERROMANCE

601—TILL SEPTEMBER
647—FATHER TAKES A WIFE
680—A MATCH MADE IN TEXAS

WEST TEXAS
WEDDINGS
Ginger Chambers

Harlequin Books

TORONTO • NEW YORK • LONDON
AMSTERDAM • PARIS • SYDNEY • HAMBURG
STOCKHOLM • ATHENS • TOKYO • MILAN
MADRID • WARSAW • BUDAPEST • AUCKLAND

ISBN 0-373-70730-4

WEST TEXAS WEDDINGS

WEST TEXAS
WEDDINGS

CHAPTER ONE

THE LAW OFFICE was intimidating, even for an adult—stuffy, somber, with uncomfortable chairs. When Christine's name was called, she paused to squeeze her daughter's hand.

"This shouldn't take long," she murmured. "Ten, fifteen minutes tops. Then we'll stop for an ice cream on our way home, and you can have a double dip of any flavor you want. Does that sound good?"

Erin looked at her with huge dark eyes and nodded.

As it had for the past eight years, Christine's heart melted. She'd loved her daughter from the first moment she'd seen her, making the trying circumstances surrounding her birth irrelevant. The only thing that had mattered was that this tiny being—so helpless, so filled with need—looked to her for protection and care.

Christine followed the secretary into Eugene Hernandez's office. A tall thin man in his late forties, he smiled and came quickly to his feet. He shook her hand and offered her a place in one of the chairs opposite his desk, then glanced at his secretary. "Mrs. Warren, if you please, some coffee? Or would you prefer tea?" he asked Christine.

"Actually," Christine said, sitting down, "I'd rather not have anything."

The secretary withdrew as Eugene Hernandez re-seated himself.

"In that case, we'll get right to it." The lawyer searched the papers piled on one side of his desk and brought forward a thick official-looking document, which he promptly flipped to a section near the back. He read it to himself, then folded his hands and looked at her.

Christine's heart beat faster. What was it? His phone call last night had told her nothing. "A matter of some importance," was all he'd say.

Eugene Hernandez cleared his throat. "The reason I called you here, Ms. Grant, was to tell you of a bequest in Mr. Ira Parker's will. A bequest to you."

Christine stared at the him. "I don't understand. I'm not a member of Mr. Parker's family, only an employee."

The lawyer's smile was controlled. "Even so..."

Color stained Christine's cheeks. She knew what he was thinking. She knew what other people thought, as well. But it hadn't been like that! Ira Parker was one of the few truly decent people she'd ever met. Through all the long hard months of his illness, he'd remained kind to both her and Erin. Christine had looked upon him fondly, as she might an elderly uncle. She said tightly, "I assure you, Mr. Hernandez, nothing like you're thinking ever—"

He interrupted her. "Of course, of course."

Christine stopped protesting. How did you successfully deny something a person was determined to believe?

"What...what is this bequest?" she asked. Just because he'd jumped to a prurient conclusion, she couldn't afford to ignore an offer of help. She was out of a job and would have to find a new home, as well.

The lawyer referred again to the document. "Yes, here it is." He proceeded to read the material aloud.

"What does that mean?" she asked, frowning. "A share in a ranch."

"Not just any ranch," Eugene Hernandez corrected. "The Parker Ranch."

Christine's frown deepened. "I don't... I've never heard..."

The lawyer's laugh contained a measure of skepticism. "Then you have a very pleasant surprise in store."

"Can I sell it?" Christine asked.

"Sell it? Absolutely not! That wasn't what Mr. Parker had in mind."

"How do you know what Mr. Parker had in mind? How do you know he didn't intend for me to sell it?"

"Trust me, Ms. Grant, that wasn't what he wanted." Like a magician conjuring a rabbit, Eugene Hernandez withdrew an envelope from a side drawer and held it out to her. Her name was on the front. "He also asked me to give you this. You're to read it in my presence."

"What other instructions do you have?" Christine asked.

"I'm to answer any question that might arise."

Christine drew a steadying breath and asked slowly, "What am I to do with one share of a ranch I can't sell? What good is it to me?"

The lawyer rattled the envelope and handed it to her.

Christine broke the seal and withdrew two pages of high-quality note paper, which she recognized instantly as belonging to Ira Parker. She paused when she saw the spidery scrawl that covered the two sheets. Growing weakness had reduced Mr. Parker's once robust writing to near illegibility. In the last few weeks of his life he had limited himself to only an occasional signature, and it had been done with painstaking care. Familiar with each phase of his physical decline, Christine realized he had written this letter, at great cost to himself, during those last few weeks.

Tears clouded her vision, but she willed them away. She was still in mourning for Mr. Parker, but she wasn't going to cry in front of the lawyer. He'd already proved he'd take it the wrong way.

"My dear Christine," Ira had written. She blinked and had to start over again. "My dear Christine, forgive me for springing this on you at the last minute, but presenting you with a share in my family's ranch is the only way I know to show you just how much you've come to mean to me. You and little Erin have given such joy to the last months of an old man's life. I want you to have something special, something that will provide for you both during the years ahead. You've had a hard life up to this point. Now don't deny it, I know it's true! Nothing can be done about the past, but everything can be done about the future. It makes me happy to think that a small gift from me can make such a difference—especially for Erin. Take her to the ranch, Christine. Take her to the Parker

Ranch and let her run wild like I was lucky enough to do as a child. My family will welcome you with open arms. Let them, Christine. No one will hurt you there. They're the salt of the earth, rock solid, with hearts as majestic as the land that surrounds them. Eugene will give you the particulars." It was signed, "Ira."

Christine lifted her stunned gaze. "He wants me to *live* there?"

"As you know, Ms. Grant, Mr. Parker could be very closedmouthed about his personal affairs. He had an accountant who took care of his finances, while my firm represented him on the occasional personal matter. I knew he was a Parker, but that was all, until the addendum to the will and his subsequent instructions." The lawyer cleared his throat. "Now, I'll be glad to answer any question I can."

Christine's mind had gone temporarily blank. She continued to stare at Eugene Hernandez. Finally, grasping at straws, she asked, "Where is this ranch?"

"In far West Texas. Mr. Parker provided two maps." He reached into the side drawer and withdrew a road map of the state, as well as a map drawn on plain paper. The shaky lines showed it to be Ira's creation.

Christine wanted to cry more than ever now, but years of controlling her emotions helped her hold herself together. "I—I can't think," she admitted.

Eugene Hernandez stood, and, coming around the desk, assisted her to her feet. "You have my number," he said smoothly. "Call me whenever you like. After the shock wears off I'm sure you'll have many questions.'' As he showed her to the door he continued, "You're a very lucky young woman, Ms. Grant. A share in the Parker Ranch will set you up for life. It's not an ordinary ranch that's hanging on by its bootstraps. This ranch is a highly successful business venture because it has good management, cattle *and* oil.''

Christine moved as if in a trance. She was aware of Erin jumping up and their leaving the law office together. But it wasn't until they were waiting for the elevator that the reality of what she'd just learned hit her. They owned a share in a ranch! A profitable ranch! And Ira wanted them to make a home there!

Going down on one knee, she gathered her daughter in her arms, gave her a hug, then asked huskily, "Erin? How would you like to live on a ranch? Mommy hasn't decided for sure yet, but...what do you think?''

"Would it have a horse?'' the little girl asked.

Christine smiled. "I'll bet it would.''

Erin looked at her, her sweet face far too serious. She seemed to have been born an old soul, with all the cares of the world already known to her. "I'd like that!'' she said.

THE HOUSE THAT had been their home for the past eight months was located in one of the older and more exclusive neighborhoods in Houston. Each time Christine drove along the tree-lined streets she expected to be stopped and questioned. What was someone from a poor section of Pasadena, a person who had grown up with an oil refinery next door, who had played in the shadow of huge storage tanks and thought it natural to breathe foul-smelling air, doing in a place like River Oaks? *Trailer trash* was the term she'd heard used to describe her prior social standing. At times it was said in jest by people in a similar situation. At others it was said in disdain.

She directed her old wreck of a car into the driveway leading to the house. The odometer had frozen at 120,000 miles, the engine wheezed and sputtered on starting, and both front doors and a fender had been transplanted from other cars. Ira had insisted she use his Mercedes while in his employ, but she didn't think Abigail and Brendan Parker—Ira's grown children—would agree to her continued use of it. So this morning she'd fired up her old campaigner and tried not to worry.

Christine glanced at Erin, who rode silently on the bench seat at her side. "Those ice-cream cones were good, weren't they?"

"Mmm," Erin replied.

Christine parked the car off to one side of the three-car garage and again glanced at her daughter. Erin was a quiet child by nature, but she'd been quieter than usual after leaving the law office. During the last few months of Ira Parker's life, Erin had grown close to him. He'd tried to explain what was happening, but at Erin's young age, Christine wasn't sure how much she understood. Christine had allowed her to go to the funeral service the previous weekend because Erin had requested it, and also because she thought it only right that the little girl be allowed to say a last goodbye. Now she wondered if she'd done the right thing.

"Mommy?" Erin said. "Do you think the ranch

will have more than one horse? They usually do, don't they? And if they do, do you think I could have one of my very own?''

Christine gave a mental sigh of relief. It wasn't the funeral that had been bothering her. "I can't make any promises, sweetheart. And like I told you, I haven't made up my mind yet that we're going.''

"Is it Ira's ranch?'' Erin surprised Christine by asking.

"You know about Ira's ranch?''

Erin nodded. "He used to tell me about it all the time. About how when he was a boy he'd go for visits and ride horses and help gather cows and look for buried treasure and—''

"Erin!''

The little girl's eyes grew large. "It's the truth! He said—''

Christine stepped out of the car. "I believe you. I'm just surprised you never told me.''

"Ira said it was a secret.'' Erin scrambled out.

"Like him giving you permission to call him Ira?''

Erin looked away. "I wish he was still in there,'' she said softly.

Christine saw that Erin was gazing at the large house. "So do I, sweetheart. So do I.''

Christine followed her daughter inside, where the white-haired housekeeper, Mrs. Tobin, took a moment to hug the little girl and listen to her excited talk of possible horse ownership before telling her that a batch of freshly baked cookies was waiting in the kitchen. Erin hesitated, unsure whether to accept the offer. Ice cream followed by cookies wasn't something she was normally allowed.

"One cookie is fine," Christine said. "If you'll promise to eat all your vegetables at dinner."

"I promise," Erin said, then skipped happily down the hall.

Once the little girl was out of sight, Mrs. Tobin's smile faded. "There's something you should know," she said. "Miss Abigail called. She and Mr. Brendan are on their way over. She asked if you were here, and when I said you weren't, she told me I should put your things out on the curb and not let you in when you came home. Now I ask you, is that any way for Mr. Parker's children to act? I told her if she and her brother wanted any dirty work done they'd have to do it themselves! She said I could leave, too, if I wanted." The housekeeper laughed. "Well, they have a little surprise coming, because I'm going to do it! They think I don't have anywhere else to live, but I'm retiring to my sister's place in the Hill Country. She's been after me for years to come live with her. I only stayed on here for Mr. Parker's sake, and now that he's gone—" her chin quivered, then firmed and lifted "—I'm *not* going to take orders from either of *them*. Not after the way they treated their father. Ignoring him when it suited them, then only coming around when they thought they'd soon have his money! It's shameful, that's what it is. Shameful!"

Privately Christine agreed. She'd caught which way the wind was blowing after her first meeting with Ira's children. They were so busy holding their noses in the air they'd have drowned if it rained! Hateful and spoiled, they were nothing like their father. Christine knew that Ira had loved them, but it was the faithful love of a parent, not because they did anything to deserve it. Whenever they were scheduled to visit, Christine would take Erin to the park, effectively removing both herself and her child from their line of fire.

"When did Abigail call?" she asked Mrs. Tobin.

"About a half hour ago. They should be here any minute."

Christine stiffened her spine. All right. It had come down to it. In truth, she had no right to stay on here. She was merely an employee, as she'd told Mr. Hernandez, and if her employer died, it was his heirs' decision what happened next. She extended a hand to the housekeeper. "While we have a moment, Mrs. Tobin, I want to thank you for being so kind to Erin and me. You didn't have to be, you just were."

"Ahh," Mrs. Tobin said dismissively, "it was easy to care for the little one—and for you, too. I hope you find another job right away, and that the little one..." She dabbed at her eyes with a tissue. "If you ever need a reference—I know I'm only the housekeeper here—I'd be glad to vouch for you. Here, I'll give you my sister's address in New Braunfels. Keep in touch."

"I will," Christine promised, stuffing the slip of paper into her pocket. "When Erin finishes her cookie, will you send her upstairs? I want to be sure not to leave anything of hers behind."

"Who could guarantee that it wouldn't end up in the garbage? Not with those two running the place."

Christine hurried to the suite of rooms she and Erin shared. She could have told the housekeeper that the time spent in this house was the most pleasant in her life, even considering Ira's decline. That she wasn't accustomed to people actively trying to make things easier for her or caring about what she thought or felt. But she found saying such things difficult.

She set about quickly packing the remainder of their possessions—folding their clothes, grabbing what was left in the chests of drawers and collecting their things from the bathroom. Fortunately she'd instructed Erin never to leave her toys outside their own rooms. She began packing Erin's collection of stuffed animals, which sat on her bed.

Erin came slowly into the room, her eyes moving from Christine, who had paused to wipe perspiration from her brow, to the open suitcase.

"Get your things together, honey. We have to leave."

"Right now?" Erin whispered.

Christine bent down to take her hand. It was cold. "You knew we weren't going to stay here forever. I told you it might be a year, maybe less. Now it's time to go."

"But I like it here, Mommy."

"I know. I do, too. But we can't stay any longer. Ira's son and daughter have other plans for the house."

Erin thought for a moment. "Are we going to go to Ira's ranch, Mommy? Because if we are, I won't mind so much."

Christine didn't have the slightest idea where they were going next or what they'd do. She'd been able to save a small amount of money from the generous salary Ira had paid her, but after settling a number of long-standing debts and paying Erin's school fees... She groaned. In all the upset she'd forgotten about school! It was only the first part of April. Close to two months of the term remained!

Erin stroked her mother's cheek. "It's okay, Mommy. We don't have to go to the ranch. And I don't need a horse. I already have one. Look!'' She ran to get her favorite toy—a miniature palomino with a flowing mane and tail that she was forever combing and brushing. She thrust it forward. "Golden Belle, remember?"

Christine folded the little girl close and smoothed her thick hair. It was like touching black silk—smooth and glossy and finely textured. Christine didn't know where hair like this had come from. Not Erin's father, or her own family. Her mother had been a natural blond, and her father—at least, the man she'd deduced was her father—had had reddish-brown hair like her own, and similar hazel eyes.

She was going to do better by her little girl than her mother had done by her. No matter what it took, no matter what she had to do to insure it. She'd already taken a number of steps. She'd gone back to school, earned her high-school equivalency diploma and gone on to business school to learn a profession. She'd moved them out of the trailer park, and Erin didn't have a procession of "uncles" drifting in and out of her life. The opposite, in fact.

"I think I've decided what we're going to do," she said, drawing back to look at her daughter. "I think we should get you a real horse and be somewhere you can learn to ride it.''

Happiness sparked in Erin's dark eyes. "Oh, Mommy, that would be wonderful!"

Someone rapped on the door. "Christine!" Mrs. Tobin called tersely. "They're here!"

Christine straightened. "Put all your things in the suitcase, honey. Quickly."

Erin hurried to do as she was told, while Christine gave another hasty glance around the room. Then she moved to help Erin close the case. As the last clasp caught, voices could be heard at the top of the stairs, then approaching down the hall. Loud voices, sharp with argument.

The door burst open, Mrs. Tobin backing in and Abigail Parker sweeping forward. Bringing up the rear was Brendan Parker, who seemed to find the whole scene amusing. A smirk tilted the corners of his well-shaped mouth and lit his eyes—the same eyes that ran over Christine with unconcealed sensual interest.

It was a look Christine had known from the time she was twelve, directed her way by some of the men her mother had entertained. Her mother hadn't liked it—not because she was upset by the unseemly notice, but because she hadn't wanted to share the attention. Later on Christine had had to deal with such looks in almost every job she'd taken. Until she'd come here.

"You weren't supposed to let her in!" Abigail Parker shouted at Mrs. Tobin. "She's probably stolen half the antiques in the house by now!"

"You're welcome to search my luggage," Christine invited with icy anger. Erin clung to her side as she threw open the suitcase, spilling some of the stuffed animals onto the bedcover.

"In there, then!" Abigail pointed to the cardboard boxes waiting by the door.

"Mr. Parker's turning over in his grave," Mrs. Tobin murmured, shaking her head.

"You shut up!" Abigail ordered. "It's all your fault that we're in this mess! If you'd helped our daddy a little more, he wouldn't have needed to hire this—"

"Me?" the housekeeper protested, her voice rising. "What about the two of you? Why didn't you give him a little help? Saints preserve us! It's you who should be ashamed. Not—"

"You're *fired!*" Abigail shouted. "Get out. Right now! Get out!"

"Abby," her brother cautioned, "you might be letting your temper get just the tiniest bit the better of you. What are we going to do about preparing the house for the sale? We'll need someone to—"

"I'll hire a cleaning service!" his sister snapped. "I've had enough of her prune face to last me a lifetime. Every time we come over she looks at us as if we're worms. As if we—"

Brendan Parker chuckled at her vehemence. "Well, in that case..."

Christine pushed the stuffed animals back into the suitcase, except for the toy horse, which she put into Erin's hands. "I think it's an insult to compare you to worms," she said. "An insult to the worms. Maggots are more like it."

Abigail lunged at her, but Brendan quickly caught

hold of her arms. "Ah-ah, sister dear," he said. "No more violence. You promised the judge, remember?"

At mention of the judge—had the woman been in some kind of trouble that Christine hadn't heard about?—Abigail deflated and looked at Christine with suddenly dead eyes. "Just get out of here," she said flatly. "Take everything you've got packed and go!"

"I want you to check for theft," Christine said firmly.

"Just *go!*"

Christine held her ground. "Mrs. Tobin is witness to my request. I want you to inspect our things and see if you find anything that shouldn't be there."

Abigail broke her brother's hold and taking a step forward, hissed menacingly, "Stop playing the sainted martyr! If you've managed to squirrel something away, more power to you. You probably earned it being at our father's beck and call all day. Not to mention having to share his bed at night!"

Christine was very aware of Erin's presence. She wanted to say something equally scathing, something that would singe the other woman's pampered skin, but she kept silent, except for a brusquely murmured, "We'll be out of the house in five minutes."

THE CAR STARTED on first try. As the engine rumbled and grumbled, Christine spoke to the housekeeper, who stood nearby. "Can we take you anywhere?" she offered.

Mrs. Tobin shook her head. "Ahh, no. I'll be fine. I've lived in this house for over sixteen years. It's going to take me more than a few minutes to pack.

Two weeks is what my contract says. Either way—me giving notice to them, or them giving it to me. And I intend to use every second, just to annoy them.'' She laughed. ''Maggots! I like that! Wish I'd thought of it.''

Erin waved as they backed out of the long drive, and Christine smiled, though she didn't feel like it.

Upon awakening, she'd had no idea what the day would bring. That by evening their car would be packed with everything they owned, and they would be on their way to a ranch in far West Texas. A large successful ranch, she'd been assured—one in which she was now part owner.

Somehow it didn't seem real.

CHAPTER TWO

"I WOULDN'T TRY IT if I were you."

The auto mechanic's words were to haunt every mile Christine and Erin covered during the next three and a half days, the time it took them to complete the nearly six-hundred-mile journey across Texas. Ignoring the mechanic's advice, they limped along the interstate in the slow lane, holding their breaths on some long climbs and laughing delightedly when they coasted down the other side. They stopped frequently to let the engine cool and to make sure that they had enough gas and water. Their worry increased as the towns grew fewer and farther between, until there were long expanses of nothing, not even a service station. At that point Christine's fingers dug into the steering wheel, as if by force of will she could make the engine continue to perform.

Only when Erin slept did Christine question whether what they were doing was wise. Would Ira's relatives truly welcome them with open arms? How would *she* feel if someone showed up unannounced on her doorstep, demanding a place to stay and a part of the action? What if instead of being kind and generous as Ira had been, they were like Abigail and Brendan? What would she and Erin do then? The answer was go back to Houston. But could the car make the return trip?

Despite her misgivings, Christine pressed on. If Ira said his people were the salt of the earth, then they were. *And if you believe that, I have a nice bridge...*

As directed, they turned off the interstate onto a narrow two-lane blacktop that seemed to go on forever. Then, also as directed, Christine made two more turns, each to a lesser roadway. The first was graded, the second proved to be little more than a rutted path. Until finally, near an old windmill, even that ran out.

"This can't be it!" Christine muttered, careful not to wake the sleeping Erin. She didn't want her to be alarmed at how truly out in the wilds they were. As far as the eye could see in any direction, there was nothing but mile upon mile of dry rocky land, low scrub and distant mountains. "Something definitely is wrong."

An X indicated the Parker Ranch on Ira's map. An X that was just as squiggly as his hand-drawn lines. But his placement was definite. The ranch and ranch house was supposed to be here. Christine looked around again. Could she somehow have missed a turn-off?

There was only one thing to do. They had to go back to the blacktop and try again. But as she began to put her plan into action, the engine wheezed pathetically, gave a violent shake, then died. Steam began to billow from beneath the hood.

"What's the matter, Mommy? What's wrong?" Erin sat up, startled by Christine's dismayed cry. "Where are we?" she asked, then became fascinated by the steam curling into the air like smoke. "Did the car finally break?"

"I'm afraid so," Christine confirmed.

"What are we going to do?"

Christine forced herself to think. She let her gaze sweep the arid landscape. The *empty* arid landscape. What else could they do? They'd walk. If they waited for rescue, all that eventually would be found of them was their bones! No one was expecting them. And no one with the exception of Eugene Hernandez, Mrs. Tobin and the garage mechanic even knew they were planning the trip. No one would check to see that they'd arrived.

The question was, which way should they walk? Back to the blacktop where cars had been infrequent, but at least there? If Christine had been on her own, she might have opted for an extended search of the area, but with Erin along, she wasn't about to take any chances. "It looks like we walk," she said. "But it could take a while. Are you up to it?"

"Can I bring Golden Belle?" Erin held the toy horse close to her chest.

They would probably be better off if Erin carried something else—something to drink or eat or cover themselves with if they had to spend the night under the stars. Christine quelled a shiver. In the city a person had to be careful about human predators. Out here, it was the four-legged kind.

"Of course Golden Belle can come," she said, giving way to her daughter's need for emotional support.

She gathered a few things, then, arms filled, pushed open her door and stepped outside.

Erin scrambled out after her, her eyes huge as she took in the windmill and the vastness of the territory surrounding them. "But, Mommy," she said, glancing back at the car, "what about the rest of our things?"

"We'll have to leave them for now."

"But—?"

"Don't worry," she said. "We'll come back for our stuff."

Christine placed a baseball cap on her daughter's head, positioning the visor forward for protection from the sun, and adjusted her own matching cap. Both were keepsakes from AstroWorld amusement park where they'd celebrated Erin's last birthday. Knowing they would need to carry as much water as they could, she placed the two remaining bottles, along with some cookies, into the center of an old cotton scarf. Then she brought the corners together, tied them in a knot and slung the bundle over her shoulder.

She couldn't be sure they would return, but her answer had appeared to satisfy Erin, and the little girl set off willingly at her side.

The first half hour gave Christine better insight into the difficulties they faced. She had no idea how far they'd come from the blacktop. Ten miles? Fifteen? Distance took on greater significance when a person was walking. Were they going to have the stamina to make it?

At the next gentle rise she paused to gauge the distance they'd come. It was depressing to find that she could still see the car. As she continued to look at it, a flash of light bounced off something near the windmill.

"Mommy, can I have a drink?" Erin asked.

Christine's gaze remained fixed on what she saw now was a slow-moving object. Was it an animal—a cow? So far, they'd seen few.

"Mommy?" Erin prodded again.

Christine slid the makeshift pack to the ground and dug inside. "Only take a few sips," she cautioned. "We have to make this last."

"For how long?"

"For as long as it takes."

Straightening, Christine once again narrowed her eyes as she stared into the distance. She didn't see any movement now. She turned to Erin. "How's Golden Belle holding up?" If there was only some way to make the ordeal easier.

"She's not thirsty yet," Erin said.

Christine nodded, put away the bottle and they started off again.

Adjusting to the dry heat was difficult. Perspiration evaporated almost as quickly as it formed. No wonder the earth was so unyielding here. Moisture was something to be prized, protected, fought for. Even the few plants displaying spring flowers seemed to do so grudgingly, guarding their blossoms with wicked-looking thorns.

When Erin skipped on ahead, Christine realized her daughter was enjoying this. It was a big adventure to her, something out of the ordinary.

Laughing, the little girl darted even farther ahead, wanting to be the first across a shallow wash.

"Erin!" Christine called, uncomfortable with the distance between them.

Two things happened at once. Erin stopped dead in her tracks to give a strangled shriek, and a loud clopping, breathing, thumping sound came up fast behind them on the other side of the rise. Christine didn't know what to do first—rush to Erin, or face down whatever it was that was coming after them. Somehow she managed to do a bit of both, and snatching up a rock, waited for what was about to appear.

Was it a mountain lion? A coyote? A wolf?

A huge dark form burst into view. It had lean powerful legs and a long face, which it shook at her. When it snorted, a flash of sunlight struck something at its mouth. It was a horse!

For a split second Christine relaxed, then she saw the rider. Dressed in traditional cowboy garb—boots, chaps, faded Western shirt, a hat pulled low over his forehead—he looked rough, uncouth, untamed. And she realized they could still be in danger.

The rider barely spared her a glance. He reached to his side, pulled a rifle from its mount, lifted it, aimed and was about to pull the trigger when Christine broke from her frozen state. He was going to shoot Erin!

With a bloodcurdling yell, Christine threw her rock at him—the same instant as the shot exploded. The cowboy gave a surprised yelp when the rock hit his arm, but he didn't lower the weapon.

Christine's gaze jerked to Erin. The little girl's face was as white as her blouse, but she was still standing.

"Run!" Christine shouted, her ears ringing from the rifle's report. She bent for another rock. "Run, Erin! Run!" she urged again.

Her daughter didn't budge.

"Stop!" Christine cried, waving her arms at the horseman. "You...you big bully! Leave her alone!" She threw her second rock.

A light touch of the cowboy's heels, a slight tug on the reins, and the big horse skittered sideways. The rock landed ineffectually on the ground.

Someone pulled on her arm. An accomplice? Christine whirled around, her eyes fierce, and discovered that the person she thought was an accomplice was Erin.

"Don't!" the little girl pleaded. "He shot it! He shot the snake! He's not a bully. He..."

The words slowly filtered into Christine's brain. "Snake?" she repeated blankly.

The man set the rifle back into place, slid off the horse and, keeping hold of the reins, walked over near to where Erin had been standing and lifted a rattler that was at least three feet long. "Here's your bully," he drawled. His voice was low, melodic—not at all what Christine had expected. "You want the rattle?" he asked the little girl.

"I thought you were going to kill her!" Christine burst out.

"You thought wrong," he replied.

"Can I?" Erin asked, excited. "Can I have the rattle?"

It had taken only seconds for Erin to forget her fright, but Christine's nerves were still twanging. And when she saw the cowboy pull a knife from his pocket and start to unfold the blade, it was all she could do not to cry out again. "I—I don't think..." She stammered to a halt when blue eyes, the same color as the sky, met hers.

He'd pushed his old dusty black Stetson to the back of his head, and as she looked at him Christine suffered another shock to her preconceived notions. He was really quite handsome, and far younger than she'd thought—in his midthirties? He had a shock of thick blond hair, lean even features bronzed by the sun and a long lithe body that looked born to the land. And those eyes! Not only a vivid blue, but penetrating. They seemed to see straight through to her soul.

Christine jerked her gaze away, angry with herself for such fanciful thinking. "No, Erin," she said. "I don't believe that would be a good idea right now."

Erin was disappointed, but Christine hardened her resolve. Just because the man was different from what she'd feared didn't mean he was no longer a danger to them.

Without a word he closed the knife, put it away and tossed the snake's remains a distance into the brush.

"I didn't see it until I was almost on it," Erin explained. "Then...I don't know what happened. There was a loud noise and..."

"It's springtime," the cowboy said. "Snakes are on the move. It's not a good time to go hikin' across land you don't know."

Christine lifted her chin. "We're looking for the Parker Ranch. And we weren't hiking. Our car broke down. I believe you saw it?"

"I saw smoke," he said. "Then I saw the car." He studied her curiously. "You say you're lookin' for the Parker Ranch? Why?"

"I can't see where that's any of your—"

"I'm the acting foreman of the Parker Ranch."

Christine swallowed the rest of her protest. He was the foreman? The "acting" foreman?

"Name's Morgan Hughes," he said, and offered them a courteous tip of his hat. But when that was done he returned to his previous theme. "You didn't answer my question," he said.

"My business is with the Parkers," Christine said. "No one else."

He stood still, watching her. She could sense the calculation taking place in his mind. The weighing of his decision. Beside him, his horse shifted its weight.

"All right," he said at last. "I'll take you there. But I still need to know your name. If you don't tell me that, we don't go."

"I'm Christine Grant and this is my daughter, Erin."

"Daughter," he repeated.

Christine was accustomed to the odd looks and surprised comments people gave when they learned her relationship to Erin. *You? You don't look old enough!* Or, *You're little more than a child yourself!* She'd given birth to her daughter at seventeen. Now at twenty-five, it was hard for people to believe that they were mother and child.

"Hello," Erin said dutifully.

The foreman smiled, and the expression changed his face, softening the hard edges. He hunkered down beside Erin. "How'd you like to take a ride on ol' Thunder here?" he asked, motioning to his horse.

Erin's face glowed. "On your *real* horse?" she asked.

His smile deepened. "Sure thing," he drawled. "Ol' Thunder's about as real as they come."

"Oh! I'd love it! I'd love it! A *real* horse!"

He swung the little girl up into the saddle, and Erin, still clutching Golden Belle, grabbed hold of the horn with her free hand.

"That's the way!" he said. Then he turned to Christine. "You're up next."

Christine took a hasty step back. "Oh, no. I'm going to walk. Erin can ride, but not—" She ended on a yip as he picked her up and hoisted her into the saddle behind her daughter.

"Now we don't have to argue about it," he said.

He adjusted the stirrups that accommodated his over-six-foot frame to Christine's five-foot-four. Then, keeping hold of the reins, he started to walk cross-country, away from the rutted path they'd been following.

After the first couple of miles Christine's sense of fair play urged her to thank him, but she just couldn't make herself do it. She'd been perfectly willing to walk. Depriving him of his mount hadn't been her idea. She kept quiet for another half mile, then said tightly, "Thank you for doing this. Is the ranch very far?"

"Another few miles," he said without looking around.

"Are— Would you like to change places?"

That gained his attention. His gaze moved up her bare leg to the line just above midthigh where her shorts started, then it moved back down again to her open-work sandal. "You aren't exactly dressed for it," he said.

She could see the way his chaps protected his long legs from the occasional stray branch or thorn. The leather was worn white in spots. Her own legs were still stinging from the scratches they'd received.

"This is so much fun!" Erin said in an excited whisper when their trek resumed.

At first glance the sudden greenness of a clump of trees in the distance was almost startling. Christine could make out a weathered set of corrals, a house and several outbuildings. Her heart gave an anticipatory leap. They were almost there! Soon she would be meeting the Parkers—and she'd get to see how they took to the news of a new partner.

Yet as she drew closer, her expectations received another jolt. She'd thought the headquarters for the Parker Ranch would be larger, built on a grander scale. This looked rather ordinary. A low stone house with a red-tile roof, an old barn, some run-down storage buildings.

A boy of about eleven, clad in snug-fitting jeans, a Western shirt and boots, let out a whoop as he ran out of the house to greet them. He stopped when he saw that strangers were in the saddle.

Was he Morgan Hughes's son? Christine wondered. He had the same full thatch of light blond hair, the same sky blue eyes. The boy waited in silence as the horse plodded closer.

Morgan Hughes handed him the reins, before turning to lift Erin from the saddle.

"Thank you," the little girl said politely as she moved off to one side.

"I can do it myself," Christine claimed, rejecting his offer of help. Her pride still smarted from her earlier unanticipated ascent. As she got down she tried not to reveal that a creaky stiffness had laid claim to her hips and legs. It had been years since she'd ridden a horse, and then only a few times one summer when a friend from school had sold rides in the small pasture behind her house.

She caught what might have been an amused twitch of Morgan Hughes's lips. He was laughing at her? Why? Did he find it amusing that she was stiff? Or was he amused at her assertion of independence? She was just about to call him on it when the screen door opened again and a woman stepped outside. Dressed in a calico-print dress covered by a serviceable apron, she'd obviously been a beauty in her youth and was still beautiful in her sixties. It didn't matter that she carried a few extra pounds, that her hair was now more silver than gold, or that her face was creased with a vivid array of lines. The good bone structure was still there underneath.

"Morgan? What's all this?" the woman asked.

"I've brought you some visitors, Mom. Lady's name is Christine Grant and that's Erin. They were on their way to the Parkers' when their car broke down."

His mother frowned. "Then why didn't you take them straight there?"

"They were on foot," Morgan explained. "I thought they might like to freshen up."

No wonder this homestead didn't match her expectations of the Parker Ranch! Morgan Hughes had taken them on a detour. Why? For his stated reason? Or because he thought, given a little added time, he might be able to weasel more information out of her? She sent him a calculating look that he returned without the flicker of an eyelash.

"We don't want to impose," Christine said.

The woman smiled. "Nonsense, you're not imposing. On foot, were you?"

"Yes." Christine urged Erin up the path and into the house. What good would it do them to refuse this hospitality? They had no means of transportation and no clear idea of the location of the ranch. If it were only Morgan Hughes here, she might have held out, demanded that he honor his agreement. But his mother was trying to be gracious.

A man was sprawled in a recliner, a newspaper lying open on the floor next to him. It was obvious he'd been asleep and that he found waking up disagreeable. He, too, was in his sixties, with graying hair and nut brown weatherbeaten skin. "What's goin' on?" he demanded gruffly. "Who're they?" His right arm and wrist were in a cast, held in place away from his body by a metal brace. Only the tips of his fingers were exposed.

"Visitors, Dub, who else?" Morgan Hughes's mother said. "Honestly, I sometimes wonder if those doctors didn't make a mistake when they said your arm was hurt worse than your head."

"There's nothin' wrong with my thinkin', Delores!" the man retorted.

Morgan Hughes, who'd taken time to remove his

chaps, nudged the boy out of the doorway. "Take care of Thunder for me, will you, Rusty?" he requested, then to the man, "I found 'em out near the border to Indian Wells, Dad. Their car had broken down."

The older man frowned. "What were they doin' out there?"

Morgan hung his hat on a hook by the door. "You'll have to ask them that."

All eyes settled on Christine, but before she could speak Morgan Hughes's mother intervened. "First things first," the woman said. "They need to have something cold to drink before you two start firing questions." She smiled at Christine. "Go ahead, sit down. We don't wait for invitations around here. You just make yourself at home. I'll be back in a second. Morgan, you want something?"

Morgan shook his head as Christine took a seat on the couch, Erin pressing tightly against her.

Morgan caught hold of a straight-back chair and, turning it, straddled it like a horse. He folded his arms on top of the backrest and studied the two of them. His father gazed at them just as closely.

"The Parker Ranch," Christine began, for something to say, "I understand it's quite large?"

The two men glanced at each other. "You understand right," Dub Hughes said.

"How...how far away is it? The directions we were given—"

"Who gave 'em to you?" Morgan Hughes asked.

Just then Delores returned carrying two ice-filled glasses of water, causing Christine to unconsciously lick her dry lips. "Now, what did I tell you two?" the woman chided her son and husband. "No questions until after they're refreshed."

"She's the one who started askin' questions," Dub defended.

Christine accepted a glass and took a sip. The cold water sliding down her throat was wonderful. She offered a fleeting smile of gratitude.

"And you, young lady," Delores said warmly a few moments later, addressing Erin. "Your name's Erin, right?"

"Yes," Erin said softly. "Erin Grant."

"What a pretty name! We have a granddaughter about your age—Jessica. She's nine."

"I'm eight," Erin said.

"And another granddaughter who's almost four," Delores continued. "Her name's Mindy. They're both over visiting a little friend right now. If you're here long enough, you'll have to come back and play. That's Rusty, their big brother, you met just now."

Morgan, looking at Christine, returned to the prior subject. "You're on the Parker Ranch right now. You were on it when I found you."

He looked different in this setting, Christine noted. In his parents' presence, he didn't seem nearly as startlingly, overpoweringly, threateningly *male*. Yet he retained an element of danger. As if he were the cat and she the mouse, and he was just waiting for her to make a mistake so he could pounce. Did he have some second sense that, from the Parkers' point of view, she might be bad news?

"Why didn't you tell me?" she demanded. "Why did you let me think—"

"Knowing the truth wasn't going to do you any good."

"Just like you didn't bother to tell me that you weren't shooting at my daughter?"

"Would you rather I let the rattlesnake strike?"

"You could have said *something!*"

"It's actions that count out here, ma'am."

"Which is exactly what I'd like right now—action! I want to be taken to the Parkers."

"Are they expecting you?" he countered.

"Do they have to be?"

"It's polite to let people know when company's coming."

Delores and Dub Hughes had sat quietly through the rapid-fire give-and-take, their heads swiveling back and forth between visitor and son.

Finally Delores murmured, "Morgan, you're the one not being very polite right now."

"Leave the boy alone, Delores," Dub grumbled. "He's doin' his job."

"Then he can do it outside," Delores flared. "I won't have a visitor in my home treated badly!"

The boy, Rusty, had come inside again. He watched from the doorway. "Are you gonna have her arrested for trespassing, Uncle Morgan?" he asked hopefully.

"Rusty!" Delores scolded him.

Christine stood up. "We've imposed long enough." Holding tightly onto Erin's hand, she added, "If someone would just show us which way to walk—"

"Morgan," Delores instructed briskly, "you take her in the truck, do you hear? Whatever business she has with the Parkers is her affair. Hers and theirs. Not ours. Not this time."

Christine smiled thinly. "Well, maybe it is just a little," she said, and then looked straight into Morgan Hughes's blue eyes. "Because as of a few days ago, I became a part owner of the Parker ranch. You work for me now, Mr. Acting Foreman Hughes."

She'd had no idea how the Hugheses would react—gasp in surprise, cry out in amazement? But she hadn't counted on a lengthy silence.

"But how...?" Delores murmured at last, puzzled. "Are you David Parker's widow? He's the only one I know who had a young wife. But she came for the last partners' meeting, now that I think about it. You aren't her."

"I'm no one's wife," Christine said levelly. "My share comes by way of Ira Parker. He left it to me in his will."

Again another stunned silence.

"But—" Dub began.

Morgan Hughes had been watching her through narrowed eyes. Something in her statement had satisfied him. Not because he'd liked what he'd heard—she could see he didn't. No, it was because she had confirmed a suspicion, an instinct he had for trouble.

He lightly touched his father's arm. "We'll let Rafe handle this, Dad," he said. "Rafe and Mae. I'm sure they'll be up to it."

A smile cracked Dub's leathery cheeks. "You bet they'll be up to it, son."

"Take 'em in the truck," Delores said quietly as she regarded Christine with a mixture of compassion and curiosity. "She's going to need every ounce of strength she has left to deal with Mae."

"Who's Mae?" Christine asked, retrieving her pack from the floor.

Delores only tsked and shook her head.

CHAPTER THREE

THE TRIP IN THE PICKUP lasted no more than fifteen minutes. The three of them sat in the cab without speaking—Morgan Hughes driving, Christine by the passenger door and Erin in the middle.

From the surreptitious glances she'd allowed herself, Christine was disquieted by Morgan's calm air of certainty. But on her side she had the knowledge that she was here by rights. It was all perfectly legal. She had Ira's letter and, after a quick stop at Eugene Hernandez's office before leaving Houston, confirmation from him of Ira's bequest.

"We're here," Morgan said, breaking into her introspection.

He'd stopped the truck on a low promontory that overlooked a wide valley. Nestled in the middle of the valley was a large complex of houses and outbuildings. It was everything Christine had expected and more. The entire setup, from the collection of corrals, chutes and pens on one side, to the grassy courtyard ringed by houses on the other, must have covered close to a mile. Even the collection of trees was impressive—at least two dozen large oaks were clustered in and around the courtyard, as well as scattered among the outbuildings.

"Sure you don't want to change your mind?" Morgan asked, seemingly willing to offer her one last chance.

"Definitely not," Christine retorted.

Shaking his head, he put the truck back into gear.

They pulled to a stop in front of a big two-story house at the head of a long U-shaped drive. They barely had time to get out of the truck before an elderly woman stepped onto the porch. She had to be in her late seventies, if not in her eighties, but Christine immediately saw that this woman was a force to be reckoned with. It was there in every line of her proudly held body, her strong features and her hawklike eyes.

"Who are these people, Morgan?" she demanded.

"Hello, Mae," he drawled, a smile flickering across his lips. "This lady has some business with you. Name's Christine Grant. And this is her daughter, Erin."

The old woman's dark eyes moved over Christine before passing on to Erin. "What kind of business?" she asked.

"Ranch business, family business," Morgan replied.

"Then you'd better get Rafe. He's over at the office." She gave Christine another once-over as Morgan went to do her bidding. "You two come with me," she said, and disappeared back inside the house.

So this was Mae, Christine thought. She urged Erin forward, but this time Erin balked.

"Mommy," the little girl whispered, "I don't want to go."

"We have to, sweetheart," Christine said. "Ira wanted us to, remember?"

"But that lady—"

Someone else appeared just inside the doorway. A far younger woman, very slender, with wheat-colored hair, friendly blue eyes and a surprised smile. "Oh!" she said, startled. "I didn't know anyone was here. Does Mae know that you're—"

Mae's voice called from the depths of the house, "Show 'em to my office, Shannon. I thought they were right behind me, then I turned around and they weren't!"

Shannon grimaced. "She sounds irritated. If you want to stay on her good side, you should hurry. She doesn't like to be kept waiting."

"Neither do I," Christine replied, before giving Erin another nudge. This time Erin didn't resist.

Christine felt the other woman's curious gaze, but refused to acknowledge it. There would be plenty of time to get to know everyone here once she had established her claim.

"This way," Shannon said, and led the way down a hall. As they followed her Christine noticed she favored her left leg.

Mae was seated at a rosewood desk in a room lined with books. "Can we offer you some refreshment?" she asked formally.

"Not for me," Christine said. "Erin?"

Erin shook her head.

"At least be seated, then." Mae motioned to the dark green leather couch and pair of cream-colored chairs set to one side. A vase filled with fresh flowers adorned a low table.

"I'd rather stand," Christine said.

The two Parker women exchanged puzzled glances.

"Morgan's gone to get Rafe," Mae said to Shannon, who nodded and perched on one of the chairs.

A moment later two men came into the room. One was Morgan Hughes, and the other... There was no way to deny this man's blood connection to Mae. He had the same strong features, the same tough edge, the same palpable streak of determination. Here was another force to be reckoned with, Christine knew, and felt her stomach clench. Maybe she should have let Eugene Hernandez place the preparatory call he'd offered. She had a bad feeling about the way the Parkers were going to react.

Rafe went to Shannon, his arm encircling her shoulders. When Shannon gazed up at him, Christine had to look away. There was something wonderful in the look they shared—love, need, a tender caring. Once, a long time ago, Christine thought she'd had that herself. It turned out she was wrong.

Her eyes settled on Morgan Hughes. He was watching her steadily. She frowned. What was he waiting around for? Why didn't he go home? He had done his job by delivering them.

Rafe released Shannon and turned his attention fully on Christine. "Morgan tells me you think you own a piece of the Parker Ranch." He said it mildly, as one might mention the time of day, but Christine could sense the steel behind his words and the shock the information gave the other two women.

"That's right," Christine confirmed, digging deep inside herself for some steel of her own.

Mae Parker sat forward. "That's impossible!" she snapped.

"I'm afraid it's not," Christine said.

"Rafe!" Mae ordered. "Tell her!"

Rafe asked a question, instead. "What makes you think you have a claim?"

From the pocket of her shorts, Christine extracted Ira's map, his letter and the confirmation letter from Eugene Hernandez. "Here," she said, "see for yourself."

Rafe's dark eyes held hers before he accepted the papers. He then moved over to Mae's desk. Both looked up with puzzled gazes once they'd finished examining them.

"I don't understand," Mae said. "Ira knew he couldn't do this. Why would he...?" Her question trailed off.

Rafe spoke into the silence. "Ira can't have willed you a share in the Parker Ranch. It's purely family held."

"Not anymore."

"Yes. Nothing's changed."

Christine tossed her head. "The will is legal. You can ask Ira's lawyer, Mr. Hernandez. His number's at the top of his letter."

Mae jumped back into the fray. "What were you to Ira?" she demanded. "His mistress?"

"Mae..." Shannon warned softly from the chair.

Mae pretended not to have heard. "Well, *mistresses* don't count for much around here, missy."

Christine smiled. "How nice for you and sad for them."

"You never answered my question," Mae said stubbornly.

"She's good at that," Morgan Hughes murmured, speaking for the first time since entering the room.

Mae shot him a look, as did Christine. Mae's was curious. Christine bristled with indignation.

Erin's hand crept into Christine's. As usual when she was disturbed, the child's hand was chilled. Christine patted it, then defiantly lifted her head. She wasn't going to allow her daughter to be cheated out of what was rightfully hers because it didn't fit in with the plans of a wealthy group of ranchers.

Her action drew the Parkers' attention to the little girl. Christine's first instinct was to pull Erin behind her, to protect her from their hostile gazes. But the antagonism they'd shown before altered the longer they looked at her daughter.

"This is your little girl?" Mae asked gruffly. "Who's her daddy?"

Direct and to the point, the way Christine liked to proceed. "That," she said crisply, "is none of your business."

"Ira?" Mae shot back, guessing.

Christine had prepared herself for the family to think that she and Ira were lovers. If Brendan and Abigail thought that, not to mention Eugene Hernandez, it would stand to reason that the Parkers would, too. But she hadn't prepared herself for an accusation of this sort. Ira was old enough to be her grandfather! That they might think she'd have a child by him...

Her mind moved quickly, making adjustments. Although if they did—even if it was only a suspicion—mightn't it smooth the way into the Parkers accepting them? The tantalizing possibility that Erin *was* a Parker?

Rafe frowned darkly and Shannon bit her bottom lip, while Morgan leaned against the doorjamb, his arms crossed over his chest. Christine flashed him another irritated look. Why didn't he just leave?

Silence was Christine's best ally. She stood quietly, holding her daughter's hand, coolly returning their inspection.

Finally Rafe said, "You understand that this is going to take a little time—"

"I don't believe it. Not for a second!" Mae spat angrily. "This is something she's made up." She rustled Christine's papers. "Just like these are."

"Call Mr. Hernandez," Christine repeated, trying to hold on to her temper.

"I think we'll do a little more than that!" Mae snapped.

"As I said," Rafe broke in again, "this will take a little time to sort out. From our point of view, Ms. Grant, you don't have a legal leg to stand on. Not the way our family trust is set up. But to be fair, while we check, you're welcome to stay here at the ranch."

"How generous," Christine murmured sarcastically.

She heard Morgan Hughes give a snort of disbelief.

"Rafe!" Mae protested. "That's not—"

"It's what I think we should do, Aunt Mae," Rafe said firmly.

Mae looked ready to protest again, but ultimately decided against it. "All right," she said. Then, surprising Christine, she added, "She'll stay in the big house with Shannon and me."

Christine's stomach clenched. Stay in the big house with Shannon and Mae? Shannon didn't look to be a problem, but Mae...

Erin must have had the same reaction because her fingers fluttered in Christine's hand and lost even more warmth.

THEY WERE SHOWN to a room on the second floor.

"You're from Houston?" Shannon asked, throwing wide a glass-paneled door that opened onto the balcony.

"How did you know?" Christine asked warily.

Shannon grinned. "The hats. AstroWorld."

Christine had forgotten about their hats. She immediately removed hers. "Ah...yes. Yes, we are. Pasadena, actually. It's a little south of—"

"I know where it is. I've been there. My father took me on one of his—" She stopped. "No need to bore you. Do you always have to explain to people from outside the state that it's not Pasadena, California, where the Rose parade is held?"

"Always," Christine confirmed.

"I'm from Austin. We're just now getting known for something besides being the state capitol—music, computers, great food."

"Aren't you a Parker?" Christine asked as Erin stepped out onto the balcony for a look around.

Shannon's grin deepened as she displayed a diamond engagement ring. "Almost. I'm marrying Rafe at the beginning of June."

Christine didn't quite know what to say. She would offer congratulations, but her tenuous presence in the house wasn't conducive to stating opinions, not even innocuous ones.

Shannon, sensitive to Christine's unease, went on with her hostessing duties. "You have a private bath through here," she said, opening a narrow door. And there's a linen closet in the hall if you need more towels or blankets. Believe it or not, it can get quite cool here in the evenings." She glanced at the twin beds. "Marie—she's the cook and housekeeper—will be up later to make up the beds. Oh, and by the way, I'm in the room next door. So if you need anything, just knock."

"Thank you," Christine said.

Erin slipped quietly back into the room and looked at them with big eyes.

Shannon seemed arrested by sight of the little girl. Then she moved to the door. "We usually have dinner around seven. But if you're hungry earlier, or want something brought up, instead, just tell Marie."

She was almost in the hall when Christine stopped her. "Why did Mae do this?" she asked. "Why does she want us to stay here in the big house?"

"You want the truth?" Shannon asked. "She wants to keep an eye on you. And what better place?"

What better place, indeed? Christine thought once she and Erin were alone. Keep the enemy in front and you'll always know what they're doing. But the strategy worked both ways. Because while Mae was busy keeping an eye on them, Christine could keep an eye on Mae.

MORGAN DIDN'T SEE the toy horse until he was almost home. The little girl had forgotten it in the truck in her mother's haste to confront the Parkers. Damned interesting afternoon, they'd all had. Mae fit to be tied, Rafe flummoxed, the rest of the ranch-based Parkers needing to be told.

Morgan turned the truck around. Whatever else, the little girl shouldn't have to spend her first night in Mae's house without her favorite toy. She'd clutched it so tightly while up on Thunder, even though her eyes had shined at the thrill of riding a real horse. It obviously meant a lot to her.

Now if there was only some way to deliver it without having to deal with her mother.

Her mother. It was hard for him to believe that they were, in fact, mother and daughter. When he'd first seen them, he'd thought that they were sisters and that the older one couldn't be more than twenty. But to have a child of eight—that was what the little girl said she was—meant that Christine Grant was...

Morgan shook his head. Today, it could mean anything. He'd seen things in some of Texas's larger cities that could curl a person's hair. Babies having babies. Young girls who should still be looked after themselves, having one, sometimes two offspring. What had made him decide that Christine Grant was older, though—probably somewhere in her midtwenties— was the way she'd handled herself under fire. Fiercely protective, with a tart tongue and a bold, give-no-quarter conviction. She'd popped him a good one with a rock when she'd thought he was a danger to her daughter, and she'd gone toe-to-toe with Mae, holding her ground, not backing down.

She was wrong, though. There was no way a person from outside the family could lay claim to any share of the ranch, unless it was through the death of a Parker spouse. And then, when that person died, the share reverted. It had been like that for the past eighty or more years. Nothing Christine Grant said or did could change that. She was out of luck. But damned if he didn't find himself grudgingly admiring her. And he had the sense, without talking to him, that Rafe did, too.

And it wasn't just because she was pretty. Morgan liked women, enjoyed their company, but that was as far as it went. Nothing emotional or lasting. And if ever he began to think differently, all he had to do was talk to his brother, Russell. It had taken Russell years to finally get free of Adell, his children dragged through it all. No, it wasn't because she was pretty. It was her spirit.

When he showed up again tonight, she wasn't going to be happy, because she'd taken a particular dislike to him. Even after he'd saved her daughter, rescued them from hours of walking in the heat, taken her to his parents' house for revival, driven her to the ranch headquarters... He smiled to himself, remembering how her eyes had flashed resentment almost every step of the way.

He turned onto the packed gravel drive of the compound and stopped in front of the big house. Old Shep, the cow-dog who'd been Rafe's friend and companion for the past sixteen years, pulled himself up off the porch and came to greet him.

"Hey, Shep," Morgan said, taking time to rub the dog's head. "How're you doin', boy?" he asked. A warm pink tongue licked his wrist. He patted the dog's side. "Gonna miss you on the spring roundup. Last time I was on one, you were right along with us. But then I guess you deserve your retirement. Sleepin' late, eatin' good food, gettin' lots of rest."

Shep's ropelike tail wagged as he looked up at Morgan.

Morgan laughed and went to the door, where he knocked and waited. How many times had he done this over the years? He couldn't remember the first time. He'd always trailed after his dad, and as foreman, his dad had virtually had a second home at ranch headquarters. And since Rafe and Morgan were almost the same age, and Rafe had trailed after *his* father, it was only natural that the two boys would be fast friends, as close as brothers. In some ways, he and Rafe were closer than he and Russell had ever been. Russell had pursued other interests and had gone on to be an engineer. To Rafe and Morgan growing up, working cattle and being on the land were the most important things in the world. As necessary as breathing.

Shannon answered the door. Although his dad thought she was "quite a little filly," Morgan had been a bit leery when he'd come home last fall to visit his parents and found Rafe head over heels in love.

"Morgan!" Shannon exclaimed. "Did you forget

something? Rafe's still in talking with Mae. I'm sure you don't have to guess what about.''

Morgan stepped inside and smiled. Much to his relief, he'd liked Shannon instantly. She and Rafe were a good match. They fitted each other perfectly. ''Actually, I brought this.'' He showed her the toy horse with the long flowing mane and tail. ''Little Erin forgot it in the truck.''

Shannon glanced up the stairs. ''They haven't come down again yet.''

''Would you give it to her?'' he asked, holding it out.

''Of course.''

At that moment Rafe came striding up to them. ''Mae was riled enough to get on the phone and call Abigail, and she got herself an earful. Seems this Ms. Christine Grant has lived in Ira's house for the past eight months—her and the girl—with her posing as his secretary-assistant. Abigail says she's never trusted her. That if she's here, we should nail everything down, because she's out for all she can get. Then Mae asked her if the child could be Ira's, which shut Abigail up pretty quick.'' He rubbed the back of his neck. ''I just wish I could stand Abigail and her brother. As it is, I'm not sure how much their word's worth. Ira was a good person, but his kids...''

Shannon leaned against him. ''Now how does Ira fit into the family tree?''

''He was one of Virgil Parker's descendants,'' Rafe said, naming one of the two brothers who had originally founded the ranch. ''Ira was a little younger than Mae. Seventy-nine, I think, when he died a week or so ago. None of us were told about it at the time, so nobody went to the funeral. Mae's still ticked off about that, and while she had Abigail on the phone, she railed at her pretty good." He paused. "Now Mae wants to hire a detective to look into Christine Grant's history. Says we'll prosecute if he finds anything useful."

"She might be jumping the gun a bit," Morgan said mildly.

Rafe's dark eyes fastened on him. "What did you learn about her?" he asked.

"Not a lot. Her car broke down out by the station-six windmill. I found 'em walking and brought 'em in. Gave 'em a drink of water at our place, then brought 'em here."

"Nothing else?"

Morgan hesitated. He knew Rafe was asking for his expert opinion. As a field inspector for the Texas Cattlemen's Association, he was trained to ferret out wrongdoers. Morgan shrugged. "It'd be a good idea to check her out of course. If you want me to, I'll—"

Rafe interrupted. "I think you have enough on your hands right now, what with Dub being stove up and giving everyone a hard time, and me needing you for the roundup. I can't afford to let you leave right now, Morgan."

"Then someone else. I can ask around for a name or two."

"Do that."

"Otherwise," Morgan continued, "I don't get the feeling she's the kind of person to take somethin' that's not hers. Now, she could be foolin' me, but—"

"That tells me what I wanted to know—for now, at least, since she's staying in the big house. It goes along with what I thought, too."

"The little girl...Erin," Shannon said slowly. "She truly does look like a Parker. All those old photographs from the family history Mae and I are compiling, not to mention Wesley and Gwen."

"I saw that first thing," Rafe said.

Morgan lifted the toy horse again, ready to hand it to Shannon, when Christine Grant appeared at the top of the stairs. Her steps halted abruptly when she saw the three of them assembled in the entryway.

She *was* pretty, Morgan reflected, no doubt about it. With her chestnut hair and her wide hazel eyes and a face that in all likelihood had haunted many a man's dreams. Not to mention her body.

Morgan swallowed, suddenly discomfited by his thoughts.

Christine's gaze went immediately to the toy horse, and she came downstairs, stopping directly in front of Morgan.

"Did you drive all the way back to bring Golden Belle?" she asked, removing the horse from his unresisting fingers.

For some reason Morgan had a hard time answering. "Yes," he finally managed.

She smiled tightly. "Then I have to thank you. Erin just realized she'd forgotten her. I was on my way—" a long glance at Shannon, a brief one at Rafe "—to ask someone to call you. Erin's in tears right now, worried she'll never see her again."

"Tell her we keep a pretty good eye on things that

are entrusted to us out here," Rafe said, his response edged.

Christine Grant had no trouble picking up on the message. "What was it Ira told me about the Parkers? Oh, yes—that you were the salt of the earth."

Then she turned to go back upstairs. Only to stop once again to glance at Morgan. "I do sincerely thank you," she said.

The three of them watched her until she disappeared from view.

At that point Shannon frowned and asked, "What did she mean by that?"

Rafe's smile was ironic. "I think we've just been told that we aren't...the salt of the earth," he explained at Shannon's continued look of confusion. Then his smiled broadened as he thumped Morgan on the shoulder. "But *you* are," he teased.

"Nah," Morgan said. "She can't stand the sight of me."

"That's not the way it looked from over here."

"Then you need to get your eyes tested," Morgan said gruffly, and went back out to the truck.

He started it and drove away. And for the first time since coming back to help out while his father was injured, once he reached the road he let himself revert to type and pressed the accelerator to the floor. Dust flew high into the air behind the racing wheels.

He'd forgotten how good it felt to let go.

CHAPTER FOUR

CHRISTINE AWOKE shortly before eight the next morning and was amazed that she'd slept at all. Unfamiliar house, unfamiliar bed, unaccustomed noises. She wasn't used to the far-off howl of a coyote or the old-fashioned twice-hourly striking of a grandfather clock in the hall just beyond the door.

Yet the arrival of a new day did nothing to change yesterday's problems. As she'd more than half expected, she was going to have a battle on her hands. The Parkers weren't at all pleased to see her. Although they hadn't shown themselves to be spiteful, like Abigail and Brendan, it might be only a matter of time before the nastiness began. She had to be prepared for anything.

She glanced at Erin, who was still asleep in the bed next to hers, and debated whether to wake her. They hadn't put in an appearance downstairs last night. Erin had already been through so much Christine hadn't wanted to heap more strain on her. The worst, from Erin's perspective, had come when she thought she'd lost Golden Belle. She'd collapsed on the bed in a storm of tears that had stopped only when the newly reclaimed horse had been slipped into her hands. Another wave of tears followed, but these were tears of happiness and relief. This morning the palomino was still clasped tightly to her chest.

Christine decided to let Erin sleep while she bathed and dressed. A return to the real would come soon enough. She gathered the same shorts and shirt she'd worn yesterday. She had no choice but to wear them again. Her suitcase was in the car and the car was out by the "border to Indian Wells." Wasn't that what Morgan Hughes had told his father? She would give a lot to be able to change into a respectable-looking skirt and blouse, and take time with her hair and makeup—to correct the negative impression she knew she'd already created. But it probably wouldn't do any good. Like everyone else, the Parkers would believe what they wanted to believe.

Erin awoke as Christine came back into the room. Her eyelids fluttered open to a moment of confusion, before she remembered where she was. She immediately sat up. "We're still here!" she said. "I dreamed we were back in Houston, with Ira and Mrs. Tobin, and—"

"We're still here," Christine confirmed, smiling fondly as she crossed to sit on the edge of the bed.

Erin frowned. "I don't know if I like this place."

"You haven't been here long enough to tell."

"That lady—the older one—I don't know if I like her, either."

Christine smoothed back her daughter's dark hair. "Why don't you go take a bath. I did and I feel great. You will, too. Then we'll go down and see about breakfast. Are you hungry?"

"Will that lady be there?" Erin asked, her expression dubious.

"Probably. Possibly. I have no idea."

Erin slid out of bed and padded barefoot and in her panties to the bathroom.

"You'll have to wear what you did yesterday," Christine called after her.

"Ew-w!" Erin replied.

Christine chuckled. "Don't fuss. That's what I'm doing."

Someone tapped on the door. Erin squeaked and closed herself inside the bathroom, while Christine went to answer it.

Shannon stood in the hall holding a tray. On it was a carafe of coffee, two cups and a glass of orange juice.

"Good morning!" she greeted Christine brightly. "I thought you might like a little help getting started this morning." She proffered the tray. "And something to wear." She tapped the suitcase at her feet with a slippered toe. "Rafe had LeRoy—LeRoy's one of his cousins—haul your car to the ranch. It's here now, in the garage out by the barn. LeRoy will take a look at it later to see if he can fix it. He's a miracle worker with engines."

Christine took possession of the tray and glanced around the room for a place to put it.

"Marie will make breakfast whenever you want it," Shannon said, "but I remember my first morning here. A cup of coffee first thing would have been welcome."

Christine set the tray on the low chest of drawers,

whose heavy dark wood gleamed with polish. "Thank you," she murmured.

"And this, too, I believe." Shannon scooted the suitcase into the room.

"Yes."

A silence fell, then Shannon asked, "Would you mind if I share your coffee? I've brought enough for two." But when Christine didn't respond, she murmured, "Then again, maybe you need more than one cup to get started in the morning. I—I'll just leave you to enjoy it. There'll be plenty of time later to talk. When you—"

"Is Rafe having the car repaired so he can get rid of us?" Christine interrupted.

Shannon frowned. "Of course not."

"There's no 'of course not' to it. I know everyone here would rather see the back of us. And the sooner, the better, I'd be willing to bet."

"Rafe told you last night that you were welcome to stay while he and Mae—"

"People have a way of changing their minds."

"Not Rafe. When he says something, he means it."

"To you, maybe."

"To everyone! Rafe is the most honest trustworthy man I've ever—"

"And how do I know I can trust you?" Christine challenged.

Shannon stared at her, wide-eyed. Finally she admitted, "You don't."

Christine allowed a small smile. "Now you understand my problem."

Shannon seemed taken aback. "You're wrong. About Rafe, about me—"

The bathroom door opened and a freshly bathed Erin came into the room. Wrapped in a large white towel that dragged on the floor, she regarded Shannon with unconcealed wariness.

Christine took the situation in hand. She swung the suitcase onto her bed and, opening it, began to search through the hastily packed clothing. "Guess what, Erin," she said with feigned brightness. "Our suitcase has arrived! Now we have fresh clothes to wear!"

Shannon went to the door. "Mae's in her office and Rafe's gone to town," she said quietly. "No one will disturb you while you eat breakfast, and I—I'll stay out of your way, too."

Christine could hear the hurt her rebuff had caused the other woman, and it pricked her conscience. They couldn't have been more than two or three years apart in age. Shannon was maybe twenty-seven or twenty-eight. But she was a Parker—or as good as. And even though she had been nice last night and had made kind overtures this morning, she wasn't on Christine's and Erin's side.

As a sop to her conscience, Christine did what she'd done the evening before when that abrasive Morgan Hughes had turned up with Golden Belle—she fell back on straightforward politeness. "Thank you for bringing the coffee and juice," she said. "And the suitcase."

Shannon's cornflower blue eyes were steady as she paused, her hand on the doorknob. "You're welcome," she said. Then she stepped into the hall, shutting the door softly behind her.

CHRISTINE AND ERIN found their way to the dining room, where two places had been set at a long table. A table whose dark heavy wood was repeated in a sideboard. Both were echoes of the Spanish flavor at work throughout the house, from the subtle undercurrent in Mae Parker's office to the more overt influences of the black wrought-iron chandelier and stair railing in the entryway to the brightly colored rugs on the gray stone floors.

The housekeeper—a plump middle-aged woman with short curly brown hair and an austere demeanor—came through from the kitchen just as Christine was seeing Erin into her chair. "So you're up," she said.

There was no subservience in her manner. Only a cool formality, which made it obvious that she knew the reason Christine and Erin were here, and, naturally, sided with the Parkers.

"Yes," Christine replied.

"And now you're ready for breakfast. What would you like? Eggs, bacon, toast?"

"Just toast for me, please" Christine said, "and cereal for Erin. Any kind of dry will do."

"Dry cereal—out of a box? For a growing little girl?" The housekeeper sounded appalled.

Christine held on to her patience. "Yes. She likes it."

The housekeeper went back into the kitchen, shaking her head.

"I would have eaten an egg, Mommy," Erin whispered.

"I know, but you shouldn't have to, not if you'd rather have cereal. The Parker Ranch is our home now, Erin. We have to start like we mean to go on, otherwise—"

The housekeeper—Marie, Christine remembered—reentered the room, carrying a larger version of the round serving tray Shannon had brought to their room earlier. Balancing it on one hip, she served the table, performing the duty as if she'd been doing it for years, which she probably had—on this ranch, in this room. She had the aura of an old retainer, a quality shared by Ira's Mrs. Tobin.

Thinking of Mrs. Tobin made Christine yearn for the time they'd spent in Ira's house and for the kindnesses the elderly housekeeper and Ira had shown them. Not once had either of them questioned Christine's motives or made disparaging remarks.

"If I've forgotten something, tell me," Marie said, standing back.

Christine glanced at the bowl of cornflakes served to Erin, along with the pitcher of milk, sugar, fresh fruit and a glass of orange juice—all within easy reach of the little girl. And closer to herself, the stack of toast, obviously made from homemade bread, along with butter and several varieties of jams and jellies. "Thank you," she murmured. "I'm sure that's everything."

Christine wasn't at all hungry, but aware that she was setting an example for Erin, she spread plum jelly on a thick piece of toast and started to eat it. Erin followed suit, adding milk and sugar to her cereal and several of the fresh strawberries.

Surprisingly, or not so surprisingly, since neither of them had done much justice to the beef stew that had been sent to their room last night, their appetites picked up, and plates and bowl were soon emptied.

At that point Christine sat back, smiling. But before she could utter a word, a man and woman, both in their early thirties, came into the room. The man had the look of Rafe and Mae Parker—thick dark hair, intense black eyes, the same familial features. But where Rafe Parker was long and lean, this man was of average height and stocky. The woman, tall and strong-looking, had short hair almost the same color as Christine's and wide-spaced gray eyes.

Her curious gaze took in everything at once—the relaxed way Christine and Erin had been sitting, their instant alertness, the clothes they were wearing. Her gaze lingered longest on Erin, though, and Christine saw her eyelids flicker.

"You're Christine, right?" the man said. The way he presented himself—shifting restlessly from foot to foot, his worn Stetson held tightly by the brim—revealed his discomfort in social situations. "I'm LeRoy Dunn, Rafe's cousin. He asked me to tow your car to the ranch this mornin'. And this here's my wife, Harriet. She wanted to come along an' meet you."

Christine started to rise.

"No, don't do that," LeRoy urged, seemingly genuinely concerned at the idea of causing an interruption. "We're only gonna be here a minute. I came to tell you I had a quick look at your car, and…well, I can't make any promises. The engine's got a lot of miles on it. But I'll see what I can do."

"If anybody can fix it, LeRoy can," Harriet said confidently. "As LeRoy said, I'm Harriet." She extended her hand, her smile friendly yet with a touch of reserve.

Christine clasped it lightly.

LeRoy spoke again. "I also came to ask what you want me to do with the stuff you've got stowed inside—in the trunk and on the back seat. There're some boxes and other things. You want me to bring them all up here?"

Christine did stand now. She felt at a disadvantage sitting down. "No, that's all right," she said. "I'll get them myself."

LeRoy frowned. "It's a long way and they're kinda heavy. I picked one up to see."

"Still, I'd rather—"

"Let her do it herself, LeRoy," Harriet said, unexpectedly taking Christine's side. "If that's what she wants."

"It's what I want," Christine confirmed.

Two more people joined the gathering, exchanging hellos with LeRoy and Harriet while at the same time eyeing Christine and Erin: an older man, in his late fifties, with salt-and-pepper hair—obviously a Parker, too—and a much younger woman, in her late teens, tall and delicately made, with a mass of copper red hair and gaminelike features. Christine began to feel overwhelmed. Just how many Parkers were there on the ranch?

"We came to see what all the hoo-ha was about!"

the older man said jovially. "I haven't seen Aunt Mae this exercised in months. Not since—" He glanced at the younger woman and shut up.

The younger woman's face froze for a moment, then with a shake of her head, she put whatever it was behind her and said, "My name's Jodie Parker. And this is my dad."

"I'm Gib," he said, and tipped the front of his hat.

Christine glanced at Erin to see how she was faring. She wasn't surprised to find the girl slumping in her chair, trying for invisibility. "Yes, well—" she murmured, then couldn't think of anything more to say.

Everyone else seemed equally tongue-tied. Then Jodie walked over to Erin's chair and, crouching down beside her, said, "I heard you had quite an adventure yesterday. That your car broke down and you ended up walking and you almost got bitten by a snake."

Erin nodded without looking up.

"And Morgan gave you a ride to his place in Little Springs on his horse."

Again Erin nodded. This time, though, she looked up, and Jodie Parker smiled.

Here was someone who didn't fit into the Parker mold, Christine thought as she watched the young woman interact with her daughter. With her bright hair, willowy frame and mischievous smile, Jodie was a cuckoo in the Parker nest.

"Do you like horses?" Jodie asked.

Scooting up in the chair, Erin nodded vigorously. Instinctively Jodie had known the right tactic to win the girl over.

"We have a horse here—Junior," Jodie went on.

"He's great for learning how to ride. I learned on him and maybe you can, too. Would you like that?"

Christine stirred uneasily, and after a quick look at her tense expression, Erin retreated to silence.

Jodie followed the direction of the little girl's glance and frowned. She slowly straightened.

It wasn't that Christine was against Erin's learning to ride. It was just...she didn't feel comfortable letting her get too close too soon to any of these people. She didn't want her to be hurt if... Christine stiffened her spine. There would be no *if!*

"So," LeRoy said, filling in the awkward silence, "how'd you end up at the station-six windmill? What road there is peters out there."

"We had a map," Christine murmured.

"Musta not been a very good one," Gib remarked.

"Who gave it to you?" Harriet asked. "Ira?"

"He hasn't been here in years." LeRoy exclaimed. "No wonder you got lost!"

"It might not have been him." Christine was quick to jump to Ira's defense. "It was probably me. I must have—"

"*What in the name of heaven...*" Mae's voice cracked like a whip, making everyone in the room jump. She pushed her way through the gathering, then turned. "I don't remember calling a meeting! Did I forget? Or did all of you just decide to come over so you could see things for yourselves? Well, now you have, so get going! Unless you don't have enough work to do..."

The room started to clear. Mae might be an old lady, but a sharp word from her got everyone bustling.

"Harriet, I'd like you to stay, please," Mae decreed. "And you, too, Shannon."

Christine hadn't seen Shannon slip into the room, but at some point she must have, possibly entering with Mae.

At the door Jodie looked over her shoulder and winked at Erin. A glimmer of a smile touched Erin's lips, only to disappear when Mae took a seat just inches away at the head of the table.

A subtle signal called Erin to Christine's side, and they immediately started for the door.

"Where are you going?" Mae demanded.

Christine's hand tightened on Erin's shoulder as they stopped and turned. "Back to our room. Do you have a problem with that?"

"I want a word with you. The child is free to go."

Christine looked down into Erin's worried face. "If I stay, Erin stays."

"That might not be advisable," Mae said darkly.

Christine felt the weight of all three women's eyes. Was Mae testing her to see what kind of mother she was? What she was willing to expose her daughter to?

"My two kids are playing outside," Harriet volunteered. "They're near the same age, so they'd probably get along fine."

Erin edged closer to Christine. Too much was happening too soon for her. Too many new people in too new of a situation, people who she realized didn't want them there.

"I'd rather take her to our room," Christine insisted.

Harriet and Shannon exchanged glances, and Mae's

lips tightened. "Little Wesley and Gwen aren't good enough for her to play with?" Mae challenged.

Christine frowned. "It's not that—"

Mae waved her away. "Oh, go on. Do what you must. But I still want a word with you."

"I'll be back," Christine promised.

Outside the room, Erin whispered unevenly, "Let's go home to Houston, Mommy. As soon as we can.... Let's just get in the car and go!"

Christine went down on one knee and, catching hold of her daughter's chin, tipped it up to look steadily into Erin's tearful dark eyes. "Honey, I know things don't seem very promising right now, but this is exactly when we have to be the strongest. It's like when you started school last term—you had to wear a uniform, and you had to get used to the nuns. You didn't like that at first, either, then you settled in and started to enjoy it."

"That lady said Ira was my daddy, but he wasn't my daddy...was he?"

Christine braced herself to answer. She had hoped, with the situation as volatile as it had been last night, that particular question had gone completely over Erin's head. It hadn't. "Ira wasn't your daddy, sweetheart," she said gently. "But he was a nice man, a very nice man who wanted us to come live on the ranch. Remember all the stories he told you? How much you enjoyed them?"

Erin wiped away a tear. "Yes. But Ira said the people who lived here were nice, too. And they're not!"

"Maybe they're just surprised by what's happened,

and it will take them a little time to get used to it—and to us."

"Like when I started school last year."

Christine kissed her daughter's forehead. "Exactly," she agreed, standing up. It galled her to have to make excuses for the Parkers, but if it helped settle Erin's mind, she'd do it.

They were just about to the stairs when the front door opened and two young children tumbled inside. One, a boy of about six or seven, with dark hair and dark eyes. The second, a girl, possibly a year younger, with the same dark hair, but with eyes a luminous shade of gray, exactly like Harriet Dunn's.

The children's bubbling laughter stopped abruptly when they saw Christine and Erin. "Who are you?" the little girl asked, being the first of the two to collect herself. "Are you a friend of Shannon's? There's gonna be a wedding, but not until June. She's already said I can be the flower girl."

"She said I can be the ring bear!" the boy bragged.

"Bear-*er*," the girl corrected.

"That's what I said!"

"You said *bear*," the girl insisted. "He did, didn't he?" She looked to Christine and Erin for confirmation.

Christine couldn't suppress a smile. More Parkers, but at least these had a certain charm.

"It's probably subject to interpretation," Christine murmured.

"What's that mean?" the girl asked.

"It means I was right!" the boy claimed.

"It means you both could be," Erin said shyly.

The little girl tilted her head to the side. "Are you gonna stay here for a while?" she asked Erin directly.

Erin shrugged.

"Do you know who our momma is?" the boy quizzed Christine. "And if you do, have you seen her?"

"'Cause if you are," the girl continued as if her brother hadn't spoken, "we could play together. Jessica's gonna be going away the beginning of summer. She's been visiting her grandma and grandpa at Little Springs. She and her brother and little sister are gonna go live with their daddy in Colorado just as soon as school's out."

Erin's reply was another shrug.

The little girl frowned. Just like the adults, she seemed puzzled by the Grants' unwillingness to be persuaded by a friendly overture.

"Wesley! Gwen! What are you doing?" The demand came from Harriet, who was coming down the hall. Her face reflected a variety of emotions—irritation, consternation, frustration. Not caused by the scene she'd come upon, Christine sensed, rather the one she'd just left.

"We were just talkin'," Wesley said.

"Didn't I tell you I'd be right out?" Harriet asked.

Both children's chins fell. "You did. And we waited," Gwen said. "But it got to be so long we thought we'd come in and see if it was okay with you if we asked Marie for some chocolate cookies. She told us she bought a tin the other day, and we should come over sometime soon to eat some."

Harriet brushed stray strands of hair away from her

daughter's forehead and sighed. "The two of you and those cookies!"

"They're really good, Mom," the pair said almost in unison.

Harriet finally broke into a smile. If Christine had known her better, she'd have said the woman looked tired and possibly a little fed up.

"I know," Harriet said, then glanced at Christine, pleading silently for motherly understanding as she gave in. "All right. Two cookies each and that's it! And be sure to thank Marie for sharing them."

The children yipped in delight and disappeared into the dining room on their way to the kitchen. A moment later Gwen came back. "You want some, too?" she asked Erin.

Erin shook her head.

"It's all right," Christine said, giving her permission.

Erin continued to shake her head.

An awkward moment followed. Harriet ended it by shrugging and saying, "Kids!"

Christine smiled tautly. It bothered her that Erin had become so solitary, that she seemed to prefer her own company to that of other children. Partly it was due to personality, partly to the life they'd been forced to lead. This was their fifth move.

She urged the little girl upstairs, and in the relative safety of their room, settled her as best she could with her toys before going back down to present herself to Mae.

Mae and Shannon sat at the table, an array of magazines spread out before them. Even from where

Christine stopped just inside the door, she could see that they were discussing the upcoming wedding.

"Pink it is," Mae proclaimed, sitting back in her chair as if there needed to be no more discussion.

"I don't like that shade of pink," Shannon said with vexed amusement. "You know that." She turned a few pages. "There. See? That's what I want."

"Looks pink to me!" Mae said stubbornly.

"Mae!"

A whisper of a smile twitched the corners of Mae's lips—the first time Christine had seen a lightening of her expression. But that look quickly disappeared when Mae's eaglelike gaze swung to her. Shannon, too, raised her head, but her gaze contained no combativeness.

"So you did come back," Mae declared, as if there'd been a doubt.

"I said I would," Christine murmured.

"And you always do what you say?" Mae scoffed.

"I do."

Their gazes locked, silently battling. Then Christine picked up an almost imperceptible narrowing of the older woman's eyes, as if Mae was taking a moment to reassess.

"Then I guess maybe you'd better sit down," Mae said at last.

Christine wouldn't do it. She wouldn't do anything the other woman directed her to.

Mae's lips tightened and she came directly to the point. "I spoke with your lawyer, Mr. Hernandez. He refuses to send us a copy of Ira's will. It would behoove you to get on the phone and straighten him out.''

"I didn't tell him not to give you a copy of the will.''

"And while you're at it,'' Mae carried on harshly, "tell him that if he's not careful, I'll have his ears pinned to the wall. I'm not without influence in this state.''

"He's not my lawyer!'' Christine denied heatedly. "I'm not responsible for the way—''

"He's acting on your behalf.''

"He's acting on *Ira's* behalf!''

"*For* you.''

Christine drew a steadying breath. She wanted to yell at the woman for being so difficult, but she knew it would do her no good. Instead, she stated crisply, "I never asked Ira to give me a thing.''

"That's not what his kids say.''

Ira's "kids''! Mae had talked to Abigail and Brendan? But then, wasn't that exactly what she'd do in her place? "If they said I did, they're lying,'' she denied.

Mae smiled like a cat happily digesting a canary. "Oh, they said that and a lot more. But I'm sure you'd accuse them of lying about everything else, too.''

"Probably, if you'd tell me what it is.''

"All in good time, my dear,'' Mae said smoothly. "All in good time.''

Shannon gathered together the magazines and stood. "I have to get back to work, Mae,'' she said quietly. "And since you don't need me here...''

"I've said all I planned,'' Mae replied. "Except to

ask for a copy of Erin's birth certificate.'' She looked straight at Christine, daring her to refuse.

"Will my ears be pinned to a wall, too, if I refuse?" Christine challenged.

"Don't tempt me," Mae murmured, a dark light glimmering in her eyes.

CHRISTINE AND SHANNON left the dining room together, their footsteps sounding hollow on the stone floor. Christine could sense that Shannon wanted to say something to her, and finally she did.

"She's not as fierce as she sometimes seems, you know. She's just protective of the ranch and the family."

Christine spun to face her. "What is she?" she demanded. "Some kind of dictator? Her word is law? Is everyone here afraid of her?"

"Not everyone, no," Shannon said quietly.

"Are you?"

"No, but we've come to an understanding." Shannon paused. "I just want you to realize…if you're telling the truth, you don't have anything to worry about. But if you're lying—"

"Ira left me a share of the ranch in his will," Christine repeated yet again.

Something in Shannon's gaze flickered. "Yes, well…" she murmured, then said nothing more.

CHRISTINE RETURNED to the guest room to find Erin stretched out on her bed napping. The past few days— the past week!—had been hard for her.

Restlessly Christine went to the open balcony door

and stepped outside. It was already hot, even though it was barely ten o'clock. Somewhere in the distance, she could hear men's voices. Yips and calls and snatches of laughter.

The Parker Ranch.

She hadn't even known of its existence a week ago. Now she and Erin were living on it, staking a claim.

Nothing had come easy to Christine. She'd had to fight hard for whatever she got. And this she was willing to fight even harder for, because it was her chance to give Erin a better life, a secure future, which a week ago she'd only dreamed about.

With that thought, Christine turned on her heel and went in search of a telephone. If they wanted a copy of the will, they would have a copy of the will. Erin's birth certificate, though, was a completely different matter.

CHAPTER FIVE

MORGAN WAITED for Rafe in the ranch's business office, his long form stretched out in the old metal chair. His hands were clasped behind his head, his hat was tipped over his face, and his feet were propped on the edge of the desk. Shep dozed on a cedar bed in the corner.

If a casual observer concluded that Morgan was dozing, too…well, he was! Last night had been a difficult one. His dad had had a lot of trouble with his arm. It had throbbed and ached, and in general, given him hell. And Dub, in turn, had given hell to everyone else.

A muscle pulled in Morgan's cheek. His mother was about at the end of her rope. She'd spent nearly a year taking care of Russell's kids, and she'd never once complained. But he could see how tired she was deep down. Keeping up with three young kids had taken its toll. The youngest had been still in diapers when she'd first arrived, the oldest starting to assert his independence—not to mention all of them being emotionally shell-shocked from their parents' long killing field that was legally termed a divorce. Then to top the situation off—his father's accident. It was a testament to his mother's pluck that she was still standing. He'd been shocked to see the fresh array of lines on her face, and the way her hands had trembled uncontrollably when he'd rushed home after learning that his father was in critical condition in the hospital. Like his father, his mother had always been a rock. But she was in her sixties now, as was Dub.

"Hey! I don't pay you to sleep on the job!" Rafe teased delivering with a solid thump to the soles of Morgan's boots.

Morgan jerked upright, swinging his feet to the floor and sliding his hat to the back of his head. "An' here I was thinkin' that's just what you'd done," he drawled. "Nice chair, nice desk, nice quiet office..."

"You're gettin' as bad as Shep." Rafe motioned fondly to the still-sleeping dog. "Hey, Shep!" he called, clapping his hands.

The big dog's head shot up. He blinked, then lumbered to his feet and ambled over to the human he loved most in the world. His tail wagged as Rafe rubbed his head and ears.

Rafe grinned. To Morgan he said, "I got the rest of the men for the roundup. Now that makes the same six extras as we had last fall. They were a pretty good group. Knew their stuff. Got along okay with the regulars."

"Dad told me they were good. Not a lot of sneakin' drinks or fighting. You set the exact date yet?"

Rafe dropped into the well-used chair behind the desk. "Well, this year, considering the wedding and everything, I thought maybe we'd get started a little early. Maybe move it up a week, say to the end of the month. That okay with you?"

Morgan rubbed his cheek with a long finger, considering all he'd done in preparation and all he had yet to do. "Sure. That's fine by me."

Rafe frowned. "There's also something else. Something I'm just catching wind of. Seems like we might have ourselves some cattle rustlers startin' to work the area. Been a few hits over toward Debolt." He named a section of the next county that could, on a relative scale, be considered neighboring ranch land.

"Ed looking into it?" Morgan asked, his professional interest caught. Ed Davis was Morgan's counterpart for the cattlemen's association in this region of the state.

"Sheriff Denton's checkin' it out. I told him to let us know what he finds. In the meantime, though, maybe you'd better tell the men to keep a closer eye out for strangers."

"I'll do that."

Rafe looked at him for a few moments, then asked, "How's Dub? I thought he was coming over with you today."

"He was, but his arm hurt him pretty bad last night."

Rafe winced, almost as if it were his arm. "Damn, I hate that."

"Yeah, so does he."

"I'll stop by and see him later. Let him harass me— that always used to perk him up."

Morgan smiled. His father had always loved to tease, and the more he liked you, the more he teased. Rafe, he considered a third son.

"I don't know what's going to happen to him,

Rafe,'' Morgan said, turning serious. "I don't know what's going to happen to either of my parents. For the first time in her life Mom seems at a loss."

"You know what she wants," Rafe said quietly.

Morgan shifted position. "Yeah, I know."

"She wants you to come home for good. She wants you here in case your daddy can't do like he used to."

"She doesn't want me taking chances and gettin' shot at any more, either."

Rafe leaned back and propped his own feet on the desk. "Which puts me in a bad position. Hell, I was at your house as much as I was here when we were growing up. Your mom and dad are almost as much my family as yours. But I can't tell you you should give up your job. What you're doing right now is a lot more than most sons would."

"Maybe it's a guilty conscience for not visiting much over the past few years."

Rafe snorted and shook his head. "You had a job to do, one you're good at. They understood. Dub sure did. He's proud of you."

Morgan went to stand in the open doorway. The office was small, an afterthought partitioned off a long narrow storage building. But it was the nerve center of the working ranch. Across the way and to the right was the long low bunkhouse, where four of the single full-time cowboys lived, and to the rear of the bunkhouse was the cook house, overseen by Axel, the housekeeper's husband. To the left was the tack room and more storage, and directly across the way were the workshops. Beyond them, the working pens and corrals.

Morgan knew every nook and cranny of the place by heart. Almost every dusty rock. He had a feeling for it he couldn't explain. Just that it went deep, to his soul. When he was away, a part of him stayed behind, creating a void nothing else could fill.

"We've learned a little more about your girlfriend," Rafe said, reclaiming his attention.

Morgan scowled. "She's not my girlfriend."

"Seems she told the truth about the will. At least, the lawyer she has in Houston says it's true. Ira did leave a will and make a provision for her—a share in the ranch."

Morgan's scowl deepened. "Like Mae said, why would he do something like that when he knew he couldn't?"

Rafe shrugged.

"Do you think she'll be able to challenge the trust?" Morgan asked.

"Our lawyer says she can try, but it won't do any good. It's airtight."

Morgan reached into his shirt pocket. He handed Rafe a folded slip of paper. "Those names I told you about," he said.

"Investigators?"

"The first one's particularly reliable."

Rafe slipped the paper into his pocket. "I'll give it to Mae."

"You, ah, you think she was old Ira's mistress?"

Rafe considered the question. "He didn't seem the sort," he said slowly, "but then, when there's a pretty face involved..." Rafe let the sentence dangle. "You did notice she's right easy on the eyes."

Morgan kept his poker face. Much to his chagrin, even after the terrible night they'd all spent, upon awakening this morning Christine's image had been the first thing that had popped into his mind. "I suppose," he said casually.

Too casually? Or did Rafe know him just a little too well? Rafe raised a dark eyebrow and continued to look at him, silently probing.

He finally gave up. He got to his feet and clapped his friend on the shoulder. "Then again," he murmured, "a man would have to be dead not to notice."

Morgan teased, "You better not let Shannon hear you say that. Or else—"

"I said *notice*."

"—or else you could find yourself standing at the altar alone."

"I wouldn't be alone," Rafe said as they walked outside. "You'd be standin' right up there with me."

Morgan grinned. "You know, Rafe, as your best friend, not to mention havin' the honor of bein' your best man, there're a lot of things I'd do for you. But marryin' you ain't one of 'em."

Shep chose that moment to trot up beside them and bark, as if lending his support to Morgan.

Both men looked down and burst out laughing. Shep, for his part, shed about five years as he trotted jauntily beside them, seemingly proud that he'd elicited such a positive response.

"DO THE BEST YOU CAN, honey," Christine urged shortly after she and Erin had found their way out to the barn and beyond it, to the garage. Their car was sitting unattended a couple of slots over from a huge black Cadillac gleaming with polish. It had taken them only a few moments to collect their loose things from the backseat and stow them in the boxes in the trunk. But in her haste to leave Ira's house in Houston, Christine hadn't realized how heavy some of the boxes actually were.

"If it starts to get too heavy, put it down," she advised Erin, who was striving to maintain her hold on the lightest of the boxes. "That's what I'm going to do."

"I'm okay," Erin said.

If it hadn't been for her daughter's presence, Christine might have sat down on the cement floor and cried. Four small moving boxes and one suitcase—the full extent of their possessions. The paltriness of the collection was almost pathetic. No wonder Ira had taken pity on them.

She lifted her chin. No. She wasn't going to think that way. And she wasn't about to cry. There was nothing and no one who could get the better of her, not when she was determined. Not heavy boxes, not the blazing hot sun, not the distance the boxes would have to be carried to the compound. And, in particular, not Mae Parker.

The woman was doing her best to intimidate them. They'd eaten lunch with her, Shannon's buffering presence unavailable since she was having lunch with Rafe at his house. Mae'd sat in near silence, but Christine had carried on as if she and Erin were alone, speaking softly to her daughter, encouraging the little girl to follow her lead and eat. If the situation proved to be the same tomorrow, she was determined to ask Marie to pack them a picnic lunch, which they could eat outside under the trees.

Hugging their boxes, they made their way to the path connecting a group of long low work buildings to the compound, the head of which was Mae's house.

"Are you doing all right?" Christine asked.

"I'm fine," Erin replied, yet Christine could hear her daughter's labored breathing. She decided to call a halt. "Let's stop here for a minute," she said.

They were just about to lower their boxes when Harriet Dunn came rushing up to them. "Oh, this is too much!" the woman protested. "I know you said you wanted to do it yourself, but honestly, I'm surprised LeRoy let you out of the garage. Oh, that's right—he's off trying to round up some parts for your car. There are plenty of other people around, though. I know I saw Morgan just a few—"

Christine interrupted her. "We doing fine. We're just taking a rest."

Harriet looked skeptical. "I saw you from my kitchen window." She motioned to the house farthest away from where they stood, yet still on this side of the courtyard. "That's not the way it looked to me. These boxes are too heavy for you."

As if to underscore her words, the box Erin had been holding tumbled to the ground. A T-shirt and several pairs of socks spilled out, and the girl quickly bent to reclaim them.

"At the very least, let me help," Harriet pleaded. "I know it hasn't been exactly, well, easy for you since you came here. But—"

"Why?" Christine challenged. She was still smarting from Mae's treatment. "Why should you want to help?"

Harriet's gray eyes never wavered. "Shannon believes you're telling the truth. And if she does, I do, too. I trust her judgment."

"You mean you admit that we have a valid claim?"

Harriet shook her head. "That's not what I said. You can't, because it's not a legal possibility. But Shannon and I...we believe *you* believe it."

Christine released an impatient breath. That wasn't what she wanted to hear. "If it's all the same to you, I'd rather not waste time playing word games. I have more important things to do."

Harriet reached for Erin's box the same instant the girl did. "Let me, sweetheart," she said.

Erin looked across at her with big dark eyes, and Harriet gave her a smile that could reassure a stone.

Erin let go and Harriet straightened. "I'm ready," she announced.

Christine resented the intrusion, but what could she do? Demand that Harriet put the box down or she'd stand there and hold her breath until she did?

Christine proceeded silently down the path, but her silence did nothing to dull the other woman's determined friendliness. Harriet chattered on, seemingly unconcerned that she received no reply.

"Your little girl is eight, right? So she's probably in...what? Second or third grade? Wesley's turning seven this summer, but he hasn't started school yet. I held him back a year because it's nearly a two-hour bus ride each way, and I thought that was a bit much for such a young child. I'll probably do the same thing with Gwen, but then, with Wesley gone for most of the day she might get lonely. Even with the new baby…''

Harriet's words fell away, and Christine glanced at her. "You're pregnant?" she asked.

Harriet's smile dimmed, but quickly brightened again. "Yes," she said briefly, then returned to the previous subject. "The reason I'm asking is, since you're going to be here awhile, do you want to see about… Erin's your name, right?" she asked, turning to the little girl. "Do you want to see about enrolling Erin in school to finish the term?"

"I hadn't thought about it," Christine said, when in fact, removing Erin from school had been one of her more pressing worries. She didn't want her held back next year because of an incompletion.

They paused where the curving gravel drive met the narrow walkway to Mae's house. "She was enrolled in school where you lived before, wasn't she?" Harriet probed.

"Yes."

"Then all I'm saying is, if you want to get her into school here so she doesn't miss out, all you have to do is talk to Rafe. Or I'll talk to him for you if you want. One word from him to the school administrator and it's a done deal."

"Why's that?"

"Because…it just is." Harriet continued on to the house.

"Because he's a Parker," Christine said, following her. Obviously being a Parker of the Parker Ranch carried a lot of weight in West Texas. What they wanted, they got. "I'll think about it," Christine said tightly.

Harriet took her answer at face value. "Yes, do that. You have more boxes you need to move, don't you?" she asked as she opened the front door and held it wide so that Christine and Erin could pass.

Christine nodded. "Yes, but as I said before, we can—"

Harriet laughed. "You're on a ranch with a bunch of big strong men. Let 'em do what comes naturally!"

Harriet's two young children came running up, laughing and screeching as they jostled each other to get inside the house first. Harriet quickly put down her box and shooed them back to the porch.

"Hush!" she ordered. "What's gotten into you two? You know you're not supposed to—"

"I'm afraid it's my fault, Harriet," Morgan Hughes confessed as he bounded up the two steps onto the porch. "We had a race to see who could get here first." His encompassing glance caught sight of Christine and Erin inside in the entryway.

Christine wanted to turn away, but she couldn't. Her muscles wouldn't do what her brain directed. Instead, she stood, box in hand, staring at him like a mesmerized rabbit. He'd shifted back to being the dangerous male—untamed, overpowering, ruggedly sensual. A man it would be impossible to escape if he took it in mind to pursue you. Christine's heart beat a crazy tattoo until finally his blue eyes released her.

"And you'll tell that to Mae if she comes out of

her office breathing fire?'' Harriet challenged, but the fondness she had for Morgan was evident.

He slanted her a smile. "I sure will."

Harriet laughed and shook her head. "Morgan, there should be a law against men like you."

"I didn't do anythin'," he drawled.

"No," Harriet agreed, "but then, you don't have to. Women must drop like flies when you're around."

Christine had heard enough. She nudged Erin and they started for the stairs. If she didn't put the box down soon she was going to drop it, and she had no intention of putting it down here. She'd come back for Harriet's box later on—in the middle of the night if that was the only time she would be undisturbed. That was also when she'd get the remaining two boxes out of the car.

"Morgan, I have a favor to ask," Christine heard Harriet say, and she had a bad feeling about what was coming next. "Would you help Christine get the rest of her things from her car? She refused help earlier, but she needs it. What do you say? Do you have the time?"

Christine's steps faltered. "No!" she protested from halfway up the stairs, but the two people on the porch didn't hear her.

"Mae's asked to see me now," Morgan said. "But as soon as we're done, I'm at her service."

"Good," Harriet replied.

There was a slight pause. "You feelin' all right?" Morgan asked. "LeRoy's told us the good news. He's over the moon."

"Sure, I'm fine. Making babies is almost my hobby."

Another pause. "Well, take care of yourself. And congratulations."

"Thanks," Harriet said. "Now, as for you kids..." Her words grew muffled as she turned to discipline her children.

Morgan stepped into the house and immediately doffed his hat. From her position on the stairs, Christine could see golden strands gleaming among the darker shades of yellow and light brown on Morgan's head, and how the thick hair had at one time been cut to accentuate its natural curl. Light played over his handsome chiseled face, caressing the high cheekbones, the straight nose and the provocatively shaped mouth.

He looked up at her, his expression unsurprised. It was as if he'd known all along that she was watching him. His glance then moved to the cardboard box Harriet had left by the door. "This yours?" he asked.

His melodic voice shimmered through Christine's bloodstream. Denying what was happening to her, she shook her head.

"It's not?" he said dubiously.

"I—I don't want any help," she finally managed.

He ignored that and swept the box from the floor. Then he moved with effortless grace to the stairs, taking them two at a time before Christine could form another protest. "Well, let's get goin'," he teased as he moved the box under one arm and just as easily scooped Erin under the other, like a sack of potatoes.

"You're holdin' up the train!" he chided when all Christine could do was stare at him.

The man was as mercurial as the wind, she realized. One moment menacing, the next drop-dead sexy, the next as playful as the boy next door. She forced herself to move, walking ahead of him to the far guest room.

Initially Erin had been just as surprised by his behavior as Christine. Now, as Morgan set on her on her feet in the bedroom, she smiled. "That was fun," she said shyly.

"Sure it was," he said. He turned to Christine, patting the side of the box. "Where do you want this?" he asked.

She shrugged. "Over there. Over here. It really doesn't matter."

He arched an eyebrow—a nicely curved eyebrow. "You sure don't take much to bein' helped, do you? Why not?"

"And you certainly do enjoy asking a lot of questions."

"It's my nature," Morgan said. He set the box down and straightened to face her.

Christine's arms were going numb, but she was determined not to show any sign of weakness. From what she'd learned so far, there were three people on the ranch who would have the most influence on her life: Rafe and Mae Parker, and this man standing so stubbornly before her. He seemed to weld an inordinate amount of power for a hired hand, foreman or not. They treated him like a member of the family.

"Are you a Parker?" she demanded.

If her question surprised him he didn't show it. "No. Aren't you needing to put that down?"

But Christine persisted. "Not even from the wrong side of the sheets?" She used the old-fashioned term for the same reason that the old-timers had used it—to keep impressionable young ears from understanding.

"No...and if you don't put that box down, your arms are going to fall off," he said.

"I'll put it down when you leave," she told him.

"What if I decide to stay awhile and visit with Erin and ol' Golden Belle over there?" He indicated the toy horse Erin had left carefully positioned on her pillow. "Did your palomino enjoy her first night on the ranch?" he asked the little girl.

"Doesn't Mae want to see you?" Christine interjected before Erin could do more than nod.

Morgan's sky blue eyes swung back to her. "Are you trying to make me believe you really care what Mae wants?"

Christine did everything she could to hold his gaze, but failed. And to make matters worse, she fumbled the box, her fingers finally losing their grip.

Only his quick action kept it from hitting the floor. Leaping forward, he intercepted it, then settled it at their feet. Upon straightening, though, he didn't move away.

Christine's heart once again started to pound as something sparked between them, something instantly recognizable even though it had been years since she'd felt such a definite stirring. Everything in her became supersensitive to everything in him. And everything about him was exciting. The way he looked, the way he moved... When he reached out to touch her, his long capable fingers threading through the hair at the back of her neck, her breathing stopped. And even though his touch was whisper light, her skin burned from the contact. She forgot about her aching arms, about Erin standing a short distance away, about why she was at the ranch. There was only the moment, only the two of them.

Then she heard him saying something and she fought to comprehend. His voice was low, husky, intimate.

"...far better," he finished.

Christine had to swallow before she could speak. "Wh-what?" she breathed.

He smiled and another torrent of feeling cascaded through her. "I said," he murmured softly, so softly that only she could hear, "a young man makes a far better lover than an old one."

The meaning behind his words—what he was intimating, what he was offering—hit Christine with the force of a lightning bolt. She jerked away from him, shocked that she could allow herself to be so vulnerable.

"Get out!" she fumed, taking refuge in anger. "Go to Mae! Go to Mae and tell her—"

"Mommy?"

Her daughter's frightened voice gave them both a start. What Christine had been about to say and what Morgan might have replied was lost.

Christine looked at Erin, who'd moved nearer to her bed, a hand reaching out to Golden Belle for security. Christine tried to smile, but the effort was less than successful. "It...it's all right, Erin," she said. "We...Mr. Hughes and I—"

Morgan Hughes broke into her stumbled explanation. "I'm going. But as for Mae, that wasn't what this was about—any of it."

His gaze bored into her. Then to Erin he said easily, "I'll see you later, Erin. Maybe then we can go for another ride."

The room, empty of his presence, might have returned to being an ordinary room. The twin beds with their white cotton comforters, the heavy dark furniture with the Spanish flair, the bright woven rugs placed between the beds and in front of the door to the balcony. Except...it was difficult for Christine to rid herself of his image, and of the way she'd felt before and during the moment he'd touched her.

She'd cut herself off from men and from all the craziness associated with them. She'd seen too much. She wasn't going to be like her mother! *He has such pretty eyes, sweetie,* her mother would excuse. Or, *Did you hear the way he talked to me? Like a poet...he called me his nightingale!* And ultimately a slurred, *He bought me a drink, wasn't that nice?* Christine had heard enough excuses to last a lifetime. None of which could justify the procession of strangers who had passed through her mother's bed, and later on, as Christine grew older, occasionally resulted in her awakening to find one of them trying to crawl into bed with *her.*

Only once in her life had she let down her guard. She'd thought what was happening between them was different. But it wasn't. She wasn't going to let her guard be breached again.

CHAPTER SIX

"I'VE BEEN THINKING..." Mae was sitting behind her highly polished rosewood desk like a reigning queen, which she was and had been for much of her adult life. At one time she'd shouldered complete responsibility for the Parker Ranch and had done the job well—during the years between Rafe's father's death and her eventual abdication because of increasing age and failing health. Morgan himself had witnessed her ability to work cattle—as good as any man, his dad liked to say—as well as her business and political acumen.

Morgan waited for her next words, standing before her as his father, grandfather and great-grandfather had done with other heads of the family. There had been a Hughes working at the Parker Ranch for almost as long as there had been a Parker Ranch.

"What would you say," Mae continued, "to seeing what you can sniff out? I know you can't leave the ranch right now. But you wouldn't have to. The woman's right here. Talk to her. See if you can get her to tell you anything she won't tell us."

Morgan thought of what had passed between Christine and him in the room upstairs only moments ago. He hadn't meant it to happen. Something had just...

clicked. And the next thing he knew, the situation had gotten out of hand. Me Tarzan, you—

"You find that amusing?" Mae demanded, catching his unconscious smile.

Morgan immediately focused his thoughts. "Actually," he said, "I was thinking that it probably won't do any good. She puts me in the same category as she does you."

"As a Parker, you mean," Mae stated.

Morgan nodded.

"But you aren't," Mae said, "not by blood. And that could come to mean something if you played your cards right. You're trained for this kind of thing. You can do it."

"What exactly do you want me to find out?"

Mae twitched in her chair. "First, who that little girl's daddy is. If it's Ira, it puts a whole new complexion on everything. And second, who *she* is. Not just where she comes from and what schools she went to. I mean the deep stuff—what she thinks, what she's made of."

"That's a tall order, Mae. Particularly right now. The roundup—"

"I know what I'm asking of you, Morgan. But if I didn't have faith in you, I wouldn't do it. I'd like to have this all resolved by family meeting time."

"*This* family meeting time?" Morgan echoed, surprised by her rush. The date she was referring to was little more than six weeks away.

"I know, I know, and there's Rafe and Shannon's wedding happening at the same time. But I have that well in hand. What I don't have in hand is the wild card this little lady's thrown us."

"Did Rafe give you the list of investigators?"

"He did, and I've already placed a call. I think we can get to the bottom of this in a week or two if we just put our minds to it."

Morgan kept his doubts to himself. Mae didn't like to have her plans questioned.

The meeting was over and he was free to go, but Mae stopped him on his way out. "Rafe tells me your daddy's arm is hurting him. Does he need a trip to the medical center, do you think?"

"Mom talked to his doctor this morning. He says discomfort is typical, but if it keeps up, to come see him."

"Dang doctors, they never tell you much." Mae gave him a level look. "I was scared silly we were going to lose him. Laying out there on the range overnight, his head busted and his arm busted. He wasn't a pretty sight when we took him to the hospital, I can tell you. Then that long wait! Delores was afraid he was going to slip away before you even heard the news. By the by, did you get that rustler you were after then?"

"We got him," Morgan said, his lips tightening.

"Good," Mae said firmly. "Too bad we can't still string 'em up!"

THE TWO REMAINING moving boxes were sitting in the hallway outside their door when Christine and Erin ventured from the bedroom later that afternoon. Morgan—it had to have been Morgan—hadn't tapped on the door or anything. He'd just left them there, waiting to be found.

"We could have gotten them ourselves," Christine grumbled as she pushed the boxes into the room.

"I like him, Mommy," Erin said softly. "He's nice."

Christine took a calming breath. Erin didn't have any idea why her mother had reacted as she had earlier. She didn't understand the trap set by sexual attraction.

"I wouldn't go that far," she murmured.

"He is! He brought me Golden Belle, didn't he? And he helped us when we—"

Christine cut her off. "Did you hear that?" she asked, lifting a hand. "Did you hear a dog bark? I wonder if it's that big one we saw earlier?"

Erin liked dogs. She cocked her head to listen, and when she heard another bark, she said excitedly, "Let's go see!"

Pulling Christine by the hand, she dragged her to the head of the stairs, where both paused to peer down to the floor below. It was quiet. No one seemed to be about. They went downstairs quickly and hurried outside.

Sure enough, the big dog stood guard beneath one of the trees in the courtyard, his tail wagging as he looked up into the branches.

"What's he see?" Erin asked. "A squirrel?"

"I don't know. I'm not sure if there are tree squirrels out here. But I guess—"

A squirrel scampered down the trunk, ran a short

distance onto the grass and flicked its tail, daring the dog to come after it.

The dog barked again, made a halfhearted leap forward, then settled onto his stomach and whimpered softly.

The squirrel flicked its tail one final time before scurrying up the next tree.

"Why didn't he chase it, Mommy?" Erin asked. "The squirrel wanted to play!"

Christine frowned. "I don't know." Then as they drew nearer, she saw the reason. "Ah," she breathed. "He's old, Erin. Look at his muzzle. See how white it is? And the way he moves?" The dog had gotten up to come slowly toward them. "Hi, boy," Christine said in greeting.

The dog wagged his tail, then went straight to Erin and gazed at her with warm brown eyes.

Erin fell instantly in love. Dropping to her knees, she wrapped her thin arms around the dog's neck. "Hi, boy. What's your name? Mommy, isn't he sweet?" She giggled when a warm pink tongue darted out to lick the underside of her chin. "You like me too, don't you?" She giggled again when she was rewarded with another kiss.

"His name's Shep." The young woman they'd met earlier in the morning had approached them unnoticed. Faded jeans encased her long legs, her body-hugging T-shirt bore the logo of a country-rock band, and her mass of coppery hair cascaded to her shoulders. Her gaze was friendly, curious. "He's Rafe's dog," she said.

Christine automatically stiffened. When it came to

any member of the Parker family, she felt the need to be on guard.

Jodie smiled at the dog's behavior. "He likes you, Erin," she said. The young woman's gaze swept over Christine. "How're you settling in? Has Aunt Mae fired up the barbecue yet and measured you for the spit?" Jodie laughed at Christine's surprised expression. "I know how it works. Make the offender squeal and squirm. You had the nerve to come here and say something she didn't like. And now you've got to pay."

Was this a new approach, or was Jodie a true cuckoo in the nest—a Parker who didn't toe the family line? Christine shrugged and said noncommittally, "We're doing all right."

"Well, if things get too hot, come over to our place." She pointed out the house on the far side of the courtyard. "My dad and I live there. I'm usually home most of the time." She saw Christine's gaze move to the house next door to theirs, nearest Mae. "That's Rafe's place. He and Shannon—mostly Shannon, because he's so busy with the ranch right now— are redoing it inside. Harriet's helping her when she can. She lives over there." She pointed to the house Christine already knew was Harriet's. "And I help, too, sometimes. So can you, if you want. Shannon's getting worried that the place isn't going to be finished in time for the wedding. Not that it's all that big a deal. She practically lives over there now, anyway."

She paused, her eyes narrowing. "You're from Houston, right? I'm thinking of enrolling at Rice University there next fall. Aunt Mae wants me to go to the University of Texas in Austin, but I don't want to. I think if I'm the one going to college, it should be my choice. Don't you?''

Christine didn't care where Jodie furthered her education, but the young woman did have a point. "The person doing the work should have the most say,'' she agreed.

Jodie broke into a warm smile. "All right! Yes! I had a feeling I was going to like you.''

"You like me because I sided with you and not with your aunt?''

"It's not just that,'' Jodie said, then grinned. "But yeah, that does help.''

They watched as Erin and Shep gamboled a short distance away in the shade of another tree.

Jodie's smile faded. "Don't get me wrong. I love Aunt Mae. She can be fierce, but she can also be... She helped raise me after my mother took off when I was a baby. So if it wasn't for her... My daddy hasn't got a clue about raising a kid.''

"Your mother left you?'' Christine asked. She was always fascinated by other people's experiences with their mothers.

"Yeah.'' Jodie looked down, clearly unwilling to go on.

Christine respected her reticence. She had plenty of that of her own. She motioned to the house just behind them, the house next door to Harriet's. "Whose place is that?''

Jodie glanced around. "That's my daddy's brother's house. My uncle Thomas...and his wife, Darlene. You haven't met them yet, because they aren't here.

They're off visiting their son in Lubbock.'' Her smile reappeared. ''Everyone held on to their hats real good after they drove off, because we thought for sure the earth was going to open up or something. Uncle Thomas just doesn't do that kind of thing! I doubt he's been more than a couple hours' drive away from the ranch since he and Aunt Darlene got married.''

Her voice lowered. ''Their son, Richard, and his wife are having marriage trouble. Aunt Mae wasn't pleased when she first heard about it, and she still isn't. She told them to go stop the divorce proceedings. As if they could! But they left, just like Aunt Mae wanted them to.''

''She's quite a woman,'' Christine murmured, her flat inflection not indicative of a compliment.

''She really is,'' Jodie agreed, her voice wry.

BREAKFAST NEXT MORNING was a repeat of the day before. Christine and Erin again managed to go down late enough to miss Mae. Only this morning the long dining-room table sported several varieties of cold cereal, an even larger choice of jams and jellies, fresh fruit, orange juice and a plate of homemade biscuits. As they were seating themselves, Marie came through from the kitchen, a pitcher of milk in one hand and a pot of steaming coffee in the other.

''You didn't need to go to so much trouble,'' Christine said as her gaze moved over the array of food.

''It's no trouble,'' Marie replied.

''But—''

''It's my job,'' Marie interrupted crisply. Her blunt features remained set.

Christine again thought of Mrs. Tobin and her warm care.

"Look! Lucky Charms!" Erin declared as she spied a box of her favorite breakfast cereal. Her enthusiasm was constrained, though, by the presence of the housekeeper.

Marie answered gruffly, "It's Wesley and Gwen's favorite, so I thought..." She hesitated, as if wondering if she'd said too much.

Christine studied Erin. With her big dark eyes and silky black hair, her resemblance to the Parkers was uncanny. She'd been struck by the similarity after meeting Harriet and LeRoy's children. Erin might truly be one of them.

Once again, the resemblance seemed to work in Christine's and Erin's favor. The housekeeper became almost friendly.

"We have some honey if you'd like that with your biscuits," she offered. "When I was a little girl, that's what my momma always used to give me for a special treat."

Erin, possibly remembering Mrs. Tobin, responded with a similar tentative step toward friendship. "Thank you," she said politely. "And thank you for the Lucky Charms, too."

A full smile brightened the housekeeper's face. "I'll go get it," she said, and hurried from the room. Seconds later the honey was on the table. "Enjoy your meal," Marie invited. "And if there's anything else you need, you just let me know."

Christine offered an experimental smile of her own. If Erin was a Parker, the housekeeper seemed to have decided, then both daughter *and* mother were due some respect. That is, unless and until this conclusion was proved wrong.

AFTER BREAKFAST Erin wanted to go outside, but she didn't want to go by herself. So Christine settled in one of the chairs set beneath the trees in the courtyard and watched as Erin amused herself with made-up games. Shep wandered over and played with her for a time, then stretched out in the grass by Christine's chair.

Christine pretended not to notice when Harriet stepped out her front door, saw them in the courtyard, hesitated, then forged ahead to offer a greeting.

She was a big woman, tall and strong, but this morning her cheeks were pale.

"Oh, gosh!" she sighed, slipping gingerly into the nearest chair. "I'd almost forgotten how bad it can be in the morning." Her hand rested weakly on her stomach.

"How far along are you?" Christine asked.

"The doctor says about eight weeks. I usually only have trouble for a week or two about this time, then I sail through the next seven months without a problem. I hope that's the way it'll be now." She glanced at Christine. "LeRoy says he thinks he'll have your car fixed in the next day or so. It's got a lot of little things wrong with it and a couple of bigger ones, but all in all, he says it's sound."

Christine sat forward. "How much is it going to cost? I don't...that is, I..." Should she admit she didn't have very much money? Was that something a person in her position should do?

Harriet shook her head. "LeRoy's got a lot of spare parts lying around, and the one or two new things he needs, Rafe's taking care of out of the ranch's miscellaneous fund."

Christine frowned. "I don't want charity."

"It's not charity. Ira drew you the map, he was off a bit, you got lost and your car broke down. It's a Parker mistake, so the Parkers will pay for it. That what Rafe says."

"But—"

"You'll have to take it up with him if you want to argue. He's not here right now. He's over at Little Springs visiting Dub. That's Morgan's—"

"I know who Dub is. I've met him," Christine said quickly, then to prevent further talk of Morgan she said, "I'm confused. Little Springs, Indian Wells...I thought this was the Parker Ranch."

Harriet smiled, a little color returning to her cheeks. "It is. Little Springs, Indian Wells, Red Canyon, Big Spur, Little Spur, Drop Creek... The ranch has nine divisions altogether. It's so the cowboys and everyone else can know what area they're talking about. It's too big otherwise. Measures in the hundreds of sections. And a section is—"

"Six hundred and forty acres," Christine supplied.

"Did you grow up on a farm or in ranch country?" Harriet asked.

"I was good at math in school."

Harriet let the nonanswer pass. "Little Springs has always been the foreman's place, and for as long as I know, a Hughes has lived there. I don't know what's going to happen if Dub can't continue. Morgan's doing the job now, but— Not that Rafe's going to push Dub and Delores out. He wouldn't do that. But if he has to name a new foreman, he's got to put him somewhere. Maybe Morgan will stay on, though. Maybe he'll—"

"What happened to Dub?" Christine interrupted. It made her uncomfortable even to think of Morgan Hughes. It had been bad enough before, when she'd thought of him merely as one of the enemy, but after what had happened yesterday… She tried to concentrate on what Harriet was saying.

"He had a really bad accident. His horse went down out on the range. It was evening before anyone knew he was missing, and by the time a search got going, it was too dark to do much. First thing in the morning it started up again, but it took most of the day. Found him in a canyon, unconscious, his arm a mess, ol' Thunder, his horse, standing not ten feet away. LeRoy said it was Thunder that saved him. There was a lot of brush in that canyon. Made it hard to search."

"I saw his cast," Christine murmured.

Harriet grimaced. "Doctor's not sure how much use of his arm he'll get back. Really messed up his wrist. Might work good enough if he retires, but Dub wasn't ready to retire yet. He's sixty-three, but you couldn't tell it from the way he did his job. He put most of the younger cowboys to shame. We're all worried sick around here about how he'll take it if he has to quit. It's not going to be easy."

"Doctors can do amazing things," Christine said.

She was thinking of her mother, and how long the medical profession had managed to extend her mother's life, even when she wouldn't do much of anything to help herself. Not even give up drinking, the activity that was killing her.

"Shannon's the one to talk to about that," Harriet said. "In fact, I was just telling Rafe that maybe she'd be the best to help Dub if he did have to give up working directly with the horses and cattle. She's been through so much herself."

Christine waved at Erin who'd stopped playing long enough to check her whereabouts. "Like what?" she asked. It didn't hurt to know something about the people you were dealing with. She knew Mae was busy checking up on *her*.

"Do you remember—it's coming up on a year ago now—when a light plane went down with six people on board, and one of the dead was Nathan Bradley? If you don't follow Texas politics, you might not recognize his name, but he was quite a powerhouse in the capitol."

"The name's familiar."

"The story was in every newspaper and all over the TV. They were flying to a political rally. Five people died, but one survived—trapped in her seat for two days. Shannon. She's Nathan Bradley's daughter."

"I remember! Shannon Bradley! But I didn't know…"

"Shannon doesn't talk about it much. She was hurt pretty bad herself, almost died, then spent months in a rehabilitation center. Her leg, her left leg, still gives her trouble sometimes."

"I saw that she limped slightly."

"It was hard on her emotionally, too. That's why I thought she could talk to Dub, maybe help him adjust. That is, if the worst happens."

Christine was silent, remembering how she'd spurned Shannon's overtures of friendship. But her position here didn't leave room for friendship, not until her claim was accepted.

"Morgan's been great about coming home to help out," Harriet went on. "Leaving his job, taking over Dub's responsibilities—"

Christine stood up. "Erin!" she called, cutting off Harriet's words. She did *not* want to hear about Morgan Hughes! "Come here, sweetheart. We're going inside."

Harriet rose to her feet, too. "I suppose I'd better get moving myself. I'm on my way over to help Shannon put up some wallpaper in Rafe's kitchen. Later on, why don't you come by? I promise we won't put you to work, not unless you're an expert. We could sure use the help of an expert right now."

"I wouldn't know where to begin," Christine murmured. Then when Erin ran up to her, she placed an arm around the girl's shoulders and they walked back to Mae's house.

MORGAN BIDED his time. He waited two days, then made sure he was in the right place at exactly the right instant.

He knew something of Christine's daily schedule from Marie—breakfast around eight-thirty, a picnic lunch outside at noon, an afternoon walk alone, dinner at seven with Mae. Certain information came from personal observation. Even though he was busy during the day, his evenings were his own, and for three nights straight, from dusk to eleven, he had kept an invisible watch.

"She puts on a good front," Marie had opined. "But underneath she's afraid. I don't know what of, but I'd guess it has to do with the little girl. She's crazy about her."

Christine Grant's life seemed to center around Erin. When the breeze drifted in the right direction at night, he could hear them talking after they went upstairs, hear the laughter they shared, the way she encouraged the little girl while also gently guiding her.

On all three nights after turning out the light at ten, she came to stand in the open balcony door, leaning against the frame, hardly moving for the next half hour.

It was then that Morgan had the hardest time not remembering the way naked attraction had sparked between them that afternoon in her bedroom. The way she'd looked at him. God, he could still feel the heat that had surged through his body! He had wanted her then like he never remembered wanting a woman before. Completely, totally, without reason.

With each day that passed he could feel himself being pulled in again. He had started to look forward to those moments when she'd come to stand in the open doorway. Work was something to be gotten through on the way to evening.

At home, in his own bed, he'd force himself to look at the developing situation clearly. What the hell was wrong with him? She could easily be a cheat, out to take from the Parkers what was rightfully theirs. Some people would go to any lengths where money was involved. It was his duty to stay objective. His duty to himself and to the Parkers. And yet, at night, in the moonlight, he waited and watched.

Her afternoon walks were designed to be solitary, her time alone while Erin was napping. And she took care to stay on a course where she'd be least likely to come upon anyone. Because she didn't want to be asked inconvenient questions?

He startled her when he stepped out from behind one of the adobe pillars that marked the head of the curving drive. She jumped, momentarily looked poised to run, but as he'd witnessed before, she quickly readied herself for battle.

"Go away!" she snapped.

"I came to apologize," he said.

She brushed past him. "I'm supposed to believe that?"

He fell into step beside her. She walked at an angry pace. Luckily for him he had longer legs.

"You could try," he said pleasantly.

She stopped to confront him, her pretty face pink from irritation and exertion. "Why?" she demanded. "Give me one good reason why I should believe anything you say."

Morgan wondered how she'd react if he did what he really wanted to do right then. And *reason* had no place in it. Most women, like most men, really weren't very attractive when they were angry. But she was. The little flecks of gold in her hazel eyes sparked as if lit by the sun. Her expression was fierce, but fiercely proud. Her clear skin almost glowed. Her lips... He dragged his gaze away from temptation.

"Because I'd like to teach Erin to ride, and if you're still angry with me, you won't let me do it."

The simplicity of his statement threw her off balance, deflecting her anger. He'd chosen his approach carefully.

She regrouped quickly. "If I don't trust you, why do you think I'd trust you with my daughter's safety?"

"Do you trust anyone?" he returned.

She glared at him and strode forward, not bothering to notice if he was keeping up—which he was.

"If you trust no one," he continued, "then I'm no different from anyone else. No better, no worse. I told you I want to apologize and I have. Now it's up to you to decide whether you want to hold a grudge."

She dismissed him. "You're not making sense."

"I'd like to start over," he said.

"By scaring me again? That seems to be your specialty."

"I had good reason to scare you that day. If I'd stopped to introduce myself, the snake would have bitten Erin. That's not what you wanted, was it?" She didn't answer and he continued, "I meant, I'd like to start over *after* that. After I brought you to my home. My mother said I was being rude to you and I was. So...I'm apologizing."

She stopped walking again and looked at him through narrowed eyes. "This is too easy," she said.

"Do you want me to do penance?" he rejoined.

"I don't believe you."

He shrugged, tapping his dusty hat against the side of his leg before settling it back on his head. "Then, I guess that answers my question." He lightly touched the hat's brim. "Sorry to have bothered you," he said, and walked away.

He moved forward naturally, not fast, not slow. Just when he seriously thought she'd called his bluff, she said his name.

"Morgan?"

He turned slowly, not letting his elation show on his face. "Yep?"

Damn! She looked even more appealing when she was uncertain. It was the first time he had seen her with such an expression. Even if it was only there for an instant.

She straightened her shoulders and said firmly, "All right. If you want to teach Erin to ride, you can."

"Apology accepted, then?"

She gave a short nod.

A smile pulled at his lips, one she didn't return. "Tell Erin I'll come get her after dinner this evening," he said.

"Us," she corrected. "I'm coming, too."

"You want to learn to ride?"

"No, Mr. Hughes. I'm just there to watch. I barely know you. I'm not about to let you take my daughter off by yourself."

"I liked it better when you called me Morgan."

"Don't push your luck," she retorted, then turned on her heel and retraced her path to the curving driveway.

Morgan had no idea whether she was going back to

Mae's or altering the course she'd previously set because she thought that was the way he planned to walk. Either way, she made it plain she'd been in his company long enough.

Morgan stood watching her. There was a nice little sway to her hips as she walked, causing the skirt she was wearing to move rhythmically against her calves. ''Mm-mmm!'' he murmured appreciatively, before he, too, went on his way.

CHAPTER SEVEN

"SHE'S A NATURAL!" Morgan said as he came to stand beside Christine at the flat board fence that separated one pen from another. He had chosen to teach Erin to ride in a pen, instead of the corral, he'd said, because a pen's smaller size was less intimidating. "She rides like she's been doing it all her life. Are you sure she hasn't had lessons?"

"Never. Not unless the nuns at the last school she attended brought in horses at recess."

Morgan shook his head, watching Erin maneuver Junior on her own. "I've never seen anything like it. Not with a kid who wasn't raised on a ranch."

Christine bristled slightly. "Are you saying you don't believe me?"

His blue gaze alighted on her face. "Relax. I'm just saying it's unusual. Hey, Erin," he called to the little girl, "take him around the other way!"

Erin grinned hugely, then very seriously urged the horse in the other direction.

Christine watched her every move. Erin did look as if she had an instinct for what she was doing. The way she sat in the saddle, the way she showed no fear. She was comfortable on top the big steed. Not that Junior could really be termed a "steed." He was big all right, but lazy-looking, and his main preoccupations seemed to be eating and resting. "All this generation's Parker kids have learned on Junior," Morgan had assured Christine when he'd first led the huge brown gelding up to them. "And they were still in diapers."

"She is good," Christine murmured softly, still watching her daughter.

"Like I said—a natural."

Morgan was on the other side of the fence, but his upraised elbow was next to hers, almost touching it. Christine moved a tiny bit away. It wasn't much, but it made her feel better. She thought she'd managed it so he wouldn't notice, but when she met his gaze, it was amused.

"How's Erin like bein' here?" he drawled easily.

Christine centered her attention back on horse and rider. "She's okay with it."

"How about you?" he persisted.

"I'm okay, too."

He didn't say anything more, but he continued to watch her. She could feel his eyes on her face. Finally she turned to demand irritably, "Why are you looking at me like that?"

"I was just wonderin' how I'd feel if I was in your shoes. Comin' to a place you don't know, havin' to deal with someone like Mae."

"Mae doesn't scare me."

"She scares most people."

"Even you?"

"No, but then I stay out of her way."

"That must be hard when you work for her."

"I report to Rafe. Anyway, I'm just doin' this temporary."

"To help out your dad—I've been told."

"To help out the Parkers, too. They're good people."

Her chin lifted. "Is that what this is all—"

"Mommy! Look!" Erin cried.

Christine looked round and caught her breath. Erin had encouraged Junior into a trot and was bouncing all over the place in the saddle. Somehow she was staying on, but from her own experience summers ago, Christine knew how easy it would be for Erin to fall. And in such a small enclosure, if she fell between the fence and the horse's hooves... "Honey, be..." she started to call. But before she could complete the sentence, Morgan Hughes had stepped away from the fence to intercept the trotting duo.

One capable hand came out to catch the bridle and slow the horse; the other reached up to steady the child. "Hey, hey," he said softly, "I think maybe we better shift ourselves to the corral pretty soon. Get a little more space to move around in. Erin, you've convinced ol' Junior here he's a colt again. I haven't seen him go this fast in years!"

Erin giggled and leaned forward to pat, then hug the horse's neck. "He's a great horse, Morgan! Almost as good as Golden Belle!"

The taste of fear was still in Christine's mouth, but by swallowing hard she overcame it. She climbed up and over the fence to stand on Junior's other side. "That was wonderful, Erin," she said, forcing a smile.

"I rode a horse, Mommy!" Erin cried jubilantly. "By myself!"

The smile remained plastered on Christine's face. She was happy that Erin had achieved one of her most cherished dreams, but as a mother, she wasn't ready for all this. She reached up to help Erin down. "Come on, honey," she said.

"Let her get down herself," Morgan instructed softly. "It's part of the lesson."

Christine's worried gaze met his. He looked so confident standing there, holding the horse steady. So strong and vital and sure.

Erin took the decision out of Christine's hands. She brushed aside her offer of help and swung from the saddle. "Can I come riding again tomorrow?" she asked.

"Mr. Hughes is a busy man," Christine said.

"Morgan," he corrected. "And I'm not too busy to take a half hour off here and there. Same time tomorrow, Erin? Unless something big comes up—then I'll have to let you know."

"Same time," Erin chirped, and took another moment to hug Junior's neck.

She looked so small pressed against the horse, but Junior's only move was to swish his tail at an imaginary fly and lightly stomp a rear hoof.

Then Erin surprised Christine by reaching out to Morgan's neck. "Thank you, Morgan," she said earnestly, hugging him, after which she quickly turned away, slipping back into shyness.

Men—with the exception of Ira—were a fairly unknown quantity in Erin's life. Christine had no broth-

ers or sisters with husbands who might have provided
a male influence. There was no father or grandfather
around. And definitely no parade of Christine's boy-
friends passing through the house.

Christine returned from her reverie to the realization
that someone had spoken to her. She looked first at
Erin, whose attention, she found, had reverted to the
horse, then to Morgan Hughes—who, it was obvious,
was waiting for an answer. "What?" she said awkwardly. "What did you say? I didn't..." Her words
trailed away.

He smiled at her, which she found even more dis-
comfiting, because there was something about him
when he smiled. Something that caught her attention
and held it, no matter how hard she fought not to let
it happen.

"I asked if that was all right with you," he repeated.

The sun was low in the western sky, lending a wonderful rosy-golden glow to the land around them. Bur-
nishing his skin, his hair, heightening his attraction to
the point that—

"I... Of course. Of course, I..." Christine stumbled.
She had to cling to reason. She couldn't let herself...

What was it Harriet had said to him? Women must
drop like flies? Yes, there definitely *was* something
about a cowboy. About this cowboy in particular. An
attitude, an assurance that you didn't see every day, if
ever. So it was only natural that when a person happened along who embodied such a difference, you responded. Only it wasn't natural for her!

Erin skipped over to clasp her hand, and Christine
used the action as a way out. "Tomorrow," she fin-

ished as firmly as she could, and turned to walk away as if nothing unusual had occurred.

She expected him to say something, to make some kind of comment. Instead, he said nothing, and that made her all the more aware of him as she wondered why he hadn't.

"YOU'RE HOME EARLY tonight, son," Dub said when Morgan, fresh from parking the pickup in front of their house, had decided to go check if his dad might still be holed up in his retreat.

On good days, Dub had taken to spending his evenings on the long narrow porch of the workshop, sometimes sitting and doing nothing, other times attempting as best he could with his one usable hand to repair ropes and bridles.

Morgan hung a foot on the weathered single step, but didn't mount it. "Yeah, I decided to pack it in early tonight." Several bridles lay out in the yard as if they'd been thrown there in frustration. Morgan motioned to the nearest. "That your handiwork?"

"Yep," Dub conceded grumpily. "Dang left hand! If I was gonna break somethin', wouldn't you think I could've managed to break my left arm, instead of my right? I do everythin' with my right. Hold the phone, eat, take a..." He shifted in his chair and laughed. "Your momma was about to skin me for a while there. Told me I better get my aim fixed or else. And she meant it."

Morgan laughed, too. It was good to hear his father crack jokes again. "Just give it a little time, Dad. Don't rush things. It hasn't been that long."

"Weeks seem like months when you're trussed up in somethin' like this," Dub complained, tapping his arm brace.

Morgan looked out over the shadowy landscape. For the past three nights he'd positioned himself outside Christine Grant's bedroom at about this time. Tonight he decided to take a break. He'd done as Mae asked and started to move in on her. But after doing it, he wasn't sure if he was totally happy about it. He understood the necessity, but...well, somehow it didn't feel right.

"Rafe rode over again today," Dub said next. "He said things are settin' up good for the roundup. Says you're doin' a fine job. Everythin's almost ready to go."

"I was taught by the best," Morgan said.

Dub grinned an acknowledgment, then said, "Havin' to do a lot of feedin' this year, too, he says."

"That rain last week helped, but it didn't come soon enough."

The weather and the condition of the cattle and the horses were the main subjects of conversation of all stockmen when they got together, even if they'd just talked about it the day before.

Dub continued, "He says there might be some rustlers workin' nearby. What've you heard? Anythin'?"

"Sheriff Denton says it looks pretty organized. He sent his deputy—you remember Tate Connelly, Emma and Dan Connelly's boy?—over to Debolt to sniff around. Seems twenty to thirty calves have gone missing at a time."

Dub whistled. "What does Ed Davis have to say about it?"

"That he's on it. He's working with the sheriff over there."

Dub looked thoughtful. "Think the cattlemen's association will involve you? Since you're already here?"

"I hope not. I'm on leave, remember?"

"I remember. The question is, will they?" He paused. "Not a word to your mother. We don't want her startin' to worry. That's the last thing she needs."

"I'm not sayin' anything."

"Grandpa! Grandpa!" a childish voice shrilled as a small towheaded girl of about four bounced onto the porch. "Grandma says you're to come inside. You're s'posed to read a story to me before I go to sleep, 'member?"

Dub pushed awkwardly to his feet. "The one about the mean ol' coyote?" he teased.

"No!" The little girl giggled. "The Vel'teen Rabbit. The Vel'teen Rabbit, Grandpa! That's my favorite." She tugged on the arm with the cast.

Morgan saw his father wince, and to prevent further pain, he swooped down on his niece and swung her high in the air, bringing her legs down on either side of his head, so that she perched on his shoulders. "Nope," he said, teasing, as well, "I distinctly remember you likin' that mean ol' coyote."

"No!" the little girl shrieked. "The rabbit! The rabbit!"

It still amazed Morgan how loud a small child could

be—and how strong. Her fingers were curled tightly in his hair and were pulling in excitement.

They made their way into the house. He lowered Mindy to the floor, and after a quick peck on his cheek, she darted ahead of his father to the bedroom she shared with her older sister, Jessica.

Because Jessica was nine, she was allowed to stay up later at night. She was in the living room, curled on one end of the couch, while Rusty, her older brother, was sprawled on the rug. Both were watching the last few minutes of a television show.

Morgan dropped down on the spare end of the couch, and when the show was over, he asked, "Have either of you talked with Erin Grant?"

"Who?" Jessica asked. Jessica liked to pretend she was far more sophisticated than her years. Especially when she was dealing with adults. She also liked to be the person in charge of whatever game was being played. Because her real life was so out of control? Morgan wondered.

"Erin Grant. The new little girl at the Parkers."

"Oh, her," Jessica said dismissively.

"I've only seen her the once," Rusty said. "The day you found 'em out walking."

"She's stuck up," Jessica said.

"Why do you say that?" Morgan asked curiously.

"Because she doesn't want to play with us. I asked Gwen, and Gwen said she didn't want to."

"That doesn't make her stuck up," Morgan said.

Jessica shrugged. "All I know is, Gwen asked and she said no."

"She's only been here a few days. Why don't you

ask again? Maybe she was shy about meeting new people."

"We could I suppose..."

"Jessica's afraid she won't get to boss Gwen and Wesley around anymore if the new girl comes to play," Rusty announced. He didn't mix much with the younger children, preferring, instead, to roam around Little Springs on his own, both on foot and on horseback. He was at that in-between age, when a boy needs to start finding what he's made of.

"That's not so!" Jessica immediately denied, sitting forward, her blue eyes flashing.

"Is!"

"Isn't!"

"Is!"

Morgan lifted a hand. "I didn't intend to start an argument. All I'm asking is for you to invite Erin to play. Do it yourself, Jessica. She's a nice little girl. You might actually like her."

Jessica retreated into her curled position against the arm of the couch. "What's the use?" she said, suddenly sullen. "We're going to be moving again soon, anyway."

"What's wrong with that?" Morgan asked. "Don't you want to go live with your dad?

"Yes," Jessica replied, but there was little to no enthusiasm.

Morgan glanced at Rusty, whose gaze slid away.

Their behavior mimicked the way they'd been when they'd first arrived at Little Springs, according to Morgan's mother. It had taken six weeks or more for the older two to start coming out of what she termed their "hibernation."

Morgan searched for something to say, something that would make the prospect of moving appealing. But they had been burned so often over the past few years, trundled back and forth from mother to father, never having a real home. This would be their last move, though. Russell had finally won full custody. Morgan didn't want to utter encouraging platitudes. A few home truths in their father's ear, though, wouldn't be out of line. Russell needed to give these kids a sense of permanence. Whatever it took.

"Grandma in the kitchen?" he asked them.

Both children nodded without speaking.

Morgan pushed to his feet and went in search of his mother. She was puttering about the room she loved best. She never seemed to tire of cooking. If she wasn't busy preparing a meal or cleaning up after, she was planning what she would cook the next day. And occasionally, like now, her mind turned to preserving for the future.

A raft of empty jars covered the tabletop and one counter. "I think we're going to need to buy more jars this season, Morgan," she said. "It's been a hard year for glass in this house."

Morgan smiled wryly. Since his arrival home, there'd been something or other break almost every day. He pulled a chair over and sat. "Dad's spirits seem to be better."

"Rafe came by and brought Shannon with him. They talked ranch business for a full hour." She smiled reflectively. "That Shannon. She's such a sweet little thing! It wouldn't hurt you to find someone like her.''

"Are you sayin' you want *more* grandchildren?''

''I want to see you settled down, Morgan, that's all. Whether or not you have kids is your business.''

''You're whistlin' in the wind, Mom.''

His mother smiled. ''One day it's going to happen to you, and when it does, you're going to be the one whistling a different tune. Some sweet little thing's going to sashay by and you're not going to know what hit you.''

An image of Christine Grant walking away from him flashed into Morgan's mind. Would *she* qualify as a sweet little thing under his mother's definition? He quickly put the thought away. ''You have to be lookin' for somethin' like that to happen, don't you?''

''Not necessarily,'' his mother replied.

Morgan went over to kiss her lined cheek. ''I have blinders on.''

''Ah, but blinders can slip off,'' she said.

Morgan laughed and gave her another kiss before heading off to bed. Even after everything, his mother remained an optimist.

CHRISTINE TAPPED LIGHTLY on the bedroom door next to hers. After a moment Shannon came to answer it. She was still in her nightgown.

Christine extended the tray on which she'd placed a carafe of coffee and two cups. ''Would you like to share?'' she asked.

She'd caught Shannon completely by surprise. The

other woman blinked, then moved out of the way. "I didn't... I never..."

Christine stepped past her. "I came to apologize. I was very rude the other day. I'm sorry if I gave offense." She placed the tray on a low chest of drawers, then turned around. "If you'd rather I leave, I will. I'll understand."

Shannon still seemed slightly stunned. As if the last thing she'd expected was an apology from Christine. "No, it's fine. I'm glad."

Christine poured coffee into the two cups. "Sugar or cream?" she asked.

"Neither," Shannon replied. She accepted her cup and perched uneasily on the rumpled sheets. Motioning to a high-backed wooden rocker near her balcony door, she said, "My only chair."

Christine went to the rocker. Sipping her coffee, she looked around. The two rooms were alike, except this one boasted a full-size bed with an intricately carved headboard and low foot posts. It also had more of the imprint of its occupant. Books, magazines, bits of fabric, notebooks, drawings—the debris of wedding preparation littered most available surfaces.

Shannon said, "It's a bit of a mess, I'm afraid. There's barely a month left until the ceremony, and there's still so much to do. Like the bridesmaids dresses. I thought we were set, then Mae comes up with something else to consider. Honestly, we're going to be lucky if the bridesmaids don't come down the aisle in their lingerie!"

"Mae's managing your wedding?" Christine asked.

Shannon grimaced. "I'd say it's about half and half. Rafe and I are holding our own."

"Do you ever think of eloping?"

"All the time! But it's to the point where we can't! The wedding's taken on a life of its own. It's like this giant monster, devouring everything in its path! If we were to just chuck it in and run off... Ahh, that sounds so good sometimes!"

Christine smiled.

Shannon continued, "And the family history is due to go to the publisher in a couple of months—Mae wants to be sure to have it printed by Christmas. She intends to send everyone a copy."

"A family history?" Christine repeated.

"That's the way Mae got me to come here. I was...well, I'd been hurt in an accident and she asked me to help her compile the Parker-family story. The family truly does have an interesting history. Two brothers, Virgil and Gibson, founded the ranch in the mid-nineteenth century, fighting off indians and bandits and the ravages of nature. It goes through the Civil War and the cattle drives to Kansas. They have wonderful photographs and letters, all kinds of records." She paused, frowning. "I still have so much to do I'm not sure..." She brightened. "Would you like to help? Can you type? Mae's put in some corrections that I just don't have the time to—"

"Do you think Mae would approve?" Christine interrupted her.

Shannon blinked again. "No, I suppose you're right. She wouldn't. Not now, at any rate." She gave a deep regretful sigh.

Christine spoke quietly. "Harriet told me who you are. About your accident. I remember seeing you on the news. Being airlifted away from the crash site on a stretcher, being taken from one hospital to another." She paused. "I'm sorry," she said inadequately.

Shannon rubbed her left knee. "That wasn't a very happy time," she said softly.

Christine finished her coffee and stood. "Well," she murmured, "I'd better get back to Erin. I think I hear her moving around. I left her a note, but she might not see it."

"Thank you," Shannon said, standing up, too. "For the coffee...and for listening to me complain."

Christine shrugged. She'd wanted to dislike the Parkers. They didn't like her, so she wouldn't like them. Only, it was hard to maintain that attitude in the face of such seemingly genuine kindness. Shannon, Harriet, Jodie...LeRoy working so industriously to repair her car.

She smiled tightly. "Sure," she said, and left the room.

ERIN HAD VISITORS later that morning as she played outside in the courtyard. Gwen, and a little blond girl Christine had never seen before, but knew instantly which family she belonged to.

"You wanna come play with us?" the blonde asked Erin. "Gwen and I are having a wedding. I'm the bride and Wesley's the groom and—"

"And I'm the flower girl!" Gwen announced.

"You can be a bridesmaid, if you want. Or the minister. We really need a minister."

Erin declined shyly.

"Gwen's mom is letting us use some of her old clothes and stuff," the little girl went on. "And makeup—lipstick and blush and powder. She's gonna take pictures!"

"We're gonna have invitations just like Shannon and Rafe's!" Gwen said.

"That sounds like fun," Christine said. She was becoming more and more concerned about Erin's withdrawal. The girl was reverting to the behavior of a far younger child—upset when Christine was out of sight, clinging when she wasn't.

As Erin yet again shook her head, the blond girl spun around and, catching hold of Gwen, started to stalk off. "The only reason we asked was because Uncle Morgan said we should," she grumbled. "I told him you wouldn't play, but he wouldn't believe me."

"Morgan's your uncle?" Erin asked.

The little girl swung around. "Yes."

Erin moved uncomfortably. She looked at Christine, then back at the two girls. A battle seemed to take place within her, then she said, "*He* asked you to ask me?"

"Yes."

Erin's troubled expression cleared. "Then I'll play," she said, and stepped away from Christine.

The other two little girls looked at each other, decided between them that this was okay and came back to collect her.

"I'm Jessica," the blonde said. "I'm nine. I'm gonna be in the fifth grade next year."

"I'm six!" Gwen piped up. "Well, almost."

"I'm eight," Erin joined in, "and I'll be in...I'll be in fourth!"

Erin's hesitation told Christine that her daughter, too, was worried about her progress in school. Which meant she, Christine, would have to talk to someone.

She thought Erin wasn't going to look back as she moved off with the two girls, but as the trio reached the curved gravel drive, heading toward Harriet's house, she glanced around, then ran back.

"You don't mind, do you, Mommy?" she asked earnestly.

Christine smiled. "Not in the least, sweetheart. Enjoy yourself."

Erin nodded and rejoined her companions.

As Christine left the courtyard her emotions bordered on bittersweet. Morgan Hughes seemed to save the day each time Erin was in danger. When they were lost, the encounter with the snake, the trotting horse—and now helping her from becoming too isolated. His name had acted like a talisman, spurring Erin on.

Should she be grateful? Or should she be worried?

One thing seemed apparent. He had a definite effect on both the Grant women.

CHAPTER EIGHT

MORGAN SHIFTED position unhappily, wishing he could be anywhere but where he was. Mae had called a meeting in the ranch office, and the tiny room was packed with Parker men. She'd specifically asked that he be present.

"The first report from our investigator is in," Mae said. "I'll read it. 'Subject, Christine Patricia Grant, age twenty-five. Born prematurely on December 28 at Pasadena General Hospital, Pasadena, Texas. Mother, Jeannette Grant. Father, unknown. Address, the Happy Trails Trailer Park in Pasadena. Mother was a dancer and a bar maid at a succession of mostly low-rate establishments, frequently on public assistance. Subject went through the public-school system in Pasadena until the eleventh grade, when she dropped out due to pregnancy. She gave birth to a daughter, Erin Margaret, now eight. Father, unknown. Subject worked as a waitress, earned her GED certificate, then went to secretarial school. Jeannette Grant died sixteen months ago from cirrhosis of the liver. Subject's work record is spotty, mostly short term. She moved into Ira Parker's house last September as his secretary/assistant. Erin was enrolled in St. Cecilia's elementary school. The girl is quiet and very smart, winning several awards in the short time she attended. Withdrawn abruptly April 8. Eugene Hernandez is a respected attorney-at-law in Houston, who did represent the late Ira Parker. Mr. Hernandez refused to be of further assistance, except to confirm the bequest.'"

Mae looked up from the sheet of paper. "That's it. Not a lot, but at least it's something. And, thanks to a little pressure from me, we managed to get a copy of the will, which is with our lawyer."

"Has he had a chance to look it over yet?" Rafe asked.

Mae shook her head. "No, but at first glance he says it seems aboveboard."

Gib removed the foil from around a stick of gum and popped it into his mouth. "Aunt Mae, you knew Ira better than the rest of us. What do you think he was up to?"

Mae shot her nephew a sharp glance. "If I knew the answer to that, Gib, I wouldn't be sittin' here wastin' my time. Or any of yours. Though in your case—"

"It's a good question, Aunt Mae," Rafe said, coming to his uncle's defense. "You did know Ira best."

"I didn't know him all that well," she replied irritably. "We played together when we were kids, when his parents came to visit. They used to skip the family meeting and come, instead, for a month every summer. We weren't all that close after they quit visiting regular."

"But you knew him as an adult, too, didn't you?" Rafe persisted.

"Not enough to know what he was thinking! Ira

kept a lot of things to himself. We'd get together once in a while when I was in Austin or Houston on business, but we never talked about anything personal. Except later, after his kids were born. I think he was at a loss with them. They took after their mother more than they took after him. Still, he didn't say much. He was more...quietly concerned.''

LeRoy snorted. ''With Abigail and Brendan for offspring, I can see why. Do you know what Abigail told Harriet the last time they got together? She told her she should have stopped havin' babies after she had one. That if every Parker did that, then everyone's share of the ranch's profits would be greater!''

Gib whistled and Mae ground her teeth.

''That must have gone over well with Harriet,'' Rafe murmured.

''She wanted to skin her. Right on the spot!'' LeRoy smiled.

Rafe reached into his shirt pocket and withdrew a letter. It was written on high-quality paper in a neat yet flowery hand. ''I guess this is as good a time as any to bring this up,'' he said. ''It's a letter from Abigail.''

Mae snatched it out of his hands, then let it fall to the desk after reading it. ''How long have you had this?'' she demanded.

''A couple of days.''

''Why didn't you bring it to me right away?''

''It's addressed to me. I wanted to think about what I was going to do with it.''

Mae glared at him imperiously. ''Why did you have to *think?* Why didn't you just—''

"It's poisonous, Aunt Mae. You can see that. How can believe anything Abigail's said? An antique writing desk, all their mother's jewelry, Ira's collection of gold pocket watches. Does it make sense for Christine to steal something like that and then come here— where everyone's eventually going to know where she is? It doesn't. Not to me."

"Of course she wouldn't bring it all with her," Mae argued. "She could have been working with someone."

"That's stretching things."

Mae stood up, signaling an end to the meeting. "Well, we'll just have to wait and see, won't we? I expect more information will be coming in soon. Now, unless someone else has something to add..." She glanced at everyone present, one by one, then her gaze finally settled on Morgan. "Morgan," she said. "I want a word with you. The rest of you, get on with your business."

As Rafe passed by Morgan, he said softly, "I want a word with you, too."

Mae got up to straighten the painting of a prize Hereford bull from the 1920s that adorned the wall behind the desk. Then she checked the calendar posted beside it, reading the notations. What she saw must have pleased her, because when she looked around at Morgan, her expression was more relaxed.

"Now," she said mildly. "What do you have to tell me?"

Morgan had prepared himself for this. "Not a lot. Not yet. I'm just getting started."

"It's been three days. Four, if you count today."

"I have to do this in my own time, Mae. If I rush her, she'll spook. She's very suspicious."

Mae frowned lightly. "This entire affair isn't exactly humming along."

"You have to have patience."

"Not exactly my strong suit," she said, a wisp of a smile touching her lips.

Morgan smiled along with her. Genuinely smiled. He'd admired Mae for years. Initially because his father did, then on his own accord. She was a strong-willed woman, hell-bent on having her own way. But her way was often what was best for the ranch and for those who relied on it. "Most times," he said quietly, "patience is the only thing that works."

Mae walked over to stand in front of him and surprised him by reaching up to pat his cheek. "You were a good boy, Morgan. Now you've grown up to be a good man. I just want you to know how much we appreciate you." She patted his cheek again, then with a bit of effort left the room.

MORGAN FOUND RAFE talking to one of the full-time cowboys on the far side of the bunkhouse. Gene, grizzled and in his sixties, had worked on the Parker Ranch for the past thirty-six years. In the city he might have been dismissed as a has-been, almost ready to be shunted to a retirement home. Here, he was respected for his cowboy wisdom and his still-lightning-fast reflexes.

"Gotta watch it, Morgan," he drawled, catching sight of him. "You get ol' Mae after you, and you're gonna wish you was back bustin' rustlers. That's gotta be easier than wrastling with her!"

"It was you she was askin' after, Gene. Wanted to know when your birthday was. Says she's thinkin' of sendin' you to Hawaii for a treat."

"Hawaii?"

"Yeah. So's you can get one of them leis. And a kiss from a pretty girl. It's the only way you'll ever get one, she said."

"What would I do with one of them leis?" Gene asked, enjoying the banter. "They're a necklace made'a flowers, aren't they? If I wore one'a them things on the range, I might have to fight off a bull who thinks I'm a heifer!"

Morgan grinned. "She means the kiss—from a pretty girl!"

"Then again," Rafe said, breaking in, "Gene wearing a flower necklace might come in handy on the roundup. All those little bull calves would be so confused they won't know what's happening to 'em while we take care of business!"

"I ain't wearin' no flowers!" Gene said stubbornly. "Never have. Never will. Never want to!" He stomped away, leaving Morgan and Rafe shaking their heads and laughing. Gene was the best of all the permanent hands. Tough, reliable, loyal, and he knew how to get the most out of a story.

"You wanted to see me?" Morgan asked.

"Mae gone?" Rafe asked, glancing behind him toward the office.

"She left a few minutes ago for the house."

Rafe pulled another slip of paper from his shirt

pocket. It matched in style and color the letter he'd given Mae earlier. "I didn't mention this," he said quietly as he handed it to Morgan. "When you read it, you'll understand why."

This script was in a neatly blocked print and definitely masculine. It was signed by Brendan Parker. "Rafe," it read, "I'm echoing Abby's warning about Christine Grant. She's robbed us blind, and now she's trying to cheat us all out of our birthright by muscling in on what isn't hers. Watch out for her. Also watch out that she doesn't get to you in another way. She's quite a sexy little number and has the scruples of an alley cat. She seduced my dad and did her best to seduce me. She'll do anything to get what she wants!"

Morgan felt a powerful anger rise up in him. If Brendan Parker were here right now, he'd— Morgan swallowed his rage and forced himself to speak softly. "You believe this?" he asked.

"If I believed it, I'd have given it to Mae," Rafe replied. "There's always room for doubt, especially when it comes to Brendan and Abigail. Something about what they're sayin' just doesn't set right. What about you? What do you think?"

Morgan hadn't told Rafe what Mae had asked him to do. She'd requested his silence and he'd honored her request. So far, at least. Morgan shrugged. "Like you said, it doesn't seem logical for her to rob them blind and then come here." He frowned. "Have they reported it to the police yet?"

"I don't know, but I doubt it. I wouldn't put it past them to have contacted the insurance company, though."

Morgan eyes narrowed. "You mean, insurance fraud? You think they might have gotten rid of—or hidden—the stuff themselves and are going to report it missing for the insurance money?"

Rafe ran a hand through his dark hair. "Lord, I don't know. That sounds pretty awful, doesn't it? I guess... I don't know."

"Even if it's not that bad, even if all they're doing is trying to ruin Christine's good name, why?" Morgan flicked the sheet of paper with a fingertip. "Why this?"

"Spite? Maybe it was the other way around. Maybe Brendan's the one who tried to seduce Christine and she—" He stopped. "Now Shannon has *me* doing it! She's been on a campaign, trying to convince me that Christine is telling the truth. At least, that she believes she's telling the truth. Shannon thinks it's Ira who's pulled the fast one—on Christine. But again, why?"

"I barely remember the man," Morgan confessed.

"We weren't exactly close, either," Rafe admitted. "His family pretty much went their own way. His daddy got involved in natural-gas production in South Texas and made a mint, then Ira ran the company until he retired. He always seemed proud to be a Parker, but it was just sort of there, in the background. Not a part of his everyday life. His kids have only been here about three times. The last was particularly memorable because they were so danged awful to everyone. You remember it, don't you? About four, five years ago?"

Both men fell silent. "Well," Morgan said after a moment, "Ira certainly did know how to cause a stir after dying."

"Do you think that's what all this is—a joke?" Rafe's lips tightened.

"Better not be," Morgan replied. "Too many people could get hurt."

ERIN WAS INVITED to lunch at Harriet's house. She'd been having such a good time playing with Jessica and Gwen that she rushed over to gain Christine's permission. Christine looked down into her daughter's flushed face, into her bright eyes, and said yes without a second thought.

"That little girl's done well by you, Christine," Mae said magnanimously from the head of the table, after learning where Erin was.

It had crossed Christine's mind to skip lunch that day or at least to have it delivered to her room, since the usual picnic had been canceled. But even though she didn't look forward to sharing the table with Mae, she knew that to do less would be viewed as weakness.

"Thank you," she murmured, spreading the napkin on her lap. She was aware that the older woman's eyes never left her.

"She has nice manners and behaves properly," Mae went on.

Christine looked up. "I don't understand why that should surprise you. Other people besides Parkers have standards to live by."

Marie served a thick rich vegetable soup. Christine tasted it. Like everything else it was wonderful. "Delicious, Marie," she said, causing the housekeeper to smile as she left the room.

"You do, too," Mae said after a long moment.

Christine put down her spoon. "You're...complimenting me?"

The corners of Mae's no-nonsense mouth pulled in a way that could possibly be described as a smile. "Well, considering," she murmured.

Christine braced herself. "Considering what? What do you mean?"

The smile disappeared. "Considering the circumstances you grew up in. A person would have thought that you'd turn out differently. But then, even a sow's ear can be changed into a silk purse, can't it? Or is it the other way around? That it can't be changed?"

What little appetite Christine had disappeared, and since Erin wasn't present, she didn't pretend. She pushed the soup bowl away, saying coldly, "Say what you mean, Mae."

"I've had a report, and it isn't very encouraging. I know where you come from, the kind of life you've lived, the kind of person your mother was, the way she made her living..."

"I've never made a secret of it," Christine said.

"You didn't tell us."

"Why should I? What difference would it—"

"We've also had a more detailed account from Abigail, listing the articles you stole from her father's house."

"I *never*—"

"Did you have someone help you? The jewelry, the desk, the pocket-watch collection—are they being held for you? Or are they already sold, with your share of the money waiting in some bank account?"

Christine could feel the blood drain from her face. "I never took anything!" she denied. Then remembering the scene that had played out the evening she left the house in River Oaks, she once again girded herself for battle. "I have a witness. Someone who'll vouch for me. Who'll tell you I would never...that I didn't—"

"Who?" The single word cracked like a whip.

"Mrs. Tobin, Ira's housekeeper. She was there when I insisted Abigail and Brendan go through our things to make sure we hadn't taken anything."

"Why would you want them to do that?"

"Because Abigail accused me to my face! I told her to look for herself. But she wouldn't. I insisted, but she still—"

"Would it have done her any good to look—if what you'd taken was already gone?"

White-hot anger burned through Christine. She'd been treated like a criminal from the first moment she'd arrived here. Distrusted, disbelieved. Her eyes flashed as she stood up.

"I didn't take anything," she repeated yet again. "And for your information, I don't have to prove it. But I will, since you're so sure I'm in the wrong. Call Mrs. Tobin. She's still at Ira's house. Talk to her yourself. She'll tell you the truth, which is something Abigail and Brendan Parker wouldn't know if it jumped up and bit them." She took a breath, but didn't back off. "Yes," she began again, "I was poor as a child. Yes, I was neglected. Yes, my mother drank herself to death. But that doesn't make me less of a human being than you! In fact, it might give me an advantage, because I don't look down my nose at people who aren't as lucky as I am, at people who've had to work hard all their lives and don't have anything to show for it! At people who are desperate!''

Her outburst had no appreciable effect on Mae. The older woman continued to sit in her chair like royalty, her white hair pulled into a smooth knot on top of her head, her chiseled features not one whit softened by age, her dark eyes as unreadable as a sphinx's. ''And are you...desperate?'' she questioned softly, after a long moment.

All Christine could do at that point was stare at her. Yes, she was desperate! Desperate to make a better life for Erin. Desperate to find a long-term safe haven for herself and her child. Desperate for what other people took for granted each and every day of their lives.

Suddenly her anger dissipated, leaving her drained. Her head drooped and her shoulders slumped. She knew it was important that she continue to fight, but the desire and the will just weren't there.

''If you'll excuse me,'' she murmured, escaping once again into politeness.

She didn't wait for Mae's answer. Instead, she walked with as much dignity as she could summon across the room and out the door.

AN HOUR LATER, Marie delivered a note to Christine. It was from Mae. The writing was strong, decisive: ''You're going to have to work a little harder at perfecting your story. The housekeeper you told me to contact, this Mrs. Tobin, is no longer employed by Abigail and Brendan. She's moved away and left no forwarding address. If she's your accomplice, which Abigail thinks she is, she's run out on you. Better check your bank account!''

Mrs. Tobin? Gone? Christine crumpled the note and held it against her churning stomach. Mrs. Tobin wasn't supposed to move for two weeks, and not that much time had gone by yet. Unless... Unless something ugly had occurred and, like Christine and Erin, she'd been forced to alter her plans.

Christine groaned, then remembered the slip of paper Mrs. Tobin had given her, the one on which she'd written her sister's address in Central Texas. But in the haste of their move and the upset in the days that followed, she had no idea what she'd done with it. Nor could she remember the name of the town. Fredericksburg? Kerrville? Neither seemed right. She searched through all the things they'd used since that day. She tore open the boxes. She had to find that address!

Erin came upon her going through the contents of the boxes for a second time. Clothes were strewn on the floor, along with most of their possessions.

Gazing into her strained face, Erin murmured, "Is something wrong, Mommy?"

Christine forced herself to smile and say, "No, I was just trying to find something, that's all. It's so frustrating when you know you packed it and then you can't find it."

Erin came closer. "What is it?" she asked.

Christine thought frantically. "You remember the book I used to like so much? The one with the funny little verses? I thought I'd read it again, only now I can't find it!"

"Isn't...isn't that the book you read to Ira?" Erin asked hesitantly. "When he couldn't get out of bed anymore? He liked it because it made him laugh."

Christine held out a hand to her daughter. "What would I do without you?" she asked. "Yes, that's exactly where it is. I left it with Ira."

"I didn't think to get it," Erin said, stepping into a hug.

"Neither did I. Oh, well. Maybe Mrs. Tobin found it for us. You, ah, you don't happen to know where Mrs. Tobin was moving, do you, when she was going to live with her sister? We could write her and ask."

Erin shook her head.

Christine held her close then determinedly changed the subject, asking about the time Erin had spent playing with the other children. While she listened she put everything back in the boxes and pretended nothing was wrong. She heard how the children were planning the wedding ceremony in Harriet's backyard, how they were going to use dolls and stuffed animals as guests, how Erin would be the minister and marry the happy couple. How later this afternoon they were going to try on clothes and play putting on makeup. Erin was almost too excited to take a nap, but after a repetition of some of what they planned to do, she sighed deeply and her eyelids grew too heavy to remain open.

Christine stood next to her daughter, gazing down at her. Erin was so innocent, so sweet. Nothing was more important than her well-being. Not pride, not shame, not fear—not lies told by vicious people.

Tears rushed into Christine's eyes, but she blinked them away. She wasn't going to cry here. Not in this house, and certainly not where Erin might wake up and see her.

Christine followed her usual routine of smearing on sun block, then she set off downstairs and through the front door. To anyone watching—to Mae—she would look carefree and out for her usual afternoon walk. No one—and certainly not Mae—would know how vulnerable she felt. How the burden of responsibility, for the past and for the future, was weighing on her shoulders.

She walked swiftly from the compound, but instead of taking the route she usually did, she continued across a wide-open field and turned down a path she'd never seen before. It led to a little rise with a view of the valley—the houses and work area, the pens and corrals, and beyond them, the range. The area was shaded by a natural grouping of trees. A wrought-iron bench with curved arms and back invited a visitor to linger. Farther on was a fenced-off area that proved to be a burial ground. The Parker cemetery, Christine concluded, after reading the names carved into tombstones—a few dating back to the previous century.

At another time Christine might have studied them. She'd always been interested in the people who came before, possibly because her mother never talked about her family. And her father—Christine didn't even know her father's name! Buck? David? Roger? Her mother had never seemed sure.

To have such an anchor in history as the Parkers had must be wonderful, Christine thought as she settled on the bench. To have a firm place in the world, with no one questioning who you were or how you'd come to be there.

Unlike her.

Tears rushed into Christine's eyes again, and this time she did nothing to stop them. She felt overwhelmed by everything that had happened over the past few weeks. Ira's death—he'd been such a kind man. In the eight months she'd worked for him, she'd come to care deeply for him. It had been heartbreaking to watch his strength decline. She remembered the quiet moments they'd shared when he no longer had any business or personal affairs to attend to and only wanted the warmth of human companionship, which he seemed to find in her. He had died in his own bed, as he'd requested, holding her hand, because Abigail and Brendan couldn't be reached. Then the discovery that he'd bequeathed to her and Erin a secure future— only to find that his family resisted even the idea that he could have done this! To be called a thief—and have no way to disprove it! All she wanted was something good for her child. A child who meant nothing to the Parkers and everything to her. Had she been right in bringing Erin here? In exposing her to people who—

Once again she heard the horse before she saw it, but this time the sounds were unmistakable. She brushed the tears away from her cheeks as best she could and reached deep inside herself for some spirit.

It was the same horse. Thunder. And the same rider. Morgan Hughes. He looked much as he had that other day: hat, vest, chaps, rough-and-ready manner. Only this time his rifle stayed securely in its mount.

She felt his eyes move over her and knew he would have no trouble detecting she'd been crying. As he swung down from the saddle and came toward her, she stood on legs that suddenly felt weak. His blue eyes were striking in his sun-bronzed face. She looked away.

When he stopped directly in front of her, he reached

out to touch her cheek. "You've been crying," he said as if the idea was foreign to him.

Christine tossed her head, rejecting his touch. "Yes," she said tightly. "Is that another crime against the Parkers?"

"Has someone accused you of something?" he asked carefully.

Christine bit her bottom lip, again forced to brush tears from her cheeks. She wanted only to get away from him—away from his prying eyes.

"You didn't answer my question," he said.

"Maybe you'd better talk to Mae," she retorted.

"I have talked to Mae."

Slowly she lifted her gaze. "Then why did you have to ask? You know what she thinks! What about you? Do you believe I stole everything Abigail says I did? That I have a partner and we planned to take advantage of a poor old man's dying days? And that I'm here now trying to get more?"

"Ira Parker, *poor?*"

"I meant, in having people near him who cared!" she snapped. Then she turned the tables on him. "You didn't answer *my* question."

His gaze remained steady. "I'm holdin' my options open," he drawled.

Christine had expected something much more definite. A definite yes.

Then he surprised her further by closing the gap between them, taking her by the shoulders, pulling her close and kissing her with a passion that could easily rob her of her senses. And promptly did.

CHAPTER NINE

CHRISTINE'S INSTINCTS egged her on, urging her to listen to the throbbing thrilling dictates of her body. It didn't matter that she didn't really know this man. Mutual attraction was enough. The way she felt when pressed against him, the way he tasted, his natural male scent, the strength of his hard muscles as he strained to bring her even closer. His hands searching, exploring. Intoxicating her.

Intoxicating. She burst free of his embrace, memory of her mother's behavior producing a very different instinctual response. "No!" she cried, shaking her head. "No!" This was the way her mother had behaved, listening only to her own needs, unmindful and uncaring of everything and everyone else. Christine had vowed she wouldn't be like that. Even before Erin was born she'd made that promise. She was a firsthand witness to the pain left by that kind of selfish thinking. Human hearts laid open, bleeding. *Her* heart.

Morgan frowned. He reached for her again, but she evaded him. Finally he drew back, appearing confused.

Christine had to steel herself against his good looks. Was he growing more handsome each time she saw him or was she just looking more closely? But what did thinking that way get her, except back where she'd been moments before? She had to hold herself aloof from everything about him—his appearance, his personality, his—

"I'll apologize if it's important to you," he offered, cutting into her thoughts.

Her breathing had not yet returned to normal, so all she did was shake her head. She didn't want an apology.

"But I can't promise it won't happen again," he said.

"I—I would think you could," she managed.

He laughed rather hollowly, glancing up to the sky as if for divine guidance before leveling his gaze back on her. "I'll try. Is that satisfactory?"

Christine shrugged, smoothing her hair and her blouse.

"Only," he drawled, his eyes narrowing, "you have to promise not to do that!" Then he gathered Thunder's reins from the ground where he'd dropped them. "One thing I should warn you about—Mae usually comes out here to sit every afternoon about this time. When I first saw you from a distance, I thought you were her."

Christine looked around as if at any second Mae might appear. "I didn't know."

He slanted a smile. "I didn't think so."

"I—I have to go," she murmured.

He brought Thunder forward. "I'll give you a ride back," he said. "We'll circle around to the right or left so you won't see her."

Christine refused. "No, I—"

"I promise I won't take advantage," he said lightly.

While she pondered his offer, he swung easily into the saddle, then leaned toward her, extending a hand. Christine looked at it. It was a nice hand—strong, capable, long-fingered.

He waited patiently, unmoving.

Finally, thinking she heard a noise, Christine grabbed his hand and, placing her foot in the empty stirrup, swung up behind him.

At a light tap from Morgan's heels, Thunder started forward, causing Christine to clutch Morgan's waist to keep from falling off. His low chuckle indicated that he was finding a certain amusement in the situation.

Ordinarily Christine would have protested, but at that moment Mae appeared, walking up the worn pathway. She'd come upon them before they'd had time to get away.

The older woman stopped and stared at them. Then to Christine's surprise, she waved them on without a word.

Christine was forced to hold on even tighter as Thunder broke into a trot, but since the pace took them quickly away from the little knoll, she said nothing to Morgan. A short time later, though, he slowed the horse to a walk and she was able to loosen her grip.

"Well, that was a narrow escape," he said over his shoulder.

"Yes. Too narrow."

It bothered her to be so close to him. Bothered her to feel the strong taut muscles of his waist and back, to feel his warmth, his every breath. It was far too intimate after their earlier exchange. Some of the feelings she'd had then returned.

To protect herself from such feelings, she concentrated on the one thing that was equally unsettling—the accusations Abigail and Brendan had made against her. She tried to remember that last afternoon in Ira's house. Mrs. Tobin had given her her sister's address just after warning her that Abigail and Brendan were on their way. Christine had then gone upstairs and, hurrying from spot to spot, collected all their things that remained unpacked. Could the slip of paper have gotten lost during that rush? Earlier this afternoon she'd checked the suit she'd worn that day, the one she'd dressed in to go to Eugene Hernandez's office. There was no slip of paper in any of the pockets. So where was it?

"Penny for 'em," Morgan said, twisting to look over his shoulder.

"They're not worth it," Christine murmured.

"Why don't you let me be the judge?"

Christine stared at his profile. Solid yet beautifully handsome. She dragged her gaze away.

"I—I was thinking about how I can prove I didn't take any of those things from Ira that Abigail says I did, when—"

"Abigail Parker's a spoiled bitch."

"—when the woman I know who'll vouch for me no longer works at the house in River Oaks. Abigail fired her the day I left, and now she's somewhere in Central Texas living with her sister, and I don't know where exactly. I did, but—"

"—you've lost the address."

Christine sighed. "That's it."

"Are you sure you haven't just misplaced it?"

"I've looked."

"Look again."

Christine cocked her head. "Why should you care?" she asked. "I thought you were on the Parkers' side."

"Nobody here likes Abigail and Brendan. They're family, but ones the rest of the Parkers would just as soon do without."

"Mae believes her."

"It suits Mae to believe her—for now."

"Are you saying—"

"Hop down and get that gate, would you?"

Christine looked ahead. There was a gated opening in the miles-long barbed-wire fence. "Sure," she said, and after a bit of shifting, she was on the ground. Morgan took Thunder through and Christine closed the gate again. She crossed to the waiting horse. "Shouldn't we be at the compound by now?" she asked, frowning. "Erin's going to wake up from her nap soon and wonder where I am. I've been out far longer than I intended."

"We're almost there," he assured her, and once again extended his hand.

Christine looked doubtfully at it, then at him. "Are you sure? You're not taking me somewhere else again, are you? Because if you are..." She was starting to work up a head of steam.

"Listen," he murmured.

In the distance, a horse whinnied and two men could be heard talking and laughing.

"Where are we?" she asked, once she was mounted again.

"Near where a part of the roundup will soon be taking place. We'll be branding, marking, dehorning, castrating, vaccinating... It's messy dirty work, so we usually keep it away from the house. There's four or five other sites across the ranch, but I thought you might like to have a quick look-see at this one, since it's so close."

"So you *are* taking me somewhere else!"

"It's on the way, and I told you we'd circle."

"Yes, but that was to avoid Mae."

"You don't want to see it?" he asked.

"Another time maybe," Christine said. "I told you, Erin might be frightened."

He twisted around again so he could see her. "You sure think a lot of that little girl of yours."

"Of course," Christine said.

"Why didn't you marry her daddy, then?" he asked. "Don't you think two parents—"

"Just take me back to the compound, would you, please?" she interrupted coolly.

He smiled. "You know, I'm never sure when you get all quiet and politelike whether you're doin' it because you think you're supposed to, or whether you're mad at somebody. In this case, me!"

Christine murmured, "The compound, please?"

Several seconds ticked by, then, facing front again, he urged Thunder on, and this time set the pace somewhere between a trot and a walk, which by necessity made Christine have to tighten her hold.

Eventually they passed the pens and corrals, then

the bunkhouse and the barn. Several cowboys paused in their work to watch them. One called out something Christine didn't understand, but she wasn't about to ask.

Bits of loose rock scattered beneath Thunder's hooves as he was reined to a halt near the path that connected the housing compound to the work area. The curving gravel drive and Mae's stone house were only steps away.

"You're home, all safe and sound," Morgan said, and as he'd done at the gate, reached round to assist her off the horse.

But this time as Christine dismounted, her foot slipped, causing her to give a strangled yelp and reach out to Morgan for support. He reacted instantly, somehow managing to catch hold of her and swing her around, until she was in his arms, balanced across the saddle in front of him.

For a second all Christine could do was blink. In her mind's eye she had seen herself crashing to the ground with Thunder's hooves dancing dangerously nearby. Then she realized that in being saved, she'd merely leapt from the frying pan into the fire.

He grinned at her. "Manna from heaven," he joked, but she could sense something more serious beneath his teasing words.

Her heart beat rapidly. All she could think was that she didn't want him to kiss her again. Or touch her again. She had to tear her gaze away, afraid he would read a message in her eyes she didn't mean. "Please let me down," she said.

"Don't I even get a thank-you?" he asked.

"Thank you," she said.

Her body was taut and growing warmer by the second. If he didn't let her down soon she was going to spontaneously combust! She wriggled, wanting her freedom. "I said what you asked," she reminded him.

"And very nicely, too." Then, to her relief, he let her slide carefully to the ground.

The earth wobbled under Christine's feet. Then she realized that the wobbliness originated in her. Not because of her near tumble, but because of her continuing reaction to Morgan! "I have to go," she said, then wondered why she'd felt the need to say it. What was wrong with her? Why didn't she just *go* if that was what she truly wanted?

He seemed as loath to break the moment as she was. "Is Erin's riding lesson still on for this evening?" he asked.

"She'll be disappointed if it's not."

"Will you be there, too?" he asked quietly.

Christine was coming to believe that he would never harm Erin. But that wasn't what he was asking. She shrugged. "Yes."

Another breathtaking smile slanted across his face, then he said simply, "Good," before he swung Thunder around and they trotted off toward the pens and corrals.

He sat the horse beautifully, Christine thought as she watched him. As if he'd been born to it. What did he do when he wasn't at the Parker Ranch? she wondered. Everyone talked about his taking leave of his job to come help his father and the Parkers on the ranch, but no one had mentioned what that job was.

Realizing she was staring after him, Christine quickly turned to follow the path to the house. Maybe she shouldn't accompany Erin to her lesson this evening. But if she stayed away, wouldn't that be like admitting she found him too disturbing?

MORGAN TRACED RAFE to the ranch office, where his friend sat talking to two uniformed visitors. One was Sheriff Jack Denton, the other his deputy, Tate Connelly.

The tune Morgan had been whistling in happy memory of the past half hour died on his lips the instant the men turned their dour expressions on him. "More trouble?" he asked, instantly alert.

Sheriff Denton, a soft-spoken man in his late fifties, shifted in his chair. A descendant of one of the Buffalo Soldiers (African American enlisted men who were members of the U.S. Army, and shortly after the Civil War were sent to some of the most dangerous outposts in the unfolding American West), the sheriff had roots almost as deep in the area as the Parkers'. Never rail thin, he had put on some weight over the past few years, but if anyone thought he was slowing down, they were very much mistaken. He still pursued criminals with as much energy as he had his first day on the job.

"'Fraid so," the sheriff confirmed. "Seems that thievin' gang's come this way. Last night the Clearys next door lost thirty calves. Fence was cut, then stood back up. Tate here says it looks the same as the ones he saw last week over at Debolt."

Morgan hadn't laid eyes on Tate Connelly in years.

One or the other of them had always seemed to be away. Himself at his job, Tate either at the university studying for a degree in criminology or gaining experience on the Dallas police force. He was a young man—twenty-four, twenty-five—but from everything Morgan had heard about him, he had all the instincts of a good lawman. Must be in the genes, Morgan thought. Come down to him from his dad, who'd died a true hero. Not to mention his mother, who worked dispatch in the sheriff's office. Morgan gave him a quick once-over and decided that he liked what he saw. Tate was a nice-looking young man, with neatly clipped brown hair and steady brown eyes. Solid. Sound of spirit.

"Did they leave anything to go on?" Morgan asked.

Tate answered, "The hand that found 'em missin' had a hissy fit right on the spot, kickin' up dirt, cussin' to beat the band. He took care of most everythin' that might've been there. And the road's been used a bunch after."

"We thought you might like to take a look," the sheriff said.

"What about Ed?" Morgan asked, mentioning his fellow inspector.

"He's comin' this evening. Said probably about seven."

"Then I'll come about that time, too. Go over it with him. I don't want to step on his toes. It's his district."

"Just thought you might like a look-see." The sheriff's smile formed deep creases in his weathered brown cheeks. "Just to keep your hand in. It must be itchin'."

"I don't need to tell you Ed's a good man," Morgan said.

"You bet you don't," the sheriff agreed. Then, standing up, he settled the hat he'd been balancing on his knee back onto his graying hair. "We been working together for more years than I care to think about. Ed, too, I'm sure."

"What's this I hear about you retiring?" Rafe asked, getting to his feet, as well.

Sheriff Denton chuckled. "Just a rumor so far. I'm waiting for Tate here to get out of his trainin' pants so's he can take over for me."

The deputy was about to protest when Jodie swept into the room.

She looked like an exotic flower in a prickly desert. She was dressed for town, in a soft cotton dress that made the most of her youthful figure. At first she looked slightly startled, as if she'd expected to find Rafe alone. Then she started to smile. "Is everyone coming or going? I'll only take a second if a meeting's about to start. Has anyone seen my dad? Rafe, have you?" She looked questioningly at her cousin, but she wasn't unaware of the impact she'd made on the other men. Morgan smiled to himself. Mae and Rafe had had trouble with her already, and if they weren't careful, they were going to have more.

"Last time I saw him he was on his way to Del Norte to do an errand for Mae," Rafe said.

Jodie pulled a face. "He hasn't left yet, has he? I

was hoping to get a ride.''

Sheriff Denton gallantly came to her rescue. ''Tate's going back to Del Norte. Would you like him to give you a ride? You won't mind, will you, Tate?''

Jodie's eyes settled on the younger man. Her lids flickered, then narrowed, and her body seemed to stiffen.

''Hello, Jodie,'' Tate murmured.

''Hi,'' she answered shortly. Then she smiled at the sheriff. ''Will I have to ride in back? Or can I share the front seat?''

''Jodie, you can ride anywhere you want,'' the sheriff assured her.

''Then if it's okay with Tate, I accept.''

''Sure,'' Tate said. ''Why not?''

Jodie glanced at him suspiciously. Had she picked up on the same offhand ''if I must, I must'' tone Morgan had? He watched them closely, curious about their relationship.

''Jim Cleary said to tell you to watch out,'' Sheriff Denton said as they all went outside to the parking area.

''We already are,'' Rafe replied.

Jodie and Tate set off uneasily in his patrol car and the sheriff set off in his, leaving Morgan and Rafe to themselves.

''I'm tellin' the men to check the stock more often and to vary the times when they do it,'' Morgan said. ''We should vary our routine, too. And maybe set up some shifts.''

Rafe's lips tightened. ''I'll sure be glad when we

get those calves branded and marked. But, like you've said before, it's still damn hard to prove a steak's been rustled.''

THE AFTERNOON went by slowly. Fortunately Erin had played so hard in the morning that she'd slept through Christine's tardy return. And as soon as she awoke, she rushed straight back to Harriet's to resume the make-believe wedding plans.

Christine used the time that followed in a fruitless repeat of her earlier search, trying to find Mrs. Tobin's address. Later she sat restlessly beneath the courtyard trees—until finally she decided to present herself at Rafe's house and offer what assistance she could to Shannon and Harriet. She'd seen them earlier carrying in more supplies.

She knocked on the front door, but nobody answered. So she let herself in and followed the sound of music and laughter to the kitchen. The room was something of a shambles, but the new wallpaper looked beautiful, as did the sections of woodwork and cabinets Shannon and Harriet were currently painting. Every window was open both for coolness and to dissipate the fumes.

"Christine!" Shannon cried, looking up. Her face was aglow with happiness and good humor. She struggled to rise from the floor, paintbrush in hand.

"No, no, don't get up," Christine said.

Harriet reached to turn off the mariachi music being broadcast from Mexico.

"And don't do that, either," Christine said. "I came to help, not get in the way."

Shannon and Harriet looked at each other, then Harriet rooted around in a wooden box and came up with another brush. She held it in front of Christine with formal ceremony. "Your level of skill, miss?" she inquired.

"Moderate?" Christine guessed.

Harriet passed her the brush. "Then you'll fit right in. That's the same as Shannon and me."

"Where would you like me to start?"

"The pantry?"

Shannon laughed. "Ooh...that's bad, Harriet. Give her the worst possible place."

Harriet grimaced. "I thought it was worth a try. All right, how about the doorway over here?"

"I'll do the pantry. I don't mind," Christine volunteered.

"Maybe you should take a look first. It hasn't been painted in years."

Christine examined it. "I'll do it."

They painted nonstop for the next hour, Christine listening to the other two women's teasing give-and-take, before Harriet called for a break. "I'd better see what those kids are up to. You've heard about the 'wedding,' haven't you?" When Christine nodded, she continued, "I told them to come get me before they start playing with the makeup, but you know how that goes. They forget. If I'm not there to supervise, there's no telling what they'll do to each other."

After Harriet left, Shannon handed Christine a soda and they went to sit at a small square table that had been moved into the dining room, along with other items from the kitchen. But now, Christine couldn't relax. Because, when she let herself, she remembered they were Parkers and she wasn't? Because she remembered why she was being challenged—that they didn't want to share their wealth? At times, that was becoming easy to forget. In fact, everyone other than Mae was going out of their way to be nice to her and to Erin. Folding her in, almost as if...

"You probably think I'm crazy, don't you?" Shannon asked. "I'd think that myself. Not content to have a monster wedding in less than six weeks, I decide to redecorate. But it's—" she paused "—like my life is starting over again, and I want everything to be fresh and new. Last year...was horrible. The plane crash, losing the people I loved most in the world. I wasn't sure I wanted to live. Then I came here."

"According to Mae's plan."

Shannon smiled wryly. "Yes, she does like to run things. But this time she was right. Rafe is...well, I love him. He loves me. And we're very happy she did what she did."

Christine fingered the condensation beading on the soda can. "What do you think she has planned for Erin and me?"

"Mae's really good about zeroing in on the truth of things. Sometimes she's off on a tangent—wanting things to work out her way, no matter what. But if the truth's there, she'll find it and she'll accept it."

"I'm not lying," Christine said.

"I never thought you were."

"And I didn't steal anything."

"I didn't think that, either."

Christine looked at her. "Why do you believe me?" she asked.

"A good sixth sense?"

Harriet returned to finish her section of cabinet, needing to hurry back to her house as soon as she did. "You should see my living room," she moaned. "Those kids! It's almost as bad as if it was the real thing. You started it, Shannon, you and Rafe. Why didn't you elope?"

"Then you wouldn't get to be matron of honor. Oh, by the way, how's the dress coming?"

"I didn't know I'd be four months pregnant at the time, that's how it's coming. Marie and I are going to be adjusting the waist seams up to the last second. I'm starting to look like a whale already."

"You aren't."

"I am! Lord, if this baby is twins, I don't know what I'll do."

"You'll have plenty of baby-sitters all hours of the day and night around here. You'll still be able to write."

"Will I?" Harriet demanded, suddenly far more serious than she'd started out. "Mae says I should get my priorities straight. Children are far more important than a hobby. But writing isn't a hobby to me. It's important, too."

Shannon squeezed Harriet's hand, and Harriet looked at Christine rather shamefaced. "I'm being overly dramatic. I tend to do that when I'm pregnant. Normally I'm a rock, but when those hormones kick in…"

"Stop worrying," Shannon advised. "Just do what you want—like you always do. Write another story and send it to the same publisher. And I'll bet they publish it, too.''

''You've written a book?'' Christine asked.

''A children's book—young adult. And it's not published yet. It won't be out until next November.''

''But it's sold,'' Shannon said.

The front door opened and two sets of boots clomped across the floor, ending up in the kitchen. When Rafe and Morgan came through the doorway, Christine instantly tensed. She hadn't expected to see Morgan again so soon. She wasn't prepared.

''Looks good,'' Rafe complimented. He smiled at Shannon and kissed her, only reluctantly breaking it off.

Christine continued to paint the outer facing of the pantry, the finishing touch. Her gaze had already met, then slid away from Morgan's.

''I see you have another volunteer,'' Rafe said.

''Thankfully, yes. Christine showed up and was willing, so we put her to work.''

Christine felt Rafe's dark gaze survey both her and the work she'd accomplished. He made no comment, merely nodded. But then, considering his position as Mae's confederate, she didn't expect more.

Harriet rinsed her brush and left it soaking in water. ''I'll be back later if I can, Shannon, but I think we just about have this room whipped. Now all that's left is the dining room, right?''

''That's it.''

As the others continued to talk about an unexpected delay in the shipment of wallpaper for the dining room, Morgan ambled over to where Christine was working and murmured, "A woman of unexpected talents."

"Dabbing paint around on woodwork isn't much of a talent."

"It is when you do a good job."

Christine glanced at the others. Morgan was standing far closer than she liked, and she didn't want anyone to get the wrong idea. But none of the others had noticed them—yet.

"It's a nice thing you're doing," he continued, "helping Shannon."

"It sprang from pure boredom."

"You're used to a more adventurous life?"

Christine shrugged. She wished he'd take a step or two back. It wasn't as if he was looming over her, but even at a moderate distance she could sense the electrical charge of his body. Remember how it felt to be pressed against him, remember the heat of their mutual need.

Christine straightened, having hurried her last few strokes. "That's it. I'm done," she announced.

Harriet had finally taken her leave, and Rafe and Shannon had been sharing a quiet intimate word. Christine's statement caused Shannon to look around, and when she did, she flashed a quick smile. "That's wonderful. Thank you so much, Christine. Another pair of willing hands has really made a difference."

Christine rinsed her brush and added it to Harriet's in the water-filled plastic tub. "Just let me know when I can help again. It— gives me something to do."

She sent a faint smile to everyone present, then hurried outdoors.

She hadn't expected Morgan to follow, but he caught up with her before she'd taken more than a few steps along the curving drive that led to Mae's.

"I have some bad news for you to pass along to Erin," he said quietly.

Christine stopped to look at him.

"Our riding lesson has to be canceled today. Something's come up I have to see to. I know it's going to disappoint her, but—"

"If it can't be helped, it can't be helped," Christine said.

"Tell her we'll do it tomorrow."

Christine had mixed feelings. On one hand, she was relieved. She wouldn't have to see him again that evening. On the other, looking at it from Erin's point of view... "I'll tell her you'll give her another lesson when you can. There's no use setting a date when you aren't sure. That way she won't be disappointed again." When he frowned, she added, "There's nothing sure about anything, is there? You're a very busy man. As foreman here you must—"

"*Acting* foreman," he corrected her. "Dad still has the title. I'm not about to take it away from him."

"Even though you do the work."

"Just tell Erin it'll be tomorrow. She has my promise."

Christine turned away. "For what that's worth," she muttered.

To her surprise she was spun back around. She had never seen Morgan angry before. She had the feeling he seldom was.

His eyes glittered. "You might come from a place

where people have forgotten what it means to give their word, where they'll lie to you as soon as look at you, but that's not the way it works out here. That's not the way my daddy taught me, or his daddy taught him. If I promise to do something, it'll get done."

"You're not doing it today," she said. "You told her you would, and you aren't."

"I warned her that ranch business could get in the way. You were there. You heard me."

Christine remembered. He had added a caveat.

"I have to go meet somebody over at—" he began, but Christine broke in.

"You don't have to explain. I believe you."

His eyes glittered again, then the anger was tamped. "Well, that's a first," he proclaimed wryly.

"I'll tell her what you said," Christine told him. She wanted to get away more than ever now. Had to get away.

This time he let her go without attempting to stop her. But for the life of her Christine couldn't resist a backward glance once she'd reached Mae's front porch.

He stood exactly where she'd left him. Not moving. Just watching her.

Christine held his gaze for a long second, then, pulse leaping erratically, went indoors.

CHAPTER TEN

CHRISTINE COULDN'T GO to sleep that night. She tried but it was hopeless. Every time she closed her eyes she started to think about Morgan Hughes. Restlessly she slipped out of bed, went to get a drink of water, adjusted Erin's covers, then finally stood in the open doorway to the balcony.

A lonely cricket chirped in the flower bed that fronted the house. Soon another answered. Christine's brooding gaze fell on the moonlit courtyard. There were so many other things she should be thinking about. Such as what was she going to do if she couldn't find Mrs. Tobin? How would she ever be able to prove her innocence? And...exactly how far were Abigail and Brendan willing to take their farciful accusation? Would they dare go to the police? Could they set everything up to look as if she'd done it? She wouldn't put it past them. But then, surely, if it went that far, someone—the police?—would find Mrs. Tobin and learn the truth. They had far greater resources than she did to investigate.

A movement under the nearest tree in the courtyard caught Christine's eye. Was it human or animal? Would a coyote be bold enough to enter the compound? An almost primal apprehension caused Christine to freeze, so as not to draw attention to herself. Breathlessly she waited. Then a form emerged from the mottled shade—Jodie!

Christine stepped over to the balcony railing and half-whispered, half-called her name. Jodie looked up and, upon seeing Christine, changed direction.

Her hair was beautiful in the moonlight, a milk-washed coppery red. She was dressed as if for day, in jeans and a T-shirt that she'd covered with a jean jacket.

"What are you doing awake?" Jodie whispered. "Couldn't you sleep, either?"

Instinctively Christine liked this oddity in the Parker nest. She was young and trying to find her way, and as a consequence refused to condemn before having uncontrovertible proof. "Hang on, will you?" Christine whispered back. "I'll come down."

Jodie grinned and waved, and Christine exchanged her gown and robe for an outfit similar to Jodie's. Only she substituted a sweater for the jean jacket.

She crept through the house and onto the front porch. Jodie was waiting near the beginning of the short walkway.

"Do you know what time it is?" Christine asked softly, conspiratorially.

"When I came outside, it was twelve-thirty."

"It's one o'clock now."

Jodie looked around them. "Come on," she said. "Let's get away from the houses." She led Christine into the courtyard and arranged two lawn chairs closer together. "This is better," she said. "We won't wake anyone up out here."

"Your Aunt Mae?"

"Anyone," Jodie murmured. "Well, Shannon's okay. She's not..."

"A Parker?"

Jodie grimaced. "It's not as bad as that. I didn't mean—"

"I think I know what you mean," Christine interrupted. She looked around at the beauty of the night. Harriet's flowers—Christine had learned that Harriet was the person responsible for all the gardening around the houses—lent a sweet scent to the air that just about, if not quite, covered the more earthy tang of wild grasses and cattle and cooling ground. "It's peaceful out here, a place you can think. Somewhere you'd rather not have disturbed by have-tos and shoulds."

"Exactly." Jodie sighed. "You do understand."

"I like to find places I can think, too."

Jodie tilted her head. "In some kind of weird way you remind me of Shannon. You're not the same at all, and yet you are. How old are you?" she asked.

"Twenty-five."

"And Erin's—"

"She was born when I was seventeen."

Jodie gave a low whistle. "I'm eighteen now, and I can't imagine..." She paused. "Would it be too nosy of me to ask..."

Christine knew immediately what Jodie wanted to ask. "I considered abortion, and then I considered giving my baby up for adoption," she said, "but in the end, I couldn't do either. They weren't right for me."

"Hasn't it been hard?" Jodie asked, wide-eyed.

"At times."

"Has her father—"

"I'd rather not talk about that."

Jodie instantly recoiled from her own curiosity. "I didn't mean... I wasn't asking because the family wants to know. I only—"

Christine interrupted her stumbling misery. "It's all right. Really." She smiled. "I know you didn't mean anything. I'd be curious, too, if I were you."

"He wouldn't...or couldn't marry you, though?"

Christine's mouth tightened. "No."

"Men!" Jodie said, and she said it with such conviction that it peaked Christine's interest.

"You sound as if you've experienced some man trouble, too."

"No one's told you? I'm surprised. I was the prime subject of conversation all last winter. 'What can we do to make things better for Jodie? How can we cheer her up?' Then eventually, 'Stop moping around, girl! Find something to do!'" She gave a sour grin. "I seriously thought about leaving home again."

"Again?"

Jodie sighed. "I ran off with my boyfriend. At least, I thought he was my boyfriend. It turned out I was just someone he could have a good time with."

"Where did you go?"

"To a ranch in New Mexico where his brother worked." She paused. "I would have gone anywhere with him. I thought...I thought we were going to get married in January as soon as I turned eighteen, but he...he caved in as soon as Rafe and my dad and

Shannon caught up with us. He couldn't get away from me fast enough!''

It still hurt, Christine could see. She recognized the feeling. Betrayal by someone you love was the worst kind. It planted a barb that was almost impossible to remove.

Jodie forced a smile. "He was a cowboy on the ranch. His name's Rio. And to me he was just the finest thing—good-looking, fun, and could he kiss!''

"Where is he now?"

"Who knows? We left him in New Mexico, but he could be anywhere—except West Texas. Rafe told him he better not come back here, and I don't think he ever will.''

"Was he your first and only boyfriend?" Christine asked softly.

Jodie thought for a moment. "Yeah, my first real one. I had a crush on someone when I was in school. It started in middle school, when he drove the bus one semester. I was eleven, he was eighteen. He thought I was a brat. He still does.''

"He lives around here?"

"He went away to college the fall after he drove the bus. Now he's back. He's been back a year, but like I said…''

"He thinks you're a brat."

"Yeah.''

"What happened to the crush?"

"I grew up. I saw how silly I was. I found Rio.''

"Well, since it didn't work out with Rio, have you thought about—''

"No!'' Jodie's voice had unconsciously risen. "I

don't want another boyfriend! Especially not Tate! He's just so... I'm not real big on men right now. I want to go to college, see something of the world. There has to be more to life than this!'' Her sweeping arm encompassed the entire ranch.

"You're tired of being a Parker?"

"I've been one all my life. I'm tired of everyone— Aunt Mae mostly—telling me what to do. What to think. How to act.'' She moved uncomfortably. "She was sweet to me when I came back from New Mexico, though. She's sweet to me most of the time now—in her own way. But then, she wanted me to go to college and I am, so she thinks she's gotten her way. But I'm doing it for me. Not for her. I finally figured out that going to college will let me be on my own, make my own decisions.''

Silence descended between them, then Jodie said, "What about your mom and dad? How did they take your having a baby so young?"

"Hasn't Mae told you? I thought the news would get around to everyone."

"Sometimes I listen, sometimes I don't. So tell me."

"I'm like Erin—my dad wasn't around when I was born. And my mother...my mother didn't really care. She, ah, had other things on her mind."

Jodie grew very still. "We're mirror images almost. My mother left, so did your dad. My dad doesn't have a clue, and your mother..."

"My mother was an alcoholic."

Jodie looked at her. "Wow," she breathed, then a moment later she said, "I guess maybe I didn't have it so hard with my dad. He is clueless at times, but I know he's there if I need him. Did, ah, you have other family nearby?''

''No.''

''Wow,'' she said again.

''I better go back inside.'' Christine stood.

Jodie got to her feet, too. She seemed at a loss for something more to say. Finally she murmured, ''What you did took courage.''

Christine shook her head. ''Courage means bravery. And I wasn't brave.''

''I think you were.''

''I met someone who was brave—Ira. To face the end of his life the way he did, with such dignity.''

''I barely knew him.''

''That's too bad,'' Christine said as she turned back toward Mae's house.

CHRISTINE TOSSED for the next hour after she went back to bed, her talk with Jodie bringing back old memories. The reaction of her mother when finally told of the pregnancy, her mother's insistence that *she* wasn't going to be responsible for the baby's care or for any of the costs. Christine had loved her mother, but she was honest enough, even then, to admit there were times when it was difficult.

She thought of Ira, wondering if he'd known about the wall of resistance she would come up against while trying to claim her share of the ranch. And why, if what Mae Parker and the others said was true and he couldn't legally leave it to her, he had done so, anyway. That didn't make sense.

It was important, though, not to think along those lines. She had to believe that it was within Ira's rights to leave his share of the ranch to her. If she thought otherwise, she'd panic, because then, she and Erin would have to leave. And they'd be back to square one, with no job, no place to live and a continuation of the hard-scrabble life they'd led up to this point. To glimpse salvation, to have it within your grasp, then to see it slip away would be the cruelest blow. It wasn't something the Ira she knew would allow.

Then once again, coming full circle, she thought of Morgan Hughes. Reliving every second they'd spent in each other's company. The way he looked, the way he moved, the way he smiled. The way she'd felt when he kissed her!

Christine moaned into her pillow. If only she could erase him from her mind!

IT SEEMED unusually bright to Christine when she awoke the next morning. She had no idea how long she'd slept, but it hadn't been long enough. She fought against the muzziness, trying to understand why everything felt so different. Then, checking the clock on the bedside table, she saw the reason. It was already after nine. They were usually finishing breakfast about this time, not just getting up!

She threw the covers back and swung her feet to the floor, ready to awaken Erin. They were making inroads with their friendship with Marie; she didn't want to harm their progress by disrupting the house-keeper's schedule. But Erin's bed was empty, and in Erin's usual fashion, mostly made up. The spread was pulled over the pillow and tucked in underneath, somewhat off kilter along the edges, but an attempt had been made. And Golden Belle claimed place of honor among the other stuffed animals and dolls.

"Erin?" Christine called.

There was no answer.

She crossed to the closed bathroom door and tapped on it. Still no answer. Erin must have awakened at their usual time and gone downstairs on her own.

Christine hurriedly dressed in the same jeans she'd worn last night and a fresh denim shirt. After a quick wash and a hasty application of lipstick and mascara, she dashed downstairs to the dining room—only to come upon Erin talking happily with Morgan Hughes. He sat at the table at her side enjoying a plate of eggs and bacon and some of Marie's delicious biscuits.

"Mornin'," he said, a twinkle in his eyes.

Christine had put on the brakes so fast upon seeing him that she had to take a little hop to keep from toppling over.

"Mommy! You're awake!" Erin cried, abandoning what remained of her bowl of cereal to come give her a hug.

"I didn't mean to sleep so late," Christine murmured, stroking her daughter's silky hair. "I usually wake up much earlier," she said to Morgan.

He'd gotten to his feet, as well. "So Erin tells me."

Christine smiled into her daughter's bright face and leaned down to kiss her forehead.

"I let you sleep, Mommy," Erin said. "When I talked to you and you didn't hear, I dressed and came down, and look who I found! Morgan says it's for sure

I'll have my riding lesson this evening, just like you said he said.''

Christine's gaze slid to Morgan's and then away again. "You'd better get back to your breakfast. You, too," she added to him as she took her usual place at the table.

Marie, who must have heard her voice, bustled into the room. "Good morning, Christine. I'll have your toast in just a few minutes."

"I'm not very hungry today, Marie. I'll munch on a biscuit. Coffee's what I need the most."

"Well, the pot on the table's fresh. I brought it in a little while ago. And there's more coming. Morgan? Do you need anything else?"

"You feed me almost as well as my momma does, Marie. I'll know where to come if she ever tosses me out."

"Delores? Toss you out? It'll be a cold day in Hades when that happens!"

The housekeeper's gaze swept the table for needed refills, then she bustled back into the kitchen.

Christine transferred a biscuit to her plate and smeared a little strawberry jam on it. She forced herself to nibble on the edge.

"Morgan said he had to see about some rustlers, Mommy! That's why he had to miss our lesson yesterday."

"Rustlers?" Christine echoed. "I thought rustlers were something from the past."

"Oh, no," Morgan said. "There's plenty of cattle thieves operating today. Sometimes they can hit a rancher pretty hard. If it's a small rancher running fifty or sixty head at seven or eight hundred dollars a head and he gets five or six head stolen, that's quite a loss."

"But this is a big ranch."

"Bigger ranch, more cattle to steal. A lot more range to choose from, too."

"Have any cows been stolen here?"

"Not here. At a neighboring ranch."

Christine frowned. "What are you going to do about it?"

He smiled. "Wait and watch."

"That's all?"

"Not much else you can do. Just keep on your toes."

Christine knew virtually nothing about cattle or ranching. Still, she'd found the discussion of rustlers interesting.

She picked at her biscuit some more, but mostly sipped her coffee. A vague headache threatened, and she still felt muzzy from sleep.

She looked up when Erin giggled at something Morgan had said. He'd finished with his breakfast and was leaning back in his chair. Erin's face was shining, and she appeared to hang on Morgan's every word.

"No, Morgan, that's not right!" she exclaimed. "The bride doesn't walk down the aisle on her hands!"

"I'm sure I saw that in one of those fancy etiquette books somewhere."

"*You* don't read books like that!"

"I do. Every evening. I read them out loud to Thunder."

"You don't! You don't! You're making that up!"

Christine was uncomfortable with the rapport developing between her daughter and Morgan. She didn't want Erin to get too attached. She cleared her throat. "Ah, Erin? Speaking of weddings, when's the big day?"

Erin turned a happy face to her—happier than Christine remembered seeing it in a long time. "Tomorrow, I think," she chirped. "Jessica said—" She stopped, her eyes growing huge as she turned back to Morgan. "Jessica's waiting for me over at Gwen and Wesley's, isn't she? I forgot!"

"They'll wait," Morgan said.

"I have to go!" Erin cried, and scrambled away from the table. Then she ran back to hug Morgan's neck before moving on to Christine. "They need me," she explained at the door. "I'm the only one who can work the tape player. It has a broken piece and you have to hold it *just* right!"

Morgan chuckled after she'd gone, his lazy glance moving over Christine. "She's quite a kid," he said. "Jessica likes her. And Jessica's picky about who she plays with."

"Jessica's your niece."

"One of my brother Russell's daughters. You met his son, Rusty, the first day you—"

"I remember him."

He smiled slowly. "That was quite a day, wasn't it?" When Christine said nothing, he went on, "Russell's kids have been staying at our place while Russell gets himself established in Colorado. They've bounced around a lot over the past few years, and I think Jessica's had enough of it."

"You drove her here this morning?" Christine asked.

He nodded. "Erin's bounced around a lot, too, hasn't she?" he asked. "You can kinda tell that about a kid."

"If she's bounced, we've done it together," Christine said tightly.

"Yeah, you can tell that, too. She's been looked after."

Christine made no more pretense of eating. "Are you trying to ask me something?" she demanded.

"Not really. I thought we were just havin' a nice conversation."

Christine stood up. "Well, you may not have anything else to do, but I certainly have."

"I didn't say I didn't have anything to do." He stood up to dig in the front pocket of his snug-fitting jeans. "LeRoy asked me to give you these. Here."

He tossed Christine her car keys. They made a gentle arc over the table before falling into her hands.

"Has he given up on it?" she asked.

"Nope. Says it's runnin' like a top, and he asked me to tell you he's sorry for takin' so long. Says there was a part he's been waitin' on and that it just got in yesterday."

Christine stared at the key ring. It seemed to have been weeks since she'd seen it. "Thank you," she murmured. "That was really nice of him. I never expected—"

"As I've mentioned before, the Parkers are good people."

She gave a halfhearted smile and walked to the door. He was right behind her.

"You told Erin what I said," he murmured as they crossed into the living room.

"Of course. I said I would."

"I thought we'd parted with a little question still hovering in the air."

"What question?"

"Whether, deep down, you ever believe anything anyone tells you. Or if you just go along, waiting for people to disappoint you."

Christine spun around to face him. "Can I help it if that's been my experience?"

The ring of truth in her reply obviously got through to him. His eyes met hers...searching.

Christine couldn't hide the multitude of hurts she'd suffered over the years. If, as he'd claimed, he could sense a child who'd been transplanted numerous times, but who'd still been well cared for, could he also sense the reverse?

A sound escaped his lips as he lifted a hand to touch her cheek. But the act wasn't so much sexually charged as it was one heart reaching out to another in empathy.

Then Mae came into the room, shattering the moment. Both Christine and Morgan moved hastily apart.

Mae's eagle eyes bored into them. She was aware she'd interrupted something. And she didn't seem pleased.

"Morgan," Mae snapped, "I was looking for you."

Christine took advantage of the moment to leave the room.

"I KNOW YOU'RE BUSY, Morgan," Mae began, "but if you can't do the job I asked you to, say so!"

Morgan was still shaken by the interlude just passed. He'd hassled Christine, she'd fought back, and the next thing he knew, he felt as if he'd been drawn into her soul. "I told you this was going to take time, Mae." He fell back on his previous excuse.

"I don't have that much time!" Mae retorted, moving irritably across the room. "I'm an old woman. I want to get this settled."

Morgan's lips twitched. "Oh, come on now. You're not so old."

She speared him with an impatient look. "Of course I am! I'm over eighty! When you're over eighty, you'll feel old, too!"

"You've never acted it."

She rubbed her right thigh, the one she'd broken some years before. A break that had put an end to her hands-on running of the ranch. "Some days I feel my age more than others." She looked at him again. "Surely you've found something out. You took her for a ride. I saw you, remember?"

Morgan's reply was careful. "Well, Christine seems to have come out of her background in pretty good shape. Seems honest. Puts that little girl's welfare before her own."

"Who's the girl's daddy?"

"I can't just come out and ask that. She'd know in a second what I'm doing."

Frowning, Mae straightened a knickknack on the fireplace mantel. "You're not listening with something other than your mind, are you, Morgan?" she asked gruffly.

It wasn't very often that Morgan experienced a spurt of anger directed against a person he liked and admired. But he felt it now. "No, Mae," he answered grimly. "It's not that."

She turned to look at him. "You sure?"

Morgan could feel the muscles in his face tighten. "I'm positive. The last thing I want—"

"What you want doesn't always enter into it. She's a pretty little thing. You're a young healthy single man. Just be careful, Morgan. She's the kind of gal that can fool you. But then, you know about that first-hand, don't you? What with Russell and Adell." Mae sighed and went back to tinkering with the knick-knacks. "Sometimes it's a blessing never to have married. You might have regrets, but they're a different sort of regrets. At least you've never had to air your dirty linen in public. Think of what's going on with Thomas and Darlene's Richard." She sighed again, shaking her head.

Morgan's anger dissipated. Somehow, looking at her today, he saw that Mae did appear to be suffering the full weight of her eighty-plus years. This was the first time he'd seen her with her guard down. He knew Richard's divorce proceedings were upsetting to her, but he hadn't realized how much. Did she see it as a chink in the Parker family's invincibility? And similarly, was that why she was working so hard to disprove Christine's claim? Did she worry that if Erin was Ira's child, it would somehow go against her ideal of the way a Parker should behave? And, as the head of the family, did she feel accountable to her ancestors for every bad thing that happened on her watch?

Morgan closed the distance between them, and almost as much to his surprise as to Mae's, he wrapped an arm around her shoulders and gave a gentle squeeze. She felt so fragile. "Everything's going to work out just fine, Mae," he said softly.

She said nothing, but she did pat his hand.

CHAPTER ELEVEN

CHRISTINE RETREATED to her room after leaving Morgan and Mae. The vague headache that had been threatening had caught up to her, full force. Stretching out on her bed, she closed her eyes.

She wished she'd never gone downstairs. She could have done without witnessing Erin's growing attachment to Morgan. Not to mention her own... What should she call that silent exchange with Morgan? All she knew was it had touched deep within her. And his reaction, his reaching out to her, not sensually, but sensitively, had made her tremble. Still made her tremble.

She jerked upright. No! This was extremely dangerous ground for her. Ground she had trod once before and didn't want to again.

All those years ago she'd been at a particularly vulnerable stage in her life, just as she was now. Filled with the need to be well-thought-of, to be believed in. To be loved.

No! She jumped to her feet and went into the bathroom for an aspirin. What was wrong with her? Had she taken leave of her senses? But then, wasn't that the problem? Her overactive senses?

She swallowed the aspirin, then stared at her reflection in the mirror. Her face still looked much as it had when she'd just turned sixteen. When she'd met the boy, a whole year older, who had come to mean so much to her. And who, when he'd learned of the baby he'd helped create, had run frightened, denying responsibility and citing her mother's behavior as her own. And to make matters worse, he'd spread nasty rumors about her around their high school.

Christine turned away from the hurt-filled image in the mirror and dragged herself back to bed. Maybe if she caught up a little on the sleep she'd missed last night, she'd feel more settled emotionally and not be so...so irrational.

CHRISTINE DID FEEL BETTER upon awakening a couple of hours later. She decided to ignore much of what had happened that morning and concentrate only on the positive.

She set out to find LeRoy, to thank him personally for repairing her car. But he wasn't around the garage or the barn, and when she stopped by Harriet's, she discovered the reason.

"Rafe needed him to help keep an eye out in one of the pastures," Harriet said. "You've heard about the rustlers working nearby, right?" When Christine nodded, she continued, "Rafe needs all the extra men he can find right now. He'd even get Gib up on a horse if he thought it would do any good, but Gib would soon be off it sketching. Did I tell you he's a painter? He used to keep it a secret—from Mae, at any rate. The rest of us knew. Mae still thinks it's a waste of a grown man's time."

"Is he any good?" Christine asked.

"I think he is. He does Western scenes. Get him to show you some of his work sometime. It'd make him happy if you did."

"What does he do around here?" Christine asked. "I rarely see him except when he's coming or going from Mae's."

"That's because Mae's the one who keeps him hopping. Jodie gets a little impatient with him because he lets Mae order him around. And she's right. He should stand up to her more. But then—" she shrugged "—it's the way he is. Easygoing."

The sound of children's voices in the backyard caused Harriet to turn. "I hate to be the one to break this up, but Delores called a little while ago. Jessica's daddy is planning to phone her after lunch, so she needs to go home." She smiled as Jessica—the only blonde in the group—ran up to get into place outside the wide kitchen window. "They've practiced and practiced this. It's set for tomorrow, you know. After Sunday dinner. The invitations will be given out this evening. Erin has yours."

Recorded music blared and Jessica stepped away from the house, her steps measured, like a bride coming down the aisle. She clutched a wilted daisy, and a little in front of her, Gwen scattered pretend flower petals. Both walked toward Wesley and Erin, who waited in front of a fan-shaped flower trellis.

Christine smiled. "They look like they have it down pretty pat."

"They do, except for the occasional disagreement or disaster. Earlier, Gwen decided *she* wanted to be the bride. Then Erin told them all that the bride should walk down the aisle on her hands." Harriet laughed and shook her head. "Honestly, I don't know where kids get some of these things!"

Christine knew exactly where Erin had gotten that particular bit of whimsy.

Harriet reached for her car keys hanging on a board by the back door, then went over to the stove to remove a pot from the burner.

"I can take her, if you like," Christine volunteered. "I mean, you're busy cooking, and LeRoy was nice enough to get my car running. Let me do it. I promise I won't get lost again."

Harriet grinned. "Well, it's a little hard to get lost going over to Little Springs. If you set off on the right road, you'll find it." She paused. "Your driving Jessica would be great, thank you. If you're sure you don't mind..."

"I'd like to help," Christine said.

THE CHILDREN'S PLAY ended on a chorus of groans and pleas to let them practice one more time, but Harriet was adamant. "I promised your grandmother, Jessica."

Of course Gwen and Wesley had to come along for the ride, as well as Erin. After they'd all trooped to the car and she'd settled them inside, Christine got behind the wheel. Someone—LeRoy?—had cleaned and polished it inside and out. It hardly seemed like the same vehicle. And when she turned the key and the old engine sprang instantly to life and actually began to purr, the impression increased. She smiled in delight.

Little Springs was just as Christine remembered it. The sudden greenness of a clump of trees, then a weathered set of corrals, a barn, a few outbuildings and a low stone house. Morgan Hughes's family home.

Christine shook her head. She wasn't going to think about him.

The front screen door opened and Delores Hughes stepped outside, frowning in puzzlement at the strange car. But once Christine got out, Delores's frown was replaced by a smile. Especially when the children piled out after her.

"Oh! So it's you!" she said, coming to greet them, wiping her hands on her apron.

"My car's just been repaired, so I thought I'd try it out," Christine said, unsure of her welcome. "Harriet gave the okay for me to bring Jessica."

"Of course," Delores said, her eyes, so like Morgan's, moving curiously over Christine.

What had Morgan told her? Christine wondered. Or had he told her anything? The woman's gaze switched to Jessica.

"Jess, why don't you take the others inside and get them a soda? And listen for your daddy's call. He talked to Rusty and Mindy earlier. This one's just for you." Jessica did as she was told, but not without dragging her feet.

Delores shook her head as she watched her granddaughter move slowly inside. "Here her daddy's calling her special, and she acts like it's a terrible trial."

She sighed. "Oh, well, they'll be together soon enough. Then Russell can try to start making up for some of the things his kids have missed along the way." She glanced at Christine. "Would you like some coffee?"

Christine's first impulse was to refuse. But as had happened the last time she'd been here, she soon found herself agreeing in the face of the older woman's resolute hospitality.

The children had taken over the kitchen, so Delores led Christine out onto the back porch. It was shaded and, even in the middle of the day, relatively cool. A round metal table with two matching chairs were set off a distance from the doorway.

"You make yourself comfortable," Delores invited, "while I get the coffee going." Then she disappeared back into the kitchen, only to reappear minutes later, nodding approval that Christine had chosen the chair farthest from the door. "I'll probably have to be up and down like a Jack-in-the-box seein' to the kids. I tell you, at my age, it's almost too much. I can barely keep up with 'em. But—" Delores leaned closer "—to tell you the truth, I'm going to miss the little rascals when they leave. It's going to be so quiet around here. Too quiet."

"When do they leave?" Christine asked.

"Their daddy's coming down for the big wedding, then he's going to take 'em back. So it'll be the first of June." Delores sighed.

A loud cry of protest made her hop up. She disappeared inside again, and Christine could hear her saying, "All right. That's enough!" Then, after a pause,

"Jessica, you pour your sister more drink than that. Now, all of you, sit at the table and behave." Finally, a few seconds later, far more sternly, "I mean *now*, Jessica!"

Delores came back bearing the coffee on a tray.

"That girl," she said, shaking her head as she sat down. "Her daddy's got a handful coming. But he can handle it, I think. Now that the worst is over." She slid a mug across to Christine. "A nasty divorce," she explained.

Christine nodded.

Delores added both sugar and cream to her coffee and while stirring it said carefully, "Harriet tells me you're holding your own over there, in spite of Mae's being on the warpath."

"What does Morgan tell you?" Christine asked, unable to stop herself. Did she truly want to hear what Morgan had confided to his mother?

"Not a lot. I wish he'd say more, but he's too well trained."

Christine nodded again. This wasn't such a good idea. She should have dropped Jessica off and kept going. She didn't want to know anything about— "Trained in what?" she heard her wayward self question.

"He's a lawman of sorts. A detective. He hunts down rustlers for the Texas Cattlemen's Association. That's a federation of ranchers who've banded together to put a stop to…"

Delores continued to talk, but she'd lost Christine. Christine was concerned with only two pertinent words: *lawman* and *detective*.

"A…a lawman?" she repeated huskily.

Delores nodded. "He's assigned to a region in the panhandle that keeps him pretty busy. Lots of activity up there, but then, I suppose there's lots everywhere. People who'd rather profit off someone else's hard work than do the work themselves. Frankly, I'm relieved he's back. I'd keep him here if I could. What he does can be dangerous. He's had more than a few close calls."

Christine stumbled to her feet. "I…we…we have to get back," she said.

Delores frowned. "Are you all right? You look a little pale. Maybe you should stay sittin' down. Drink some of your coffee."

"I—I had a bad headache earlier. I thought it had gone away, but suddenly…"

"Then you shouldn't be driving, that's for sure! Come on." Delores moved around the table to collect Christine, placing a strong arm around her shoulders. "You come inside out of the heat and lie down for a little while in the cool. You can use mine and Dub's room."

"No, no…I'm fine, really. I'd rather—"

"Just for half an hour. That'll probably make all the difference. And don't worry about your little one or Wes and Gwen. They'll be fine. I'll give them lunch along with my crew and call Harriet to let her know what we're doing." She took Christine through to a small bedroom where she quickly pulled the curtains and fluffed a pillow. "You just rest for a while until you feel better."

Once she was alone, properly lying down as Delores

had insisted, Christine stared blankly at the ceiling. This short excursion to bring Jessica home was going from bad to worse. Her excuse of a headache—which she didn't have—had only gotten her in deeper.

What concerned her most, though, was why learning that Morgan was a professional investigator had created such havoc inside her? She had no reason to be afraid of him or of what he might find even if he did take it in mind to investigate her. She wasn't trying to pull a fast one on the Parkers. She hadn't stolen what she'd been accused of stealing in Houston.

Only, why hadn't she heard about his profession before this? Why had no one thought to tell her? Had there been a conspiracy to keep her in the dark?

Also, why would hearing that his mother worried about his safety cause her to—

No! No! *No!* It wasn't that! She didn't care for him. Not even the tiniest little bit. Not in any way.

She hopped off the bed, straightened her jeans and shirt, ran a hand over her hair, stiffened her spine and marched from the room. She had no idea how much time had passed since she'd gone in there, but it had been more than enough.

Dub Hughes, Morgan's father, was now in the kitchen with the others. While the children finished their lunch at the table, he perched on a stool at the narrow bar just off the kitchen work area, munching a sandwich. His right arm, held in place by its brace, was unusable. "Well, well, look who's here," he drawled when he spied her standing in the doorway.

Christine smiled tightly. Erin, she noted, had eaten

very little, and when she looked up and saw her
mother, she ran over to her.

"Are you all right, Mommy?" Erin asked worriedly.

Christine smiled. "I'm fine. Much better now. I
think it was the heat."

Delores studied her, pausing while dishing up several small bowls of ice cream. "Are you sure?" she
asked. "You don't look all that well."

The phone rang and Delores hurried to answer it,
then she called Jessica from the table. "You can have
your dessert later, Jess, after you've talked with your
dad. Why don't you use the phone in our bedroom?
It'll be quieter."

The girl mumbled something that sounded like as-
sent and left the room.

"You want a sandwich?" Dub asked. "It's from a
good side of Parker beef."

Christine declined, then said, "I think we should go
just as soon as the children have finished their ice
cream."

"What do you have to rush?" Dub asked. He
looked better than the last time Christine had seen him,
not as drawn. "Mae keepin' you on a tight rein?
How'd you like meetin' her? She a surprise to you?"

Christine met his seemingly placid gaze, but she
could sense the sharpness of the mind behind it. She
answered slowly, "I think Mae could surprise anyone."

"Well, you must be holdin' a pretty good hand,
since she ain't sent you packin' yet."

"Dub!" Delores warned.

"It's the truth!" Dub declared. "If she wasn't, Mae would've seen her off the ranch after the first five minutes."

"That's the Parkers' business," Delores maintained. "Christine, would you like some ice cream yourself? Or something else to eat?"

Christine refused again as Dub continued, "The Parkers' business *is* our business."

"Not about who gets a share in the place," Delores retorted.

"It's been the same all my life. If you're a Parker by blood, you get your one share when you turn twenty-one. If you're not, you don't. And the shares can't be passed on to an outsider."

Christine spoke up. "By that reasoning, doesn't that mean you're an outsider, too?"

Dub's eyes narrowed. "We've never claimed to be family."

"But you consider yourself a part of the Parker Ranch."

"By virtue of several generations' blood and sweat, yes. But there's a difference. We don't claim to *own* any of it."

"That's enough, Dub," Delores said. "You forget—little pitchers have big ears. Now," she said to the children at the table, "anybody for seconds?"

Of course they all agreed, their attention quickly turned to the unexpected treat and away from what the adults had been talking about. Even Erin's attention.

Christine met Delores's gaze, and the two women shared a silent affinity.

AFTER RETURNING to the compound and leaving Gwen and Wesley in Harriet's care, Christine and Erin walked up the curving drive to Mae's house. Erin had been quiet throughout the drive back, breaking her silence only when she'd said goodbyes to her friends. Now she spoke what must have been on her mind.

"Mommy," she asked, "are we going to get to stay here?"

Christine had been preparing herself for such a question. "I seem to remember, not too long ago, you wanted to leave."

"That was in the beginning. Now I like it here, Mommy. It's like Ira said. I know I haven't gotten to go riding outside the corral yet, and I haven't helped gather cows like he did. But I'm learning to ride. And I'm making friends."

Christine stopped where the drive met the pathway to Mae's house. She knelt down on one knee so she could look directly into Erin's eyes. "Honey, I wish I could say yes and mean it, but...I'm not sure. There are things I can't control. Things that maybe I won't be able to change."

Erin's dark eyes had tears in them. "Don't they like us, Mommy?" she whispered.

Christine's heart flooded with love for her child. She wanted to protect her from all hurt. Keep her safe, keep her whole, keep her just as sweet and innocent as she was at this moment. "If we have to go, it won't have anything to do with you, sweetheart. Or with me, either, really. It's just that Ira...tried to do something nice for us, and he may not have been able to, because some rules were made a long time ago that say he can't."

"Didn't Ira know about these rules?" Erin asked softly.

"I don't know. Most important, though, is that he really cared for us, so he tried." She rubbed her daughter's thin arms and forced her tone to be brighter. "But we don't know what's going to happen, do we? Everything might work out fine—the rules might not count—and we can stay here forever. That's a better way to look at it, I think."

Erin gave her a watery smile, then nodded. "I think so, too," she murmured, and slipped her hand into Christine's as they turned to go inside the house.

THE RIDING LESSON that evening went so well that Morgan told Erin he'd saddle up Thunder next time and they'd go for a ride together in the holding pasture. Erin, of course, after letting out a shriek of pleasure, immediately had to share the news with Gwen and Wesley.

"I've never seen anything like it," Morgan said, shaking his head as the girl ran off toward the compound.

Christine murmured something and turned to follow her.

"Hey!" Morgan said sharply. In a few steps he caught up with her and grabbed her arm. "What's the matter with you? Why are you acting this way? What have I done?"

Christine tried to shake his hand away. "You? You haven't done anything," she said.

He frowned. "You've been acting weird since I got here this evening. Don't tell me nothing's wrong."

"Have you been home?"

"Not since this morning. Why?"

"I have. I brought Jessica back. Your brother wanted to talk to her."

"So?"

"So I learned something I didn't know before. And isn't it funny I didn't know it."

His frown increased. "I won't have any idea until you tell me."

"You're in law enforcement. You arrest people. You put them in jail."

"So?"

Christine let a little of her cool and contained facade slip. "So...why did no one tell me? Why didn't *you* tell me?"

"I arrest cattle thieves. Are you a cattle thief?"

"There are some here who might think I am!"

He smiled. "If you are, you're the best-lookin' cattle thief I've ever had the pleasure of comin' across!"

Christine succeeded in jerking her arm free and started to walk away again. She didn't know why this had been gnawing at her all afternoon, but it had. A part of her still believed she'd been kept in the dark on purpose.

Once again, he caught up with her. He was still smiling, but when he took in her unhappy expression, his smile died.

"You're angry because you didn't know?" he said. "But how was I to know you didn't know? It's common knowledge. I don't make a secret of it. I catch rustlers for a living. What's the big deal?''

Put like that, her anger did sound unreasonable. Still...

''I'm commissioned as a special Texas Ranger,'' he went on. ''I work with the county sheriffs of the districts where I'm assigned to catch rustlers. We talked about it this morning, didn't we?''

''We talked about rustlers, not about you catching rustlers and arresting them.''

''You have something against that? Against *me* for doing it?''

''No,'' Christine had to admit.

He tried that smile again. ''Some people call us 'cow cops.' I kinda like it.''

Christine resumed walking, but this time in concert with Morgan. ''Why don't you work this area since it's so close to home?''

''Someone else is already assigned to it. Fella named Ed Davis. He knows the whole area like the back of his hand. Which is how I've come to know my section of the panhandle.''

''How did you ever decide to do something like that? Your mother says its dangerous.''

''Do you care?'' he teased.

Christine was having a hard enough time adjusting to the fact that he was in law enforcement. Anything else was...unwelcome. ''It's—'' she shrugged ''—interesting. Tell me...is it dangerous?''

''It can be. Depends on who you're dealing with. Rustling cattle has many forms. You get the people inside—the cowboys or foremen who put a few calves aside for themselves, or the seasonal help who know the best way to case a place is to work it. They've been known to come along later with a truck and use the exact-soundin' horn the cattle are used to as a signal for feeding. Sometimes they use the same cow cake—that's the sweet cubes of grain the cows are used to eatin' when they're bein' fed—and they just move the cattle out through the gates and up ramps into a truck. Easy as pie when you're a professional cowhand. Other times it's city boys who don't want to have to work at it real hard. They steal cows that're already on trucks or near loading ramps at feedlots. I've known a couple who used a cow-dog to do most of the work for 'em. So it just depends.''

"You mean cowboys are rustlers?''

"It's the other way around. Most times rustlers are cowboys. At least, they have been at one time. It takes a lot of skill to maneuver cattle into a truck. Particularly on ranches like this one, where the cattle are mostly wild—they fight.'' He paused, smiling. "Sometimes it's a family tradition. Several generations of a family make their living rustling. They're so good at it a cowhand or a cowman never know they're gettin' stole from.''

"Then how do they get caught? How do you...?''

"Sometimes they don't. Sometimes they get careless or sometimes someone spots a brand on a hide or at a cattle auction. That's how we catch up with a lot of 'em. We have a computer at headquarters in Fort Worth that lists missing cattle. Happens twenty-two cattle show up across the state that match their description exactly. Fella hustlin' 'em swears he got 'em off someone who didn't tell him his name. That's a pretty standard alibi.''

"How did you learn to do this?"

"I grew up workin' cattle."

"So in your job it's best if you've worked cattle, too."

Morgan nodded. "You have to know more about it than the other fella."

They completed the walk to the compound in silence. Christine didn't know what else to say. She needed to be by herself. To absorb everything. She could see now why Rafe and Mae Parker relied so strongly on Morgan. Why he had stayed in the room during her initial reception. Why he had been so suspicious of her, questioning her. Why she'd felt he had quickly sensed she was something more than a casual visitor. It was his training, his job...his nature, as he'd once told her.

Morgan saw her onto the porch. At the door she hesitated.

"Are you coming in to see Mae?" she asked.

"No."

The sun was starting to set. It was near the end of what must have been a hard day for him. And she had no idea, what with the threat from rustlers, whether he was on his way home or going to spend some of the night on watch.

"Are you going back out?"

He nodded. "For a while."

"Aren't you tired?"

He shrugged.

Christine looked at him—really looked at him. And

this time she could see past his physical attractions to the steady look in his eyes. To the strength of his character. He was a man on whom responsibility settled comfortably.

He took a step closer and she didn't move away. She even knew what he was going to do next before he did it. He reached for her, bringing her closer to him, then touched his lips to hers. Lightly at first. Softly, tentatively, and when she didn't stiffen and draw away, the pressure increased.

Moments later the kiss broke off, and Christine gazed up at him wide-eyed. It reminded her of her first kiss—filled with wonder and exhilaration. Yet at the same time this kiss had deeper shadings of maturity.

He smiled at her slightly dazzled look, then without another word, left the porch.

Christine watched him walk away. Two kisses from him in two days. Both so very different. One, all flame and demanding passion. The other? Spine-tingling, but executed with self-control.

Then that smile. As if he enjoyed keeping her off balance.

And even more troubling to her peace of mind, why had she so enjoyed both? To the point that, this time, she hadn't even bothered to protest.

DUB AND DELORES were still up and sitting in the living room when Morgan let himself into the house. It was late. He'd tried to be as quiet as he could, cutting the truck's engine and letting it roll to a stop, then closing the door with care. He'd even removed his boots at the doorstep and carried them inside.

Dub looked up from the book he'd been reading—Russell had sent him a box of books shortly after the accident, knowing his father would go crazy if he didn't have something to do with his time. Delores was doing her usual knitting. She made sweaters for everyone on the ranch—from lowliest cowhand to Mae herself. Nice warm sweaters that kept the chill away in winter.

"What are you two doing up?" Morgan asked, his voice remaining hushed.

"Couldn't sleep," Dub answered shortly. "Dang arm. I don't think it's ever gonna heal."

"Give it time, Dub," Delores said quietly. "That's what I keep telling you."

Dub shifted irritably in his chair.

Morgan looked at the dusty boots still in his hand. He swung them nonchalantly. "I understand you had a visitor today."

"Yeah, that little filly makin' the claim on the ranch," Dub replied. "She's sure somethin', all right! Sharp as a tack and won't back down. Maybe it's Mae we should be feelin' sorry for!"

"What about you, Mom? What do you think?"

Delores answered after a long moment. "I like her, from what I've seen. She's not a big talker, but she's good with kids. That little girl of hers means a lot to her. It's not just show." She narrowed her eyes. "Why?"

Morgan shrugged. "I was just wondering."

"You gettin' sweet on her?" Dub teased.

Morgan smiled. "Might be."

Dub jerked upright in his chair. "Aw, hey! I was

just teasin'! I didn't mean—'' But when he saw that his son continued to smile, he relaxed. "Aw, you were just teasin', too. For a minute there, you had me goin'. I thought you meant it."

"Good night, Dad. I'm off to bed."

Dub shook his head. "Sure wish I could help with things."

Morgan patted his dad's shoulder as he passed by, then stopped to kiss his mother's cheek. "You, too, Mom. Good night."

Delores caught the hand that rested on her shoulder, detaining him. "I know what's happening," she said quietly, making his heart take a funny little dip. "Did you think I wouldn't hear about the rustlers? I couldn't take two steps in town without someone saying something. You just be careful, Morgan."

The rustlers! For a second Morgan had thought— Then he met his mother's gaze again, and he knew he hadn't fooled her in the other regard, either. She knew his teasing hadn't been teasing. It had been an honest answer.

"Take care with that, too," she murmured, then added, "Make sure you're sure," before she let him go.

Morgan left the room shaking his head. His mother's intuition had always been impressive.

things.

CHAPTER TWELVE

ERIN WAS SO EXCITED about the play wedding that she
woke up at first light the next morning, ready to rush
over to Harriet's house to begin the day. All the invitations had been handed out, and only the final re-
hearsal had yet to be performed. Even Mae had gotten
into the spirit and invited all the guests to an afternoon
picnic that was to take place shortly after the ''ceremony.''

Christine called a halt to her daughter's immediate
plans. ''Gwen and Wesley's daddy has been helping
Morgan and Rafe. He might have been up late last
night and he's probably going to work part of today,
too. I heard Mae say something about the men taking
guard duty in shifts. You wouldn't want to wake him,
would you? Or Harriet? You'd better wait until after
ten o'clock.''

Erin agreed and calmly accompanied Christine to
breakfast, but when she went out to play on the front
porch, Christine knew it was with the idea of keeping
watch on the Dunn house hoping for signs of activity.

As Christine lingered over a cup of coffee, she
heard a commotion in the kitchen. Curious, she went
to peek inside. A big burly man dressed in a white
T-shirt and well-worn jeans was standing with his

back to her, a bag of onions braced over his shoulder. In front of him, barring his way out the door, stood Marie.

"You're not leaving this house with those onions!" the housekeeper said firmly. "Use your own."

The man's voice was surprisingly thin and high, but he was so big and bulky no one in their right mind would dare comment on it. "I've told ya. I can't! You know everythin's planned down to the last bean 'cause of the roundup. This here picnic is a house doin', not mine. Even if I am the one s'pose to cook it! Anyway, I'm not goin' to use 'em all. Just a few."

"Then take a few, only a few. You're not goin' to run me out. I won't stand for it."

"Outta my way, woman!"

Christine stepped into the room. "Marie?" she said. She had no idea who the man was, but Marie had been nice to her. If she needed help...

Marie saw her concerned expression and started to grin, which, in turn, caused the man to swing around. His face was just as round as his body, and his hair was cut so short it was almost nonexistent. When he saw Christine, he, too, started to grin.

Marie playfully lashed him with a dish towel. "See? You've worried Miss Grant. You're a bully, Axel Douglas. And all because of a few silly onions."

"You won't think it's so silly when Miss Parker asks why the barbecue sauce doesn't taste like it should. Mornin', Miss Grant," he ended with a friendly dip of his head.

"Then for heaven's sake take them—but bring back what you don't use. And I mean it. You probably have tons squirreled away in that chuck-wagon grub you have packed, and you're just too lazy to look for 'em.''

"Why should I do that when I have such a sweet and generous wife?"

Marie went over to him, pulled his balding head down and gave it a huge smacking kiss on top. "You remember that," she instructed. "Particularly when I come lookin' for a few onions myself someday."

Axel bolted for the door. "Nice to meet you, Miss Grant," he called, then he was gone before Marie could change her mind.

She chuckled. "I don't care if he takes the onions. I have more. But if I make it too easy, he'll think he can do it anytime, and we have to keep it straight about what is whose between the house and the cook house."

Christine placed her cup on the counter. "It must be a monumental job to prepare a meal for all those people."

"Axel loves it, especially roundups. He's considered the best camp cook in West Texas. And he is!"

This new view of Marie completed her transformation in Christine's eyes. Rather than being austere and remote, as she'd shown herself to be when Christine and Erin had first come to the ranch, the housekeeper was warm and caring, humorous and spirited.

"Is there anything I can do?" Christine asked, wanting to be helpful. She wasn't accustomed to being among those waited on.

Marie had gone back to scrubbing a baking pan, but at the offer, her labor stopped. She flashed Christine a look, then shook her head. "Not a thing. It's all being taken care of. Anyway, I don't think Miss Parker would be very happy if I..." She paused. "This is what Axel and I get paid to do. Get paid *well* to do. You're a guest here, Miss Grant. You're not supposed to be put to work helping the cooks." Then, to take any offense from her words, she smiled and said, "We appreciate the thought, though."

Christine smiled. Add "diplomatic" to Marie's list of attributes.

Afterward, she wandered around a bit, watching, as time went by, the preparations for the picnic. A long wooden table materialized and was placed in the shaded courtyard. Bench seats were added. Chairs of all sorts joined the lawn chairs already there. A touch of smoke wafted on the air, and when Christine tracked it down, she found Axel standing over a huge barbecue pit at the cook house, across from the barn.

"Had to get this started early, so's it'll be smoked just right," Axel said, motioning her over to show her the joints of beef cooking slowly. "My secret sauce," he murmured, stirring the contents of a pot. It smelled delicious, all peppery and spicy. Even though she'd just eaten, Christine's mouth watered.

As she walked back to Mae's house, she heard the children outside at Harriet's. At promptly ten o'clock Erin had gone to knock at the door, and a sleepy-eyed Harriet had waved from the doorway when she'd seen Christine. Now, preparations for the play wedding were going full steam. The toy audience was being assembled, a few flowers, with Harriet's permission, were being picked—although, from Harriet's cry of dismay once the children had gone back inside, they must have chosen the wrong ones.

Shep got up to amble toward her as she neared Mae's house again. When she'd left earlier, he'd been sleeping on the porch.

"Hi, boy," she said, sitting down on the top step.

The old dog's warm brown eyes were accepting, his tail wagging. She stroked his head and neck and rubbed his ears in a way he seemed to like. He then curled up beside her, apparently content to stay there forever.

Christine had been heading for her room. On a day like today when everyone else seemed to have someone to be with or something to do, she felt the ache of loneliness. But suddenly she had something to do, too, and a companion to do it with. She leaned back, still stroking the dog, and began to talk to him.

"How did you manage not to have a role in the wedding?" she asked him. "I'm surprised they didn't try to dress you up and make you walk down the aisle. As father of the bride or something. Or did they try and you ran off? And now you won't go near in case they catch you and try to make you do it again, right?"

Shep thumped his tail, then rested his chin on Christine's thigh. Suddenly the door behind her opened, and Shep's head—and hers—jerked up.

It was Rafe. By himself. No Shannon, no Mae, no Morgan. Christine struggled to her feet. She had never talked to him on his own, and she wasn't quite sure what he...how he...

"I—I was talking with Shep," she said defensively, like a child caught in a questionable activity.

"What'd he have to say for himself?" Rafe drawled. He and Morgan were like bookends in everything but their coloring. Both long and lean and confidently masculine. He bent down to rub Shep's head.

"Not a lot," Christine said.

"You do most of the talking?" Rafe straightened, and his dark eyes zeroed in on hers. It was clear he was taking her mettle.

Christine smiled slightly. "He's a dog of few words."

Like Mae, Rafe's smile took some of the edge off his strong features. Made him seem less fierce. "He's a good ol' boy," Rafe said. "Been my buddy for a lot of years. Slowin' down a bit now. But he's still a good ol' boy."

Christine had run out of things to say to Rafe. He knew everything about her that Mae knew and, like Mae, probably held strong views.

That was why it surprised her when he said, "Shep's seldom fooled about people. He likes you and he likes your little girl. That should be taken into account."

Christine looked at him warily. "Into account for what?"

"The eventual outcome of what we've been dealing with. Whether your little girl is or isn't Ira's, and whether or not you've been taken advantage of—or taking advantage yourself. Shannon seems to think it's you who's been victimized. That you were sent out here on a wild-goose chase for who knows what reason. Me? I'm not sure. I want to know a little more.

But if Shep likes you, there must be somethin' to you.''

He gave her a slow smile, then settled his hat back on his head and, calling to Shep, set off for his house.

Christine sank back on the upper step and watched them go. He certainly didn't mince words. You knew where you stood with Rafe Parker. And if there was a question, he told you that, too.

THE GUESTS at the make-believe wedding assembled in Harriet's backyard at the appointed time. Dub and Delores, along with Rusty and Mindy, Gib and Jodie, LeRoy, Harriet, Mae, Shannon, Christine. The missing men—Rafe and Morgan—would take turns coming in as the afternoon progressed.

The children had worked hard. Stuffed animals and dolls, dressed in their best, had been seated on over-turned boxes and chairs. A crayon-drawn stained-glass window was hung on the trellis behind the box representing the altar. Flowers were tied to the hands of some of the dolls.

There was a slight holdup at the beginning. Wesley had to be pushed out from behind the side of the house, LeRoy's jacket almost swallowing him, a neck-tie, inexpertly knotted, hanging almost to his knees. Erin followed directly behind him, looking somber and ministerlike in what had to be an old blue robe of Harriet's. Only no minister would dare wear the amount of lipstick, blush and powder she'd layered on. And this minister carried a flower, instead of a Bible. Wesley, embarrassed by his participation in such a girlish affair, didn't stop at the altar, forcing Erin to make a grab for him and haul him back.

With Wesley finally in place, Erin mounted the box, then, reaching into the folds of her robe, switched on a portable tape player. The music blared and was quickly lowered—something formal and recognizable, but definitely not Mendelssohn's "Wedding March."

In spite of this, Gwen, standing behind the crowd of well-wishers, started forward. She was wearing one of her own fancy dresses, which she'd accessorized with heaps of scarves and jewelry. She, too, had bright cheeks and lips. And as she walked down the aisle, she scattered zinnia petals.

The bride, Jessica, had chosen a frilly pink party dress that undoubtedly had once been worn by Harriet. Because it was sleeveless and scoop-necked, Jessica wore it over her own white blouse. It was caught at the waist by a narrow belt and the extra folds allowed to hang over Jessica's hips, giving the illusion of a period costume. In back the hem dragged on the ground. A wide-brimmed summer hat almost obscured her face, but a momentary glimpse showed that she'd had just as much fun as the other girls experimenting with makeup.

Jessica milked the moment for all she was worth, moving slowly, enjoying the attention. She held the bouquet of flowers dramatically in front of her, almost like an offering.

The music stopped before she'd finished her entrance, but that was ignored. Everyone had to wait until she was in place.

Erin spoke clearly. "Do you, Wesley, take Jessica…'' But Wesley had other plans. Instead of waiting to say his line, he flipped Jessica's hat off, stole one of Gwen's scarves and plucked the flower out of Erin's hand. Then he ran away, laughing maniacally.

All three girls were outraged, and after a stunned moment, gave chase, screeching their anger.

The guests couldn't contain themselves any longer. They all burst out laughing, having enjoyed the spectacle, but most of all, it's slapstick end.

''I took lots of pictures,'' Harriet told everyone. ''I'll have copies made.''

LeRoy said, ''Wes isn't goin' to thank you for it when he gets older.''

''He isn't going to thank me now!''

The children made a return sweep around the backyard, Wesley now running for his life.

Mae chuckled. ''Boy's gonna regret it when those girls catch up with him.'' Then to everyone at large she said, ''Come on. Let's go see what Axel's managed to pull from his sleeve for our dinner.''

Christine sidled up to Harriet as the others started off for the courtyard. ''I'll help you clean this up later if you like. After all, Erin—''

Harriet shook her head. ''Nope. That's one of the promises the kids made me. If I let them have their wedding here, they'd have to clean up. And I'm holdin' 'em to it.''

Christine nodded. ''A good idea.''

By the time everyone arrived at the courtyard, food was already being served at the table. A long white cloth covered the wood planks, and places had been set. Christine saw carrots, fresh green beans, mounds of potato salad, steaming squares of cornbread, a thick chili sauce, green chili peppers and at the foot of the table—with Axel in place holding a sharp-pronged fork and a long knife for carving—the charred chunks of barbecued beef.

"Wonderful!" Mae declared, taking the honored position at the head of the table. Everyone else filed in after her.

Christine looked around for Erin, then saw her and the other two girls walking dejectedly toward them.

"We couldn't catch him," Erin complained, edging close to Christine, in need of a hug.

"He went into the barn and we looked and looked," Gwen contributed, doing the same thing to Harriet—getting close, needing sympathy.

Even Jessica hung on her grandmother's neck. "Wasn't he awful? Boys can be so…" Words seemed to fail her.

Delores patted Jessica's hand. "It was beautiful, anyway. You girls in particular. It looked like a real wedding."

"Just like Shannon and Rafe's is gonna be," Gwen said.

Jodie giggled and Shannon smothered a smile.

"Why don't you girls go wash up," Harriet said, "then come back and eat with us. You can clean up the backyard later."

"Wes has to help us," Gwen stated firmly. Then not so firmly, "Doesn't he?"

"Definitely," Harried agreed. As the girls started to run off, she called after them, "Use lots of soap to get that makeup off. You want to keep your skin pretty.'' Then added to the table, ''And save my towels.''

''You probably should have your head examined for agreeing to let them do this in the first place,'' Mae said. ''Especially in your—''

''My condition is fine, Mae. And it wasn't that hard. The kids enjoyed it.''

Mae shook her head and said no more.

Everything was delicious, Christine decided after her first few bites. Axel truly was a superior cook. In some quarters he'd be referred to as a chef, but this wasn't one of them, and Christine didn't think he'd appreciate the title. Camp cook was good enough for him.

There was lots of lively conversation. The children—including Wes, once he'd apologized—were scattered among the adults, and the atmosphere was very relaxed, very comfortable.

Even Christine, talking mostly to Harriet and Shannon and Jodie, found the time enjoyable. She noticed when LeRoy left and Rafe returned to have his meal, then she noticed Rafe leave a short time later as everyone abandoned the table for the lawn chairs. It was only when she saw Morgan's approach that she felt her insides tighten.

There was something so elemental about him. Other men she'd known paled in comparison. They'd been concerned with things that didn't seem important. Who they were going to get to go to bed with them. Who they were going to best financially. And, in her younger years, how they could find someone to give them money and do nothing in return. Morgan Hughes wasn't like that. That must be why it'd be so easy to—

What was she *thinking?* That that must be why it would be so easy to love him?

Oh, God, no, she thought wildly. Not that! She didn't want to feel that deeply for anyone again!

He greeted some of those present, had a word with his parents, sent a long look toward her—which she evaded as best she could—and settled at the table.

Erin, seeing he was alone, went to join him.

Christine couldn't move. She could barely breathe!

WHAT NOW? Morgan wondered. She'd seen him looking at her and quickly turned away. The last time they'd been together he'd thought they'd made some progress. At least, moved away from being sworn enemies. Now this!

Erin popped up at his side.

"Hi, Morgan!" she chirped.

"Hi, little lady," he responded, smiling.

"You've come in to eat lunch?" she asked him, more as a conversation starter than as a true question.

"I'm the cow's tail," he teased. "Last one in."

"Do you mind if I sit beside you?"

"I'd be honored."

"You want more to eat, honey?" Marie asked, hovering nearby, ready to bring out another plate.

Erin giggled, shaking her head. "I'm stuffed!"

A short time could make a huge difference in a little girl, Morgan noted. Erin was starting to bloom here. It would be too bad if she had to be uprooted. If she and her mother had to leave the ranch.

He glanced up and caught Christine looking at him again. At him, not at Erin. Something deep inside him shifted, but before he could identify what it was, Christine looked away.

He helped himself to almost everything at the table. It had been a long time since breakfast. He tried not to shovel it in, conscious of Erin watching him with shining, almost worshipful eyes.

If only her mother would look at him like that, he thought, then immediately pushed the thought away. He didn't want to be worshiped by Christine. Just—

"—until Wes decided to be silly." Erin was earnestly trying to tell him something, but he hadn't absorbed a word.

"That's awful," Morgan said, gambling that it would be an appropriate response.

Erin sighed heavily. "It was. Why do boys have to be like that, Morgan? Why can't boys be more like girls?"

Morgan had to smile. "Aw, you wouldn't really want 'em to. Just think how much fun you had gettin' mad at him."

Erin giggled. "We did have fun. We chased him to the barn, then when we couldn't find him, we came back here and he showed up."

Morgan nodded.

Erin sighed again, and this time it was a little longer before she spoke again. "Did you know Ira?" she asked.

"I met him, but I didn't know him."

"He was nice. He used to tell me stories about the ranch. About how when he was a boy he used to help with the cattle, and how there's a treasure of gold coins buried somewhere on the ranch and he used to dig with a little girl cousin of his to try to find it.''

Morgan nodded. ''It's supposed to be here, all right. One of the old-time Parkers buried it during an Indian attack, only he couldn't remember later where he buried it.'' Morgan looked at her. ''Do you know who that little girl cousin was?'' he asked and when Erin shook her head, he motioned to the lawn chairs. ''Mae,'' he said.

''Mae?'' Erin echoed, as if it didn't seem possible to her that Mae had ever been anything but what she was now—an old woman.

''Uh-huh.''

Erin considered the revelation for a moment, then said, ''She's a lot older than my grandma. My grandma's dead, too. Did you know that?'' She didn't wait for a reply. ''My grandma didn't like us very much, either. She was grumpy and fussed a lot. She slept a lot, too. And she smelled funny. Mommy said it was Grandma's favorite perfume, but I didn't like it. We didn't see her very often, just every once in a while.''

Knowing the truth behind the tale Erin was telling him made giving a reply difficult. Morgan settled for a safe ''That's too bad.''

''Mommy said Grandma loved us, she just didn't know how to show it. Is that the way it is with Mae, too?''

Another thing about children, Morgan reflected, they sometimes had the uncanny ability to cut straight to the heart of a situation. Mae wouldn't like it if she heard him agree, but he did. "I suppose," he murmured.

"Ira wasn't like that at all," Erin said, smiling in remembrance. "He was nice to Mommy and me. After school, he let me play in the room where he and Mommy worked. He played games with me, read to me. And when he got sicker, he let me listen when Mommy read to him. He liked funny stories. I do, too." Her smile wavered, disappeared. "I liked him a lot," she added simply.

Morgan met her dark gaze. It was so much like a Parker's it almost took his breath away. He'd met this same look all his life—from Rafe. This little girl *had* to be a Parker. But the way she spoke about Ira, the way she spoke about her mother's relationship with Ira...well, it didn't add up. Something was off center. Something—

"—do you?" Erin asked, breaking into his thoughts again.

"Do I what? I missed what you said." There was no way he could pull himself out of that one, not with such a direct question.

"Do you think that when people die they go to heaven? That's what the nuns at my school said. If the people are good, of course. But what if they're good *and* bad? Do you think my grandma was good enough to go to heaven? And Ira—was he? Do you think they're in heaven together right now this very minute? And that they can look down and see us sitting here? See you and me talking? See—"

"Whoa, whoa," Morgan said soothingly, just as he

would to a highly strung colt. He smiled. "You're takin' on quite a lot for such a nice quiet Sunday."

"But do you? Could they?"

She wasn't going to let the subject go, not until she had an answer. He took a breath and said, "I look at it like this. People should do the best they can with what they're given, and if they do, they should end up with something good in the end. If that's heaven, great. And if while they're up there they want to look down on the rest of us and eavesdrop once in a while...well, I guess they've earned the privilege."

Erin sat very still, thinking about what he'd said, then her face broke into in a huge grin and she pressed her head against his arm, hugging it tightly. "I like you, Morgan," she said happily. "I really like you!"

For a second Morgan pulled her closer. "I like you, too," he returned. "You're a pretty special kid."

And while he ate peach cobbler for dessert, she sat beside him, continuing to chatter lightly about this and that, until Jessica and Gwen came to get her and they went off to play.

CHRISTINE HAD KEPT a surreptitious eye on Morgan and Erin as they sat together. She'd seen how deep in conversation they were. She'd recognized the expression Erin got when she had hold of something she was determined to get an answer to. She saw how, when Morgan had obviously come up with a satisfactory answer, Erin had reacted. And how Morgan had responded to her. It was unsettling to see them growing so close. She worried how Erin would be affected if, yet again, they were forced to leave the place—and the people—she was starting to feel a connection to.

At this point, though, Christine didn't know what she could do about any of it. About Erin and Morgan, or Morgan and herself. She couldn't be thinking in terms of *love*. She'd sworn it would never happen to her again. The vulnerability associated with love was too dangerous. And yet, here she was.

She stood up. She'd rather be alone and miserable than miserable in a crowd. Especially a crowd of Parkers. But Harriet stopped her, Harriet who was sitting next to Delores Hughes.

"Christine, just a minute. There's something…"

Christine smiled and stepped over to Harriet, who immediately launched into a subject she'd touched on before.

"Delores and I were talking," she said, "about Erin and school. This couldn't have come at a better time, you know. The kids are just coming off spring break. If you want her to, I'm sure Erin could enroll."

As Harriet spoke, Erin, Jessica and Gwen came running up. Christine couldn't help glancing toward the table where Morgan and Erin had been sitting. Sure enough, he was gone. Had he already left for the range?

Jessica had overheard. "School?" she asked. "Erin's gonna come to school with us? Oh, that'd be great!" She turned to Erin. "I could show you—"

"Quiet, Jessica." Delores tried to quell some of her granddaughter's excitement. "It hasn't been decided yet."

Erin looked from her new friend to her mother. "Could I, Mommy? Could I?"

The only one disappointed was Gwen, until she thought of a solution. "Could I go, too?" she begged. "Mom, could I? Please?"

Harriet shook her head slowly. "Not yet, honey. It's not time for you. You have to wait until next year...or maybe the year after."

Christine gazed into her daughter's still-upturned expectant face and knew that this was a problem she *could* do something about. Erin enjoyed school and got good grades. "Well, I don't see why—"

The two older girls couldn't wait for her to finish. They whooped and danced with excitement, with Gwen trying to join in.

"We'll show you everything we do," Erin promised, trying to cheer up the younger girl. "And you can help me with my homework. Every night!"

Gwen brightened at that and the three girls skipped away.

Harriet grimaced. "It looks like Gwen's going to start school next year, doesn't it? Whether I'm ready or not. LeRoy and I aren't going to have any peace, otherwise."

"I'd say it looks that way," Delores agreed. Then the older woman focused on something over Christine's shoulder, and she smiled.

Christine twisted around and saw that Morgan had come to stand right behind her. She froze. All except for her nerve endings, which clanged like warning bells. She tried to step out of the way, but he caught hold of her shoulders and didn't let go.

"I'm sorry to interrupt you ladies," he drawled easily. "I just came by to see if Mom needs help gettin' Dad home—before I head out again."

His hands seemed to burn through the material of Christine's shirt. She was consumed with the need to turn around and dissolve against him, to feel the assurance of his kisses, to become a part of him.

She caught Delores's long look—at the positioning of her son's hands, at what must have been, for anyone even remotely sensitive, the dead giveaway of Christine's expression.

Delores's eyes fluttered, then without revealing anything of what she was thinking, she answered mildly, "We'll be fine, Morgan. Rusty can help him into the truck. He's done it before."

"And *we're* all here," Harriet said. She, too, was looking at Christine and Morgan a little oddly. As if something unusual and unexpected was taking place before her eyes and she was trying to decide if what she was seeing was real or not.

"I won't worry, then," Morgan murmured, and let go of Christine.

"No, I think you already have enough to concern you," his mother said.

Morgan paused for a second, as if he'd picked up a message in his mother's words. Then he tipped his hat and left them.

Harriet whistled lightly under her breath and lifted her eyebrows. "Has something been going on that I don't know about?" she asked curiously.

Christine's cheeks pinkened. Something they rarely did.

Delores got to her feet. "Don't you think it's time we make sure those kids clean up your backyard? Jessica told me your arrangement."

"Oh, yeah, sure," Harriet agreed, getting to her feet, as well.

Christine knew her curiosity had not been satisfied.

As she hopped into bed that night, Erin sighed happily. "This was fun today, Mommy. I really do like it here."

Christine tucked the covers under her daughter's chin. "I know you do."

"I even like most of the people. Do you know what Morgan told me? He told me Mae was the little girl Ira used to play with when Ira visited the ranch as a boy. Isn't that funny?"

"It is."

"And he said Mae's like Grandma—she doesn't know how to show people she loves them."

"My, my, you two certainly did have a nice talk."

"We did!" Erin responded enthusiastically. Then she grew quiet for a moment. "Mommy?" she said eventually. "Who's my daddy? Gwen's daddy lives with her, and Jessica's going to go live with her daddy in Colorado. But I..."

Christine's heart contracted. Erin's words were an echo from the past. Her mother had always put her off; she wouldn't do the same.

"You've never asked me before," she murmured.

Erin wriggled under the cover.

Christine smoothed her daughter's hair away from her forehead and said softly, "Your daddy was a really nice boy I went to high school with. He had brown hair a little lighter than mine and dark blue eyes, and he played on the varsity football team.''

''Why didn't... Why isn't...''

Erin wasn't mature enough to form the proper questions or to receive the stark truth for an answer. But Christine knew more questions would follow as the years went by. For the time being, though, Erin deserved some sort of answer. There was no telling how long she'd been wondering.

''We were both very young. I think...he was too young to know what to do. You can understand that, can't you? When something scares you, you pull the covers up over your head and hide?'' She put action to her words by playfully covering Erin's face with the sheet.

Erin giggled, as Christine had hoped she would. But the girl quickly returned to her subject. ''But why was he scared? I was just a little baby!''

Christine shrugged. ''People are funny about what scares them. Do you remember how Mrs. Tobin was afraid of frogs?''

Erin giggled again. ''I know. It was so silly. A frog wasn't going to hurt her!''

''Exactly,'' Christine said.

Erin let her mother readjust the covers under her chin, then, smiling, closed her eyes. ''Sing to me, Mommy,'' she requested.

Christine started to hum. Then, in a soft clear voice she sang a song she'd learned in elementary school, one that Erin had always loved. She sang it until she thought Erin was asleep, then started to move away.

But Erin wasn't asleep yet. She opened her eyes after Christine stood up. "You know what I wish, Mommy?" she murmured.

Christine sank back onto the side of the bed. "What?" she asked, smiling.

A moment passed, then in a sleepy voice the little girl whispered, "I wish Morgan was my daddy."

CHAPTER THIRTEEN

IF CHRISTINE HAD FELT at loose ends when Erin first went to Harriet's house to play, it was nothing compared to how she felt after dropping her daughter off at Little Springs to catch the school bus with Jessica and Rusty. She was consumed with misgivings and wanted to drive Erin into town herself, but Erin had rebelled. Half the fun of the day seemed to be the long ride with the other children. And in the face of Harriet and Delores's confidence that everything would be fine, Christine found it difficult to refuse her.

"Don't worry, she'll enjoy herself," Delores had assured Christine, standing by the car.

"But her teacher... I should meet her teacher, shouldn't I?"

"There'll be time for that in the next few days. Rafe called the principal last night and I spoke to Erin's teacher this morning, so that part is under control. And Erin will get the lay of the land quicker and feel better about the other kids if she meets them on equal terms. No other child is going to have their mother bring them to the classroom today."

"But her papers... At her other schools I've had to fill out—"

"Rafe's word is good for a few days. Don't you worry about that."

Rafe's word, Morgan's word… These people were big on going by a person's word.

So she'd driven back to the ranch with a memory of Erin setting off with Jessica and Rusty, talking happily, almost bouncing as she walked.

Very different from the little girl who'd arrived here. And part of the credit had to go to the Parkers. They might doubt her mother's story, but they'd never made an unkind comment to Erin. They attached no blame to her. Because they believed there was a possibility she was a Parker? Or because that was just the way they were, and they'd treat any child in a similar manner? Christine was coming to believe that it was the latter. As Morgan had said, they were good people, at least in that regard.

She thought about telling them the truth about Erin. That Erin wasn't Ira's child. But she knew they'd find out soon enough, anyway. A good investigator would surely learn everything there was to know about her and her past.

In the meantime, let sleeping dogs lie. Wasn't that the saying for what she was doing? For the moment it made perfect sense.

SHANNON, CHRISTINE realized over breakfast later that morning, was restless, too. Rafe and some of the hands had gone out to the far reaches of the ranch for a few days to gather the horses that would be used in the roundup. The final countdown for all the big events—the month-long spring roundup, Shannon and Rafe's wedding, the annual Parker family meeting—was beginning. And Shannon's nerves were beginning to fray.

"I don't know why I let Mae talk me into a June wedding," she said. "I could have put my foot down and said no. And she'd have listened—I think. Rafe certainly didn't care. It wasn't his idea to have a wedding this big right when everything else was happening." She groaned, chasing a strawberry around on her plate before successfully capturing it. "I thought, get it all over with at one time. Let Mae have her way, make her happy, and then Rafe and I can settle into our place with everyone's blessing. But I didn't know quite how…difficult it was all going to be!"

Shannon hadn't appeared at breakfast in the main house since Christine's arrival. Was it because, as she'd promised, she was staying out of the way? Or was it because she usually breakfasted with Rafe? Christine had no idea what kind of living arrangement the two of them had. If they stayed together nights, they were very discreet. But then, under Mae's eagle eye, who wouldn't be?

"I'm sure everything's going to be fine. It wouldn't dare not be, would it? I mean, since Mae has a hand in all the arrangements."

Shannon's eyes crinkled in a smile. "You're beginning to understand how things work around here."

"I was left in very little doubt."

A silence followed, then Shannon said, "I asked you this before, but at the time…" She took a breath. "Do you type? Because if you do, I could certainly use your help. With everything that's happening, the family history just isn't getting done. And I promised Mae—''

"I type. What do you want me to do?"

"Help me put in the corrections! Mae's changed her mind about three different times, but I made her promise this was it. That is, if she wants the material to get to the publisher in time for a Christmas-gift printing."

"I'll be glad to help," Christine said. "It'll give me something to do, other than worry about Erin."

"Oh, that's right. She started school today, didn't she?"

Christine nodded, unable to prevent a frown of concern.

"She took the bus?" Shannon asked.

"Yes. I'm not worried about her in school. Erin loves school, enjoys learning. It's just…I didn't expect… It all happened yesterday afternoon at the picnic. One thing led to another and today's she's gone. I don't even know where, really. Or what the school looks likes. Or who her teacher is…" Christine's voice faded momentarily. "And I won't see her again until the bus lets her off out front sometime this evening."

Shannon gazed at her from over her empty plate. "I have an idea," she said. "Why don't we go into Del Norte ourselves? We can drive to the school and let you have a look around. We don't even have to get out of the car if you think it would embarrass Erin. But you can see the school and the town, and maybe that'll help you feel better. Would you like that? Then in the afternoon we can work on the history."

Christine brightened.

"We'll take Mae's Cadillac," Shannon continued. "That way, if the kids are out on the playground, Erin won't recognize the car. You wouldn't want her to wonder if something's wrong."

"Mae won't mind?"

"Not unless she has some plans for the car I'm unaware of. I'll go check." Shannon smiled at her as she left the room. Within minutes, she was back. "Mae says its fine. So. When do you want to go? Now?"

Christine stood. "Why not?"

THE ROUTE THEY TOOK leaving the ranch was the reverse of what Christine should have used on the day she and Erin got lost. The roads turned this way and that, the same as indicated on her map, but Ira had mistaken which road to turn onto from the main highway. She could see now how very off course she'd been.

"Erin likes school?" Shannon asked.

"She loves it. Gets all As."

"I was weird that way, too." Shannon grinned. "The teachers loved me, because I didn't cause any trouble and my homework was always done on time."

"Sounds familiar," Christine said. "Sometimes I wish Erin would get into a little trouble once in a while. Just to show she's asserting herself."

Shannon laughed. "If she hangs around Jessica long enough, you might get your wish. If ever there was a little girl who asserts herself—"

Her words broke off as she sat forward and slowed the car. Up ahead, a dark pickup truck that had been towing a livestock trailer was parked on the side of the road. A man with a friendly smile emerged from some nearby rocks as they drew closer. "I suppose we should see if he needs help," Shannon murmured, frowning. "Let's just pull up alongside and ask."

The man ambled over and propped his elbows on the open passenger window. Close enough for Christine's nose to twitch at his sour smell of perspiration.

"Do you need some help?" Shannon asked, leaning across Christine.

His smile broadened. He was a young man, but already weatherbeaten. And his rather unkempt brown hair could use the same wash as his clothes. "Well, I s'pose that could depend on what kinda help you're offerin'," he replied in a broad drawl.

Shannon's mouth tightened. "I meant with your truck. Has it broken down? Do you need us to send someone to look at it?"

"Naw, I just had some trouble with a tire, but I got it fixed. No problem. But can you tell me... You live around here?"

Christine didn't like the way he looked at them.

"Reason I'm askin' is," he continued, "you didn't see no truck carryin' ten, twelve steers on it in the past few days, have you? Probably comin' from this way and goin' that?" He motioned from his left to his right.

"I'm afraid not, but we don't get out here a lot. What's the problem?" Shannon asked.

He grimaced. "Fella stole 'em off me, that's what! I'm runnin' 'em for a friend of mine, and the next thing I know, when I go to check 'em they're gone!

Fence posts cut and then put back up, pretty as you please. Nobody'd knowed it happened, 'cept for me checkin'."

Shannon and Christine looked at each other. That sounded exactly like the work of the rustlers Rafe and Morgan were watching out for.

"What you need to do," Shannon said, "is talk to Sheriff Denton or his deputy, Tate Connelly. One or the other of them should be in Del Norte—that's the next big town up this road. You just keep going and you can't miss it. What you're describing is something I'm sure they'd be interested in. Maybe they can help you find your missing steers, too."

The man smiled again. "I'll do that," he said, straightening away from the car. "Sheriff Denton, you say?"

"Or Tate Connelly," Shannon repeated.

He nodded, then waved them on. "Thanks for stoppin'," he said, as they rolled forward slowly, so as not to smother him in dust.

Once back up to speed, Shannon murmured, "He reminds me of someone—Jodie's Rio. Not as handsome and definitely not as clean, but something in his attitude's the same."

"Jodie told me about Rio."

Shannon nodded. "Rio hurt her a lot. She's just now getting over it—at least, enough to start thinking about the future."

"It takes a while," Christine murmured, remembering her own past.

Shannon's gaze left the road for a second to join hers. "Yes," she said softly, "it does."

THE DRIVE TO DEL NORTE took well over an hour and a half to complete, even at speed. They then relaxed over a cold drink at a local café, and briefly toured the rather quaint downtown area before driving into a nearby residential area where the high school, middle school and elementary school all shared the same large block.

Each redbrick building—the high school being the largest—looked solid and well cared for. Young children played in the fenced-in elementary school yard, older children were shooting baskets on an outdoor court, and a few teenagers were doing laps on a track. It was an ordinary scene, safe and secure, and Christine felt much better.

On the way back to the ranch she turned to Shannon. "I really appreciate this. I know it seems silly now, seeing how normal everything is, but..."

"I know all about the games a mind can play. I had nightmares for months after the plane crash. Terrible things. Finally, after I came here, they went away. Well, mostly went away. I still have the odd bad dream, but they're nowhere near as frightening."

"Still, I appreciate—"

"I enjoyed it. Getting away from the ranch and all the weight of what's coming up is a relief. Rafe's been so busy lately we haven't been able to go anywhere."

"I'll help out anywhere I can," Christine volunteered. "The wallpaper for the dining room, when it arrives... I've never put any up before, but I'm willing to learn."

Shannon smiled. "If you can help with the typing, that'll take a huge load off my shoulders."

Christine smiled back. "Now that's something I *can* do."

"I WONDER IF WE SHOULD tell Morgan," Shannon said as they turned into the road leading to the garage.

"About the man who had his cows rustled?" Christine asked.

Shannon nodded, then answered her own question. "We probably should."

When the car was parked and Shannon was ready to set off for the ranch's business office to find Morgan, Christine said, "I think I'll go on to the house. There's something I forgot to do. You don't mind, do you? Telling him yourself?"

Shannon frowned, obviously puzzled. "No, of course not."

Christine tried to smile, but knowing she was acting like a coward made it difficult. She had worked hard not to think about Morgan all morning, but Erin's whispered confidence had rung in her ears for hours last night. *I wish Morgan was my daddy.* Now, confronted with the prospect of seeking him out, she just couldn't do it!

Christine returned to the house and after closing the door safely behind her leaned against its bracingly cool surface and released a long sigh.

MORGAN WAS OUT at the corral talking with a cowboy who'd just returned from one of the pastures when he looked up and saw Shannon approaching. The last he'd seen of her, she'd been behind the wheel of Mae's big Cadillac, taking off somewhere with Christine. He'd wondered where they were off to, but with Rafe gone, he didn't have a way of finding out. Christine was nowhere to be seen now, though.

He finished with the cowboy and moved forward to greet her. "How's it goin'?" he asked. "Missin' Rafe already?"

"Terribly." She grinned.

"Yeah, it looked like it. I saw you goin' off for a joyride in Mae's car."

"I took Christine to Del Norte to see the elementary school. You know Erin started today. She rode the bus with Jessica and Rusty."

"I heard somethin' about it, yeah."

"Christine was worried since it all happened so suddenly. She didn't even know where Erin was going. So I took her there, let her have a look around, and now she feels better."

"You like her, don't you?" Morgan asked.

Shannon nodded. "Yes, as a matter of fact I do." Then, with a narrowing of her eyes, she added, "And you do, too, don't you?"

"Why are you askin' me that?"

"You Parker men!" Shannon said impatiently. "You're all so darned slippery about being pinned down!"

"I'm not a Parker."

She flashed him a wry look. "You're just as good as. I'm asking because I'm curious. Harriet said something that made me—"

"Ah, Harriet."

"She said she picked up on something yesterday that surprised her."

"What?"

"She thinks you have feelings for Christine."

Morgan smiled. "Harriet's hormones are playin' games with her imagination."

"So, you're denying it?" Shannon pressed him.

"I didn't say that."

"Oh!" She stamped a foot in frustration. "I don't know why I bother!"

Morgan felt like a stallion caught in a box canyon. "Yeah, I like her," he admitted after a moment.

Shannon rolled her eyes and sighed. "Now was that so hard?" She hooked her arm in his and walked with him back toward the compound. "I truly do like her, Morgan. I don't know how this is going to end up— I know she can't inherit a piece of the ranch—but little Erin is so happy here. And I think Christine is, too— as much as she'll let herself be. I think—" Shannon bit her lip "—she's had such a hard time in her life that she doesn't know what a real home is. She hasn't said anything, but..."

"Yeah, I know what you mean," he said.

Shannon switched subjects. "We met someone out on the road to town today. A man."

Morgan raised one brow. "Am I the one you should be telling this to?"

She ignored him. "He said he was looking for some steers he'd had stolen. And what he described sounds a lot like what's been happening around here. Fence posts cut down and then set back up as if nothing had happened. He said he's lost ten or twelve head."

Morgan stopped walking and turned to face her. "On the road, you say?"

"He was having trouble with his car—his pickup truck, actually. He was towing a livestock trailer. Something was wrong with one of the tires."

"Did you see something wrong with one of the tires?"

Shannon shrugged "No, but by the time we got there, I think he'd already fixed it."

"Did he say he was from around here?"

She frowned. "He didn't say, but I got the feeling he wasn't. Morgan, what is it? Why are you—"

"One more thing. What'd he look like?"

"Dirty. Needed a bath. Youngish—late twenties? Brown hair... Morgan, tell me, what is it?"

"Well...it's kinda strange for someone to be out on the road tryin' to track down a rustler himself. And carrying a trailer. Did he think he'd find the cows standin' around and just be able to chute 'em up and take 'em home?"

"I told him to go talk to Sheriff Denton or Tate. That maybe they could help him." She eyed Morgan closely. "But you don't think he's going to do that, do you?"

Morgan shrugged. "He could be on the up-and-up. Strange things happen all the time. We'll know if the sheriff gets a call."

"I didn't like the look of him," Shannon said. "I don't think Christine did, either."

"Where was this?" Morgan asked.

"Off the ranch. About three miles down the road to Del Norte."

"That's pretty close by."

"He wasn't there when we came back."

Morgan laughed. "It would've been strange if he was. Then we'd really start askin' some hard questions. You didn't see him in town, did you?"

"No, but then we weren't looking for him, either. What are you going to do, Morgan?"

"First, call the sheriff. Second, call Ed Davis."

"You think he was one of the rustlers, don't you?"

"I think…we need to wait and see."

"Oh, Lord," she murmured.

"Keep it under your hat, okay? No use causin' an uproar if we don't need to."

"Don't tell Christine, you mean?"

"Don't tell Mae," he clarified.

Shannon understood completely. With Rafe away, he would be the one to catch the full force of Mae's worry.

CHRISTINE AND SHANNON worked on the family-history corrections for most of the afternoon, and Christine found herself becoming caught up in the stories. She was working on the early history, which told how the two Parker brothers had come to what others considered a godforsaken land and through hard work and dedication carved out the beginnings of what came to be known as the Parker Ranch. How they and their offspring had held on to it through Indian and outlaw attacks, through the Civil War, through numerous droughts.

"This is amazing," she murmured as she leafed through the pages. "I mean, every family has a history, but so very few can pass it on—especially all these letters and documents and photographs."

Shannon looked up from her work. "I was amazed by it, too. And captivated. You can see why this land means so much to the Parkers."

Christine grew still, and Shannon, seeing it, was quick to say, "I didn't mean it like that. I only meant—"

Christine shook her head. "No, it's exactly as you say. The ranch does mean a lot to them. That's why...that's why they don't take kindly to someone from outside making a claim."

"Christine, truly, I didn't mean..."

Christine pushed away from the computer and stood. Then she wandered over to Mae's desk and lightly fingered the brass pen-and-pencil set that was its only decoration. With her new knowledge she could see that her and Erin's prospects were dim. The Parkers would never let her have a share in the ranch. By hook, by crook or by sterling truth, she would never see any profit from it—not money for Erin's future, not a place for them to continue living. She should never have allowed Erin to start school. She should have held firm, not let herself be swayed by anyone, even Erin. Because, in all probability, they would soon have to pick up and move again.

But there was nothing left in Houston for them to return to. Nothing anywhere, really. What if, when the Parkers had finally had enough and tossed them out on their ears, they found a little place in Del Norte? She could find a job in an office or a café. That way Erin could remain in school here, with her new teacher and her new friends, and continue to—

Mae entered the room and stopped short, her gaze

fastening on Christine's handling of her pen. Christine immediately let go of it.

Mae's dark gaze instantly picked up on what Christine and Shannon were doing, but she took her usual place behind the desk and proceeded with what she had come to say. "You've had a call," she informed Christine tersely.

Christine's head jerked up. Her first thought was of Erin. Had something happened to her?

"It was that person you told me about," Mae continued, "Ira's housekeeper, Mrs. Tobin."

"Mrs. Tobin?" Christine echoed.

Mae's strong features were tight. "Yes. She called to check on your welfare. She said she was worried about you."

Christine's heart gave a tiny leap. Mrs. Tobin. Dear Mrs. Tobin!

Mae's set expression didn't crack. "I confronted her with what you told me—that she could confirm you didn't steal any of the articles Abigail and Brendan swear you did."

"And what did she say?" Christine asked faintly. Was there room for a small ray of hope?

"She confirmed your story. She also explained that she left the week after you because Abigail was so nasty to her and made life so miserable she couldn't stand it any longer. She said it was impossible for you to have stolen any of those things because she'd seen them in place herself when she dusted for the final time—a week to the day after you moved. She saw the jewels, which were in a clear case, all the pocket watches in their showcase, and she rubbed furniture oil on the desk itself." Mae paused for breath and for effect. "Of course," she continued levelly, "that's exactly what would be expected of an accomplice."

Christine started to tremble with anger. To be exonerated of guilt, then to have that acquittal pulled out from under her was too much to handle. Her first instinct was to strike back. But Mae lifted a hand to forestall her.

"There's something more," she said. "I called Abigail. She blustered and blathered, saying some more things I won't tell you about. But in the end she admitted it was all a lie. You never took anything. She'd made it all up—she and that brother of hers. They're not fit to be Parkers, and I told her so. I also told her that if ever they took their charges further, I was going to see to it personally that they were charged themselves." She paused to let all that sink in. Then, stiffly, she said, "I owe you an apology, Miss Grant. This changes nothing about where we stand on the ranch issue, but...fair is fair."

Christine was stunned. Seemingly, with a flick of her hand, Mae had disposed of most of the charges against her. She didn't have to worry anymore about defending herself to the police or trying to prove something was a fact when her only witness had disappeared.

"Mrs. Tobin..." she murmured.

"She left her number in New Braunfels. Asked me to tell you to call her as soon as you have the time."

Getting up, Mae walked with a straight back to the door. It was only when she was about to step into the hall that Christine managed to find more words. "Mae?" she said. "Thank you."

The old woman paused and, turning her whole body, gave a curt nod before proceeding into the hall and closing the door behind her.

Christine sank into a chair. Her relief was enormous. It felt wonderful to be vindicated. Particularly in Mae's eyes. Yes, Mae's, most of all. Because it was Mae who'd been so quick to doubt her.

Shannon swooped down to give her a hug. "That's wonderful, Christine. Wonderful! Do you know what it means to have Mae do that? She's probably doubted Abigail and Brendan's story all along. From everything I've heard about them they're terrible people. Brendan's always getting into some kind of woman trouble, and Abigail—Rafe discovered this only recently—has gotten into trouble with the law! It seems that not too long ago she shoplifted a necklace at Neiman Marcus. The store detective caught her, the police took her in, booked her, and when she had to appear before a judge, her temper got the better of her and she tried to attack the store detective. The judge gave her six months' probation and told her the next time she assaulted someone she'd go to jail." Shannon laughed. "Right now Mae's probably trying to figure out how she can disown those two."

Christine smiled, still slightly stunned. So that was why, on the day she and Erin had left Ira's house, Brendan had warned his sister about attacking her. He'd mentioned a judge. "Poor, poor Ira," she murmured, shaking her head sadly. "He didn't deserve children like that."

Shannon wordlessly nodded agreement.

CHAPTER FOURTEEN

ERIN HAD CHATTERED happily, well past her newly determined eight-thirty bedtime, about the school and all the children she'd met that day. She liked her teacher, she liked the food in the cafeteria, she liked the long bus ride. There wasn't anything she didn't like about the day. Except—Christine was sure she'd added this as a sop—she'd missed her mother on occasion. Christine had listened patiently, letting her wind down, then after the little girl was asleep, tried to wind down herself.

She hadn't realized she'd been so successful until her predawn awakening to Erin's alarm clock. As she helped her daughter get ready for the day, she found herself feeling better than she had in ages. The extra rest, combined with the lifting of suspicion, allowed her a new sense of optimism. Not everything had worked out yet, but at least she wasn't still being considered a thief!

When she drove Erin to Little Springs that morning, it was Morgan who came out to talk with her.

"Mornin'" he drawled, leaning down to fold his arms on the sill of her opened window.

Unlike the man she and Shannon had met yesterday—who, Shannon later confided to her, Morgan suspected might be an actual rustler—Morgan, this close, disturbed her senses rather than offended them. He was a perfect specimen of a man in his prime—wide-shouldered, slim-hipped, suntanned, vigorous. She'd responded to his innate virility right from the first.

A smile slowly crossed his face. "I understand you're to be congratulated," he murmured.

"I didn't do anything."

"I know—that's what I mean."

Christine waved at Erin, who was setting off with Jessica and Rusty for the bus stop. She knew she should restart the car and be off herself, but she couldn't make herself move. Not as long as Morgan was willing to stay there and talk. She had this crazy need to be near him.

"I did tell everyone I didn't do it," she reminded him.

"You did."

"You didn't believe me, either."

"I wanted to believe you."

"That's not the way you acted."

"Oh?" His blue eyes moved over her, delivering a message of remembered intimacies.

Christine swallowed. She was dancing dangerously close to the fire. To pull back a little, she said, "Shannon told me about that man yesterday—what you suspect about him. What are you going to do?"

His smile told her he knew exactly what she was up to. But he played along. "Ed Davis has an idea or two he's been working on. I might be givin' him a little help."

A chill ran up her spine. "You mean, to help catch the man?"

Morgan nodded, his blond hair glinting in the early-morning light. "Him and anybody else he might be workin' with."

"And that can be dangerous, right?"

"It's my job. It's what I do." His smile turned tender as he reached into the car and tipped up her chin. "Would you care," he asked softly, looking directly into her eyes, "if something did happen to me?"

"I— I—" But he didn't give her time to finish. Instead, he leaned in and claimed the kiss she'd been longing to give him.

"I won't get hurt," he promised quietly, "but I will come back and ask that question again. Think you might have an answer for me by that time?"

Christine smiled tremulously. But she already knew the answer. Yes, she'd care! That was the trouble. She'd care a lot!

He straightened and, with a short wave, watched her pull away. *Later,* his stance seemed to say. *We'll sort this all out at a time and in a place that offers more time and far more privacy.*

Christine's grip tightened on the steering wheel. It seemed the only solid thing in her world.

AFTER BREAKFAST, Christine again offered to assist Shannon with the history, and they worked straight through till noon. It was when they broke for lunch that the front doorbell rang. Shannon went to see who the caller was while Christine waited.

"Package, miss," a man's voice said. "For Miss Mae Parker?"

"I'm not Miss Parker," Shannon replied, "but I'll sign for her."

A clipboard was exchanged, Shannon signed her name, then the package was handed over. More of a packet, really, in a next-day-delivery mailing envelope.

Shannon closed the door and rejoined Christine, and the two of them entered the dining room where Mae was already seated.

Shannon handed her the envelope. "This just arrived for you," she said.

Mae took it and, after studying the mailing label, clasped it to her breast and swiftly left the room.

Shannon lifted an eyebrow. "My goodness," she said. "It must have been something she needed right away."

Christine shrugged and smiled at Marie, who was carrying a tray containing three chilled tuna salads on beds of lettuce.

Mae didn't return during the lunch break. Marie had to carry her salad back to the kitchen. She tsked at the empty chair each time she came to check on their progress.

Christine and Shannon were passing the front door again, ready to go back to work, when Gib burst in. He looked more energized than Christine had ever seen him.

"Where's Mae?" he said quickly.

Shannon frowned. "What is it, Gib?"

He shook his salt-and-pepper head. "Mae called

and told me to do something, but I don't think I heard her right. She wants me to go find Rafe and bring him in.''

"Bring Rafe in from collecting the horses?" Shannon said incredulously. "But I thought... Wouldn't it take something like the end of the world for her to do that? I mean, he'll be back day after tomorrow. Possibly even tomorrow—that's what he told me.''

"That's why I want to check. I don't want to go off half-cocked, bring him in and then get both of 'em mad at me for doing the wrong thing. Where's she at?''

"Maybe her office," Shannon guessed. "Christine and I were working there earlier, but she disappeared at lunch to—''

Gib didn't wait for her to finish. He called a quick "Thanks!" over his shoulder and set off down the hall.

Shannon frowned at his back. "I'm not sure I want to go in there right now, do you?" she asked.

Christine shook her head. "No.''

"Let's wait out on the porch, and if Gib does have to go get Rafe, we might as well call it a day. Mae'll probably want her office for the rest of the afternoon.'' She paused. "I wonder what it is?''

Gib was out of the office in less than five minutes. His expression, when he came upon them on the porch, was even more strained. "Gotta go get him. She says no one's answering the radio and what she needs to talk to him about won't wait.'' Gib ducked his head and jogged off.

"That answers one question, then," Shannon said. "We get the rest of the day off."

CHRISTINE DECIDED the best place for her was her room. She lay down for a while, trying not to think about what was happening downstairs, trying not to wonder if it could have anything to do with her. She also tried not to think about what Morgan was doing, if he was in any danger or would be in danger while helping to deal with the rustlers. But she did let herself think about *him*. Wondering, enjoying, daydreaming about what would happen when once again they met.

She drifted off to sleep, only to be awakened sometime later by a knock on her door.

She sat up, slightly bufuddled. "Yes?" she called, searching for her shoes with her toes, while at the same time trying to straighten her shirt and smooth her hair. She crossed to the door and swung it open to see Shannon standing there. She looked...odd. Strained, white-faced, her eyes filled with concern.

"I'm sorry to wake you," she apologized, "but Mae wants to see you. Rafe's here now. So's Morgan."

"Morgan?" Christine repeated stupidly.

Shannon nodded. "Come on. We have to hurry. Otherwise, Mae..." She didn't finish. Instead, she grabbed Christine's arm and pulled her downstairs.

Christine's mind slowly cleared as they hurried down the hall to Mae's office. "What is it?" she asked. "Something to do with the packet Mae received?"

Shannon didn't answer. And when the door opened

to reveal the people inside, Christine felt like an aristocrat being presented at the guillotine. Mae, Rafe, Morgan and Gib waited for her.

Shannon accompanied Christine inside and, once there, remained beside her, a stubborn look on her face. *I'm not leaving,* her expression said.

Mae was seated at her desk. She looked as if she'd shrunken and aged since Christine had last seen her. The lines on her face were deeper, she'd lost color, and her eyes... Her dark eyes almost burned when they fixed on Christine.

Christine glanced at Morgan. She'd been looking forward to the moment when she'd see him again, but she hadn't planned for it to be like this. What could possibly have happened? He, too, looked shaken, like the rest of them.

"Sit down," Mae directed her, her words clipped.

"I'd rather not," Christine said, just as she had the first time she'd gone through one of Mae's interrogations. She wanted to scream, demand she be told what was going on. But she wouldn't do it. Intimidation was a huge part of Mae's repertoire, and if she pretended not to be intimidated, Mae would lose a large portion of her control.

"I should have known it from the beginning," Mae muttered. "From the way you stood up for yourself." Then she was silent a moment before finally collecting a sheaf of loose papers and shaking them at Christine. "I don't know what kind of game you and Ira have been trying to play—" her voice shook on the last word "—but it's come to an end with this! This is the biggest, most unmitigated—" Her voice shook again, then cracked, and finally she dropped the papers back on the desk.

Christine was scared. She didn't understand. What kind of information had reached Mae that could result in such a complete breakdown of her usual control?

She looked around, her gaze skipping from face to face, begging silently for information. It stopped on Morgan. He took a step toward her, but Rafe held him back.

"This has to be settled," Rafe said quietly.

Morgan shook off Rafe's hand and crossed to her, anyway.

"What?" Christine said to him as Shannon slipped quietly into Rafe's arms.

"You might ask that, yes," Mae said, having regained her strength. "Why didn't you tell us you were Ira's daughter?"

"But Erin's *not* Ira's daughter," Christine said. "I know I let you think she might be, but I don't see how you can—" She stopped. "What did you say?" she asked.

"I said—"

"Mae, be kinder," Shannon pleaded, "please. Don't you see she—"

"I *said*, why didn't you tell us you were Ira's daughter in the first place? It would have saved us all a lot of time and trouble!"

Christine looked at Morgan again, standing close beside her, his hand clasping her arm. She needed him to translate. She was having trouble understanding.

Mae thrust a sheet of notepaper directly at her. It

was filled with a familiar spidery scrawl—Ira's handwriting.

"Read it," Mae commanded. "We all have. It was written to me."

Christine took the notepaper, but stared at it unseeingly. "Did you say Ira's daughter? But Abigail is Ira's daughter."

"Ira's *other* daughter. Read it. Like I told you." Mae's voice had grown less angry, as if even she could see that Christine had entered a state of shock and couldn't quite grasp the significance of what was being said. If Christine was acting, it was a great performance.

Christine felt Morgan's arm move to her shoulder. Felt him lead her to a chair and heard him urge her to sit down. Which she did. Still, her fingers wouldn't function properly. Nor would her brain. The notepaper fluttered to the floor.

Morgan picked it up.

"Give it to Shannon," Mae ordered. "Read it out loud, Shannon."

"No, Mae, I won't." Shannon stood her ground. "I think this is something Christine should be told on her own, without witnesses."

"We're family here," Mae snapped. "Morgan included. And *her* included, it seems. Or so these blood tests say." She rattled more papers. "Parker blood. Ira's blood. Unless they're faked."

Rafe took the notepaper from Morgan. "I'll read it," he said quietly.

"Read this, too," Mae commanded, "so she'll know who sent it."

Rafe accepted a more formal letter. "Christine," he said levelly, "this letter is from Eugene Hernandez. It's on his letterhead, has his signature and is dated yesterday." He began to read. "'Dear Ms. Parker, please find enclosed a sealed collection of material entrusted to me by my deceased client, Ira Lee Parker, before his death. The seal is intact and unbroken. As instructed, it is being sent to you exactly one week after confirmation that Ms. Christine Patricia Grant and her daughter, Erin Margaret Grant, are in residence at the Parker Ranch. Upon completion of this duty, my entire responsibility to my late client is terminated.'

"Now the other," Rafe said after a quick glance at Christine. "This is from Ira to Mae, signed by him, and dated March 25 of this year. 'Mae, I know this is going to come as a complete surprise, but the young woman I sent to you, under the guise of inheriting a share in the ranch, is in fact my daughter. A daughter I had no knowledge of until her mother contacted me as she lay near her own death almost a year and a half ago. I didn't tell Christine who I was for fear of having her hate me. By this time you'll know that I have died. But I couldn't leave things as they were, with her struggling, alone, trying to raise my only grandchild. I sent her to you with the knowledge that you wouldn't rest until you learned the truth, which I'm now providing. And that once learned, you also won't rest until Christine and Erin are treated fairly. Proof positive is in the blood tests. If you want to recheck the tests, I've made provisions for a sample of my blood to be maintained at the laboratory. Christine's you can get from her. The tricky part of this entire undertaking is Christine herself. She's very proud, very independent—having had to be independent from a young age. Please, Mae, help me make her understand. Please tell her for me—as many times as it takes—that I love her, and that she and Erin made my last months in this world worthwhile. Also, Mae, please be sure that she's given her rightful inheritance, and that she accepts it. For Erin's sake, if not for her own. And, again, that she knows I love her.'''

The effect of Rafe's low voice reading Ira's words echoed through the room. Mae twitched, Shannon wiped away a tear, Gib looked down at the floor, and Morgan's fingers, which were gripping her shoulder, tightened.

"So," Mae continued, seemingly undaunted, "is it true?"

Shannon came to stand by Christine's chair. "Mae. This has to stop. Rafe, please!"

Rafe, shaking off any lingering doubt, took command. "That's enough for now, Mae. I think we have our answer. Let's allow Christine to have some time on her own to get used to it. We'll talk later. Does that sound all right with you, Christine?"

Christine looked up at him. *Ira? Her father?* But how? When? He and her mother had never...

Rafe stepped over to the desk and extracted from the myriad papers another envelope. This one had her name on it. "Ira asked us to give this to you, too," he said quietly, and placed it in her hands. Then he went to the door and motioned for everyone, including Mae, to leave.

Soon, only Morgan and Christine were left in the room. Without a word, Morgan knelt beside her and pulled her close.

She shut her eyes and tried to experience only this moment. To be aware of his strength and his kindness and his desire to make things better for her. And his wish to take away some of her pain.

"Morgan, I don't understand. How could Ira be my..." She couldn't say the word out loud.

"Maybe the answer's in there," he said, nodding at the envelope. Then he smoothed her hair away from her face and kissed her temple, her forehead.

"But I can't be Ira's child!"

"Hush," he advised, pulling her closer. "For now. For a minute. Just breathe steady. Relax."

Christine did as he said, and slowly, some of the blood that had frozen in her veins began to flow again, and her mind didn't seem as unable to cope.

She returned his embrace, holding him as tightly he was holding her. His strength, his steadiness, was helping.

Finally he broke away. "I'll leave you, too, now. So you can read what Ira—" He stopped. "I'll be out in the hall. I won't go away," he promised.

Christine nodded, burning both with curiosity and dread.

Morgan hesitated, then bent to kiss her full on the mouth. Smiling slightly, he left.

Christine glanced at the envelope. She still didn't know what she felt. Everything within her seemed to be on hold. She ran her finger over the spidery letters that formed her name.

She opened the envelope and sliding out a sheet of paper began to read. "My darling daughter Christine, by now you know the truth. I can't begin to make everything up to you, to erase the past. If only I'd known—but I didn't know. And coward that I've proved to be, I couldn't tell you once I did. I was afraid that, in your pride, you'd reject me, as well as what I offered. Your mother contacted me shortly after she'd entered the hospital for the last time. She said—and this I think she *wouldn't* mind me telling you—she felt remorse at how bad a mother she'd been, and how bad a grandmother. I met Jeannette when she entertained at a private club where I was a member. We met two or three times after that. I can't say it was love. I also can't say that it wasn't—at least temporarily. I had no knowledge of the pregnancy, and I don't know why she didn't contact me for money to help raise you. She wouldn't say. She refused even to tell me where you were. Just that you were out there somewhere—my daughter! I hired someone to track you down. Then I became ill again. Christine, take what little I offer. Take it for Erin. And forgive me. Please. All my love, your devoted father, Ira Parker."

Her father. Her *father!* How many times had she wondered who her father was? How many days and nights had she ached to know something about him, to the point of scouring her mother's photo albums and counting back the months and years until she settled on a likely candidate? And all that time—her fingers tightened, crumpling the notepaper—and all that time her mother knew Ira was no more than fifteen or twenty miles away! Living with his two other children, showering on them everything that she...

Christine started to shake. Why? Why hadn't he told her? She'd liked him! She'd admired him! She'd held his hand as he died!

It was too much. All she wanted to do was rail and cry and throw things. *Why* had her mother kept his identity a secret? Why had Ira sent her here to what he knew would be certain rejection? Because he was afraid she'd refuse his delayed gift of inclusion? Well, she *would* reject it! Just as she'd reject him. She didn't need him or his money or his love. She'd been on her own taking care of herself all her life! She didn't need anything from him!

Morgan. She did need Morgan. To help her think. To help her wade through this morass of lies and partial truths.

She went to the door and, opening it, heard Mae say, "I appreciate all you tried to do, Morgan, even though now it seems that checking up on her didn't really matter. She's a Parker, and as a Parker, she—"

Christine must have made a sound. A strangled gasp. Morgan turned, and from the way the blood drained from his face, it was clear he knew he'd been found out.

The crumpled note tumbled from her suddenly nerveless fingers. Morgan had been checking up on her for Mae? That was all their budding relationship had been? Another subterfuge? Another out-and-out lie? And if that was so, who could she believe—ever?

He reached for her as she lunged past them. "Christine!"

She wouldn't stop. She ran down the hall and to the stairs, passing Shannon and Rafe on the way, but she wouldn't look at them, not even when Shannon called her name.

She ran on, pounding up the stairs and into her bedroom. Boots pounded after her, but she slammed the door shut and leaned against it, hoping to keep Morgan on the other side, away from her.

His fist beat against the wood. "Christine!" he called. "Open the door! It's not what you—"

"Go away! Go away!"

"I have to talk to you, Christine!"

"No! I don't want to talk to anyone! Leave me alone, all of you!"

"Christine, I love you!"

She closed her ears against him. It didn't matter what he said, because it wasn't the truth. No one told the truth, here or anywhere. No one *cared* enough to tell the truth. Morgan in particular.

He rattled the doorknob. "You had a hard hit just now. Christine, please, let me explain."

"I hate you! I hate you all!" she shouted. She knew she sounded like a child, but that was exactly the way she felt, betrayed by those she cared most about—yet again.

"You don't mean that," he said tightly.

"Yes, I do! I really do!"

Her breaths were coming in gasps. Her heart thundered in her ears. Tears streaked her cheeks. She waited, listening, for him to go away, and when he finally did, she dragged herself, stumbling, to the bed.

She wanted to cry. She wanted to fill the world with

her tears. Only, now that she was free to give in to her emotions, when no one would see her or hear her, she couldn't.

She lay there, unmoving and dry-eyed, for what seemed like hours. Then, finally, she cried.

MORGAN CAME DOWNSTAIRS slowly. He felt like death warmed over, his emotions drained. All he could see was the look on Christine's face. All he could hear were her anguished cries of betrayal.

Rafe and Shannon were in the living room on the couch. Rafe was holding Shannon protectively, as if she'd been crying. Mae stood at the window staring out at the courtyard beyond.

"She won't talk to you?" Rafe asked quietly.

Morgan shook his head and collapsed into a chair.

"I should've known she was a Parker," Mae muttered again, her back turned to the room.

"That was a pretty brutal way to handle things, Aunt Mae," Rafe said, his lips tight.

"She didn't know," Shannon murmured sadly.

"Which was what we had to find out, wasn't it? What was I supposed to do?" Mae demanded, spinning around. "Pussyfoot about? No. I asked and we found out the truth." She frowned. "I don't know why she's acting so huffy all of a sudden. It's an honor to be a Parker, not a tragedy!"

"Maybe she doesn't see it that way," Rafe said.

"Then she'd be wrong!" Mae snapped. "Ahh! I've had about enough of this. Tell her when she's over her snit to come see me. We'll get all the paperwork started to give her her share in the ranch. And as far as staying here goes, she can keep on doing that, too. Shannon, you'll be living at Rafe's place in a month. The two of them can take both guest rooms, as far as I'm concerned. Give 'em a little space to spread out.'' Her shoulders twitched as she added uncomfortably, "I didn't mean to hurt her feelings.''

Morgan said nothing. He couldn't. Everything he knew about Mae told him that she truly hadn't meant to hurt Christine—or him. But she'd said exactly the wrong thing at the wrong time more than once that day. *Bull in a china shop,* he recalled hearing his dad describe her years ago. Dub was right.

Mae left the room, her head held high, but with a giveaway hitch in her walk. She wasn't quite as invincible, or as uncannily right, as she wanted everyone to believe. She knew it, only she didn't like to admit it.

"It's more than learning she's a Parker, isn't it?'' Rafe said, once Mae was gone.

Morgan nodded. "Mae had asked me to find out what I could about her, and she was thankin' me for it when Christine opened the door and heard her.''

"And that matters?'' Rafe asked.

"We heard what you said upstairs,'' Shannon told him.

"Oh, hell!''

Shannon pulled away from Rafe to pat Morgan's arm. "Just give it time,'' she consoled him. "Give her time.''

"I'm afraid she'll head for the hills, before...'' He glanced at his watch and was surprised to see it was after five. "Damn, I have to meet Ed Davis in less than an hour."

"And I have to get back to the muster," Rafe said, sitting forward. "Gib came drivin' up like a crazy man. We lost several horses we probably won't see again until fall, if then."

Shannon looked at both men. "And what am I supposed to do? Hold everything together?"

Rafe flicked the tip of her nose with a long finger. "You bet you are," he said, grinning. "You're capable."

"Could you keep an eye on Christine?" Morgan asked. "Not let her take off anywhere?"

Shannon frowned. "It's almost time for the school bus, isn't it? Didn't they let Erin off out front yesterday?"

"I remember seein' it stop," Morgan said.

Shannon got to her feet. "Maybe what I'll do while you're both still here is have a little talk with Harriet. See if Erin can stay over at her place for a while. Just until Christine pulls herself together. I doubt she'd want her daughter to see her all upset."

"Good idea," Rafe murmured, still eyeing his best friend.

Morgan glanced at his watch again and silently yet energetically cursed the cow thieves who were taking him away from where he most wanted to be.

CHAPTER FIFTEEN

THE HOUSE WAS QUIET when Christine left her room, carrying her one suitcase. In it, she'd packed as much as she could of her and Erin's things, being sure to include Golden Belle. The rest of their possessions...well, it didn't matter. Suddenly nothing mattered but getting away from here.

She crept down the stairs, not wanting to make any noise. She had no idea what time it was, but it was dark outside. In the house, the only light came from the living room. Mae? Christine's insides quivered. She didn't want to see Mae again.

She was at the front door when someone came into the entryway.

"Christine?" Shannon said, her voice alarmed.

Christine turned.

"What are you doing?" Shannon asked. "You're not leaving. Tell me you're not leaving. Not when—"

"I don't want Ira's charity. I don't want any of your charity," Christine stated tightly.

"It's not charity when it's your right by birth. If you're a Parker—"

"*If!* Even with everything there still seems to be a doubt!"

"No! You didn't let me finish. I was trying to say,

if you're a Parker you get your share of the ranch at age twenty-one. That should have been given to you, too. You have a lot of money coming, Christine. Four years' worth!''

"I don't want it."

"No one still has doubts! Not even Mae! She said..." When Christine's face froze, Shannon changed her tack. "Morgan asked me to keep you here, not to let you leave. He had to go out— Something about the rustlers. But he really cares for you, Christine. And Morgan's not a person to advertise his emotions. He—''

Christine interrupted her. "Where's Erin?"

"She's at Harriet's. I didn't think you'd want—''

"Thank you," Christine said coolly, then, remembering how Shannon had consistently stood up for her, she repeated, far more earnestly, "I truly do thank you, Shannon. And tell Rafe...tell Rafe he should definitely appreciate you."

Then she let herself out the door, tears falling, unheeded, down her cheeks.

Shannon followed her outside. "Christine! Morgan—just let him explain. It's not what you think!"

Christine continued walking.

Harriet, of course, like Shannon, tried to talk her out of reacting so quickly. "Think about it," she advised.

As she had with Shannon, Christine thanked her, but she continued to hold to her plan. She had to get away from the ranch!

Erin was totally confused. "Mommy? I don't understand," the little girl said in a small voice as she climbed into the car and Christine started the engine. "I thought we were going to stay here. I thought if I made friends and started school, we'd—"

For the first time in her child's life Christine shushed Erin harshly. "Don't talk! I can't explain right now." Tears hovered on her lashes. "Just believe that what I'm doing is right for us. Please, Erin. I— I'll tell you everything later."

Erin gave her a look that mixed fright with regret. "I like the ranch," she said quietly.

"I know," Christine said, her fingers working anxiously on the steering wheel as she directed the car away from the ranch.

Erin grew quiet. She'd shrunk into her seat, her chin on her chest, her hands clasping her schoolbooks.

Christine experienced a moment of disquiet. Was she doing the right thing again by leaving? But how could they stay?

They drove on and on, and as time passed and only the moon and the headlights illuminated the road ahead, she began to realize that she must have made a wrong turn again.

This time, at least, she knew she was still on the Parker Ranch, but where on the Parker Ranch? Which division? She glanced at Erin, who still sat hunched away from her.

"Honey, I think..." she started to say, when the headlights flashed on something up ahead. She instantly slowed down, rolling forward cautiously. It was a livestock trailer, off the road, backed up to what looked like a downed fence. Immediately she knew what it was. "Rustlers!" she said, alarmed.

Erin's head popped up and she strained to see.

The next thing Christine knew, someone had jerked open the driver's door and was dragging her outside the still-moving car. She cried out and heard Erin shout, "Mommy!"

"My little girl!" she managed, fighting the arms striving to control her.

The car veered to the opposite side of the road and came to a stop. Christine didn't breathe freely until she saw Erin hop out, unhurt, and run toward her.

"Where the hell did you come from?" a rough voice asked in her ear while his fingers cut into her arms.

A second man ran up, intercepted Erin and brought her over. "What's goin' on?" he demanded gruffly. "Harry's got those calves just about— Hey, I know her!" he said, squinting at Christine. "She's the one I was tellin' ya about last night. Her and that other one. They sure grow 'em pretty out in this part of the state." His teeth flashed as he smiled.

"Shut up and help me," the first man growled.

"What are we gonna do with 'em?" the younger man asked.

"Tie 'em up's all I can think to do right now. Here, get that rope in the back of the trailer."

A background noise Christine now realized she'd been hearing all along became clearer. The muffled sound of hooves, of lowing cattle, and a "suc, suc, suc" call by a man on a horse, who was driving them forward.

"Better hurry," the first man said, and roughly forced Christine to an upright fence post. He made her sit down and tied her arms to it behind her back. The same was done with Erin.

"Maybe sometime we'll meet under other circumstances," the young rustler said to Christine, grinning. "I'll buy you a drink and maybe you can—"

"Get over here, Rowdy!" the first man barked, hurrying back to the trailer.

It was odd, Christine thought, but after seeing that Erin was safe she had no other qualm or fear. Possibly because she'd been through so much that afternoon. This was just one thing more.

Erin wiggled her arms, testing the strength of the rope at her wrists, which proved to be very strong and expertly tied.

"It's okay, sweetheart," Christine said mildly. "Mine are just as tight. I think…if we just sit here, they'll be gone soon. They don't want us. They want the cattle."

The back gate of the livestock trailer was open and a ramp was arranged over the downed barbed wire. The man on the horse urged the calves closer, the horse working back and forth to cut off any calves with thoughts of freedom. And with the help of the two men on foot, some of the cattle started going up the ramp into the trailer.

Suddenly from out of the night, other figures emerged, running toward the trailer.

"Hold it!" a loud voice commanded.

There were more shouted orders as about a half-dozen men, some in uniform and others not, converged on the startled rustlers. The younger man—Rowdy—tried to run, but was quickly cut off by one of the newcomers. The man on the horse wheeled around and tried to kick his mount into a gallop, but another newcomer caught the reins and dragged the man from the saddle. The third rustler, seeing what had happened to his confederates, lifted his hands in the age-old signal of submission.

The calves began to scatter and some of the ones in the trailer scrambled back out to join the other animals.

One of the newcomers hurried over to Christine and Erin and, falling to his knees, whipped a knife out of his pocket and began to cut their bonds. Morgan!

To Christine, the whole thing was like a crazy dream. That they'd gotten lost again, this time when trying to leave the ranch. That they'd happened upon the rustlers who had been causing so much trouble. That Morgan would be the one to rescue them.

He made a low sound deep in his throat and, still crouching, gathered them to him, one in each arm. "My God," he said huskily, "when I saw the two of you—"

"Morgan! Morgan!" Erin cried, holding on to him for dear life, burying her face in his neck.

An older man came over. "All right!" he said gleefully. "We got 'em, Morgan! Caught 'em red-handed with their pants down!" He eyed the trio. "You, ah, know these two ladies?"

Morgan stood up, bringing Christine and Erin with him—Erin straddling his hip, Christine leaning against him. "I'm goin' to get 'em home now, Ed. Their statements can be taken tomorrow, right?" He glanced at another man walking by, leading away two of the rustlers, both in handcuffs. "Sheriff Denton? That okay with you?"

"Sure," the man in uniform said. "Just so's they don't forget what they saw."

A second uniformed man, younger and thinner, followed the first, with the third rustler—Rowdy—in cuffs, as well.

"You may have to wait on that drink, sweetie," Rowdy called to Christine. "I might be out of commission for a while. Will ya wait for me?"

"Tate," the sheriff grumbled over his shoulder, "keep that polecat quiet!"

Christine turned her face away. Emotionally she was completely empty. Erin seemed happy and relieved to be in Morgan's arms, and Morgan seemed happy to be with them, and she herself? She felt nothing.

Morgan saw them into Christine's car and got behind the wheel. "I won't ask what you were doin' way out here," he said, starting the engine. And he was as good as his word. In fact, he didn't say anything all the way back to the compound.

MORGAN TOOK THEM to Mae's house, even though he wanted to bring them to Little Springs so he wouldn't have to leave them. Erin had been afraid, but it was Christine who worried him most. She seemed past the point of being merely detached. It was as if nothing was getting through to her. She was moving on automatic.

When Shannon came running out of the house to the car, with Harriet following closely behind, Christine barely blinked. When Harriet offered to help Erin get ready for bed, reasoning that a return to routine would be good for the child, Christine again barely responded.

"Should I go get the doctor?" Morgan asked Shannon worriedly after telling her everything that had happened.

"I think what she needs is rest, Morgan. She's been through a lot today. She's more in shock than anything. I recognize the signs."

Morgan gazed at Christine, who continued to sit like a zombie, an untouched cup of tea in her hand.

Shannon smiled encouragement. "Come back tomorrow to talk with her," she said. "Let her have tonight to rest and think. I know it's hard, but—"

"If it's what she needs, she'll have it," he said. Then he bent to scoop a freshly bathed and pajama-clad Erin into his arms. She clung to him.

"I was afraid, Morgan," she said simply. "Mommy said we were leaving here."

"Your mom was upset, honey," he replied huskily.

"So we're not leaving?" Erin asked.

"I hope not."

Everyone understood now why Erin looked so much like a Parker. She *was* a Parker, only not in the way they'd expected. Her looks ran true to the blood, where her mother's did not. Only, the little girl didn't know it yet. And, Morgan acknowledged, it wasn't his place to tell her.

He summoned a smile and swung Erin around to ride on his back. "How about if I tuck you in?" he asked. "I know you're gettin' to be almost grown, but since I'm here, what do you say?"

"Yes!" she said, giggling.

He took her upstairs where he saw that Harriet had already turned down her bed. "You sleepy?" he asked once he'd pulled the covers up to her chin.

"Yes. No. I don't know." She giggled again, only this time more softly. "I sounded just like Mommy. She says that sometimes."

Morgan sat on the side of the bed. It surprised him how much he had come to care for Erin. He liked her shy sweetness and intelligent independence. In no time at all he could come to love her. In no time at all... Hell, he already did!

"Morgan?" she said, turning serious. "Those were bad men who tied us up out there, weren't they?"

"Yes. They take things that aren't theirs."

"What's going to happen to them?"

"They'll be charged, have a trial and go to jail."

"For how long?"

"For a long time. You don't need to worry about them, honey."

"Is that what you do? Catch bad people who steal cows?"

"It's what I do."

"Here?" she asked.

Erin and his niece and nephew must have talked. "Not here. Somewhere else."

Her big dark eyes darkened even more. "Does that mean," she almost whispered, "that you're going to go away one day? When your daddy's arm gets better?"

Morgan couldn't lie to her. "Probably," he said.

Erin surprised him by tearing up. "I don't want you to go, Morgan. I want you to stay right here. With us!" And then, somewhat improbably, but perhaps logically enough, considering what she'd just been through, she added, "And I want to stay here, too!"

With her last words, her arms encircled his neck and pulled him close. He could feel her warm tears on his face. He held her for a time, as she seemed to need, then gently extracted himself. "I have to go home now, Erin. But I'll see you tomorrow, okay?"

She bit her bottom lip and nodded.

CHRISTINE DIDN'T REMEMBER going to bed that night, who had helped her upstairs, what had been said. Nor did she remember stretching out between the cool sheets, whether Erin was asleep or awake, or when she herself had gone to sleep. It was as if, to protect itself, her mind had finally switched off, just like her emotions.

She awoke sometime before dawn, once again fully sentient. She remembered everything that had happened yesterday in painful detail. Starting from the time the packet had been delivered.

She was Ira Parker's daughter. She, Christine Grant. Or could she now call herself Christine Grant Parker?

She moaned and turned on her side to stare at the first muted rays of sunlight. She'd always wondered who her father was, always longed to have roots. And, considering the family she now found herself to be a part of and its history, she definitely had roots.

Oh, Ira!

Then there was Morgan. Her eyes fluttered shut. His betrayal of her hurt most of all. Every time he'd talked to her, been with her, it had been at Mae's behest. Getting to know her, getting her to trust him, had been his assignment. Had she instinctively perceived that? Was that why she'd reacted so strongly upon learning his occupation? Unconsciously had she sensed the need to question his motives?

He was an investigator. And he had been secretly investigating *her!*

She moaned again and sat up, her knees raised, her head resting on them, her hair covering her face like a veil. A veil she wanted to keep between herself and the rest of the world. Particularly the Parkers—and Morgan.

She had actually started to think that she might be falling in love with him. *Ha!* That she could trust him. Another *ha!* She could trust him about as far as she could trust that rattlesnake Erin had come upon their first day at the ranch. And *love* him? That was a joke. A huge, terrible, unfunny joke—on her!

She threw herself back against the pillow. What should she do? Her first instinct had been right, she believed, even if it had failed. She had to get away.

Ira had been wrong to send her here. She was like a square peg trying to force itself into a round hole. She didn't fit in. She would never fit in!

Maybe she and Erin could go to New Braunfels and stay with Mrs. Tobin and her sister for a time. She could find a job and a place for them to stay and pretend that none of this had ever happened. She could forget about Morgan and Mae and Rafe and Shannon—and all the others. She could erase from her mind the fact that she was a Parker. That Ira Parker and her mother had...

Ira Parker and her mother. It still didn't seem real. She knew her mother had at one time entertained in some exclusive clubs in downtown Houston. She'd seen some photographs taken at the time. Her mother had been young and strikingly pretty then. Christine lifted her head. There had been men in suits clustered around her mother in the photographs. She hadn't paid much attention to them because she'd always been so taken with the brightly colored sequins and feathers her mother had been wearing, and how happy and carefree she'd looked. But what if...

"What if one of those men was Ira?" she whispered, completing the thought aloud. She tried to imagine what Ira might have looked like twenty-five years before, then tried to remember what the men had looked like. But it was no good. She couldn't create a memory where none existed. Ira might have been pictured in one of the photographs, then again he might not. She had no way of knowing. Not now. The photo albums eventually had been burned in one of her mother's drunken fits.

So her mother had felt remorse at how bad a mother she'd been, how bad a grandmother. Wasn't that a case of too little, too late? Why had she waited all those years to tell Ira? Why hadn't she told *her* even as an adult?

It hurt that her mother hadn't told her. It hurt that Ira had kept the truth from her. It hurt that Morgan...

Christine closed her eyes and listened to her daughter's soft rhythmic breathing. She needed to stop thinking for the moment. It wasn't helping. It was far and away better to go back to feeling nothing.

ERIN AND CHRISTINE slept well past the time for the school bus that morning. When Christine came to, somewhere around ten o'clock, Erin was just waking.

They looked at each other.

"Are you okay now, Mommy?" Erin asked, her fingers curled around the edge of the sheet.

Christine tried to smile. There was so much she had to tell her daughter, but the time wasn't yet right. "I'm fine, sweetheart," she said.

"You were... It was funny last night. I got scared."

Christine knew Erin wasn't talking about the rustlers. She was talking about being hurried out of Harriet's house and into the car. "I know. I'm sorry."

"Did something scare you, Mommy? Is that why we...? We're aren't going to go away from here, are we? I don't want to. I like it here. I like the ranch, I like my new friends, I like the school. I like riding Junior..."

"What about Mae?" Christine asked, thinking about the last time she'd seen Mae—angry and suspicious and accusing, as usual.

"Is she the one who scared you?" Erin asked.

"We had...words," Christine conceded.

"Gwen and Wesley say she barks louder than she bites—that's what they said when I told 'em she makes my tummy nervous. They said she's told Marie to always keep a supply of their favorite cookies, and sometimes she has one with them."

"Then she can't be all bad," Christine agreed. *If only it was as simple as sharing a cookie.* But Erin was trying her best to help.

"What if we had to leave, sweetheart?" Christine asked, adjusting the pillow under her head. "What if...we didn't have a choice?"

Erin's eyes widened. "You mean, because of the rule Ira broke?" She worried her bottom lip, then said, "I'd ask Mae if we could stay, anyway. I really don't want to go away from here, Mommy."

Christine continued to nod. She had her answer. A Parker on Parker land. Erin, unconsciously, had become one of them.

CHRISTINE HELD her head high as she went downstairs into the dining room, Erin at her side. Marie hovered around them. Shannon showed up, then Harriet, then Jodie. All of them solicitous.

Then someone else appeared in the doorway—Morgan.

Without her being quite sure how it happened, everyone else faded from the room. Even Erin.

It was just she and Morgan, both standing now and facing each other. He was dressed in his usual jeans and shirt, looking as good as he always did. With that smile that normally created havoc in her bloodstream. But not today.

"You look a little better this morning than you did yesterday," he said.

"What do you want, Morgan?" She cut to the chase.

"To talk to you."

"We have nothing to say to each other."

"I disagree."

She tossed her head. "You told me something once that I've never forgotten. You said, 'It's actions that count out here.' Do you remember that?"

"I think I do."

"I think I do, too. And you know what? I think I believe it."

He took a few steps toward her. "Christine, what you overheard... Mae did ask me to see what I thought, but I didn't do it the way you—"

Christine's hand jerked out to stop him. Her face was turned slightly away. "No! I think it's exactly the way I heard it. But—" she shrugged "—there's not really all that much to get excited about, is there? I mean, we never—"

"I do love you, Christine," he said quietly, as if he'd said it before. She had a vague memory that rang through her pain.

"I don't love you," she insisted.

"Christine—"

"You're just like all the others, aren't you? I thought you were different and then you turn out to be exactly the same."

He closed the distance between them, taking her arm, pulling her to him. "Stop it," he ordered. "If by the others you mean Erin's father—"

"I thought you believed Ira was her father."

"I never believed that."

"'A younger man makes a better lover'—I can tell you everything you've ever said to me!''

He looked at her for several long seconds. She could see that he wanted to kiss her, that he wanted to do more than kiss her, but he held back. "Why?" he questioned softly. "Why can you remember so much?"

She jerked out of his hold. "It's all a lie. Everything's been a lie! My mother! Ira! My coming here! You!"

"So, what are you going to do?"

Frowning, she hugged her arms over her breasts.

"Erin doesn't want to leave here, does she?" he asked. "She's told me that."

"Is that the way you work it?" she snapped. "Turn my daughter against me?"

"I'm not working anything," he said. "I'm trying to talk sensibly, calmly—"

"Even Mae's doing it—with cookies!" Christine knew she was scraping bottom for something to use against him, but she would wield whatever she had.

"Then you won't object if I use something from my own arsenal," he said, moving toward her again.

She backed up until she hit the wall. When she tried to duck to the side, he put out a long arm to stop her. When she tried to duck the other way, he did the same thing, effectively trapping her.

"You listen to me for just a minute, okay?" His voice was low, firm. "Mae Parker is my employer. She asked me to do a job for her. She asked me to get to know you. I believe her exact words were 'to see what she's made of.' I did that. But I didn't do it only because she asked me to. I would've done it on my own, anyway. *Not* because I was suspicious of you," he forestalled her protest, "but because I was attracted to you. I still *am* attracted to you."

"That doesn't make any difference," she blurted, "because I'm…"

His eyes glittered, then he bent his head, his lips moving smoothly up her neck, from her shoulder to just behind her ear, making her tremble in spite of her intention not to.

"You were saying?" he drew back slightly to ask. He was smiling again—that slanted devil-made-me-do-it smile—and his eyes twinkled.

Christine caught her breath. She wasn't going to be persuaded this way!

"No!" She gave a mighty heave, freeing herself. "This is more important than that. My mother might have been putty in a man's hands, but not me. I'm *not* her!"

His smile disappeared. "I never thought you were."

Christine raked a hand through her hair, shaken. Not only from the kiss.

"The only man—boy, really—I ever went to bed with was Erin's father. Plenty of others have wanted to, believe me. But I wouldn't! Because I refuse to be guided by glands and hormones and—" She stopped herself abruptly, knowing she was divulging too much. "I haven't wanted that kind of life for Erin," she finished as strongly as she could.

"The kind of life you were forced to live."

"Exactly."

"So does that mean you're cutting out the possibility of ever falling in love?"

Christine pressed her lips together. She wouldn't look at him.

He came to her again. They might have been doing a slow-moving dance. He forced her chin up between his thumb and forefinger. "Because that's not what it's all about, either. Being promiscuous and being in love are two very different things."

"Being in love didn't do me much good," she said.

"How old were you? You had to be sixteen, right? And you say he was a boy?"

She refused to answer. He was taking too much on himself. Delving into places he had no right to be.

"Are you the same person you were when you were sixteen?" he challenged softly.

When she still wouldn't reply, he said, "I'm not coming back here again for a month. Our roundup starts in a few days, so I've got plenty to keep me busy. You can have all the time you want to think. About being a Parker, about whether you're going to stay here or go, about whether you'll ever let yourself believe I'm telling you the truth." He studied her face. It was as if he was burning every feature, every errant freckle, into his memory.

Then, without giving her the kiss she expected, he turned away and left the room. Without looking back.

CHAPTER SIXTEEN

WEDDING PREPARATIONS switched into high gear after the start of the roundup. As the month went by it seemed there was never a day that some problem didn't crop up. And to add to the complications was the preparation for the Parker family meeting—where the majority of the Parkers from around the state enjoyed a get-together and thrashed out any business concerns.

From everything Christine had heard, business took a distant second to fun. "Everyone comes in trailers and parks in the pasture nearest the compound," Harriet had told her. "We have barbecues and dances and old-fashioned ice-cream socials. We just kinda catch up on everyone else's news."

To combine the family meeting and the wedding had been Mae's idea. And in a way it made sense. But the actual management of it all, especially near the end, was an ordeal.

Shannon was relieved when Rafe was available again, and after a few days off, the cowboys, too, helped with the last-minute dribs and drabs.

Wedding gifts had been arriving by the ton, from everyone who felt close to the Parkers or to Shannon or to her mother and father. Gifts even came from the governor and both state senators. Not to mention numerous state representatives and affiliates of both political parties.

"My heaven," Shannon had said almost helplessly, looking at the presents that took up most of a downstairs room.

Finally the day arrived, clear and bright and, thankfully, several degrees cooler than the days preceding. Taking into account the expected June heat, the ceremony had been set for early evening. Electrical power had been strung to a pair of huge white canvas pavilions, under which the vows would be exchanged and the catered dinner and reception held. A raised wooden dance floor was set up outside and to the right. The party was expected to last far into the night.

Guests and family members had started to arrive several days before, and travel trailers sprouted like mushrooms in the nearby pasture. Everyone in the compound, particularly those in Mae's house, was happy and excited as they helped Shannon get ready on the big day.

Christine participated as best she could, but as evening drew near she retreated to her room. It was difficult not to be happy in the face of all the merriment. And she *was* happy—for Shannon and for Rafe, who she'd come to decide was more than acceptable for a newfound relative. He'd treated her fairly all along.

But Morgan's continued absence was trying. He'd said he would leave her alone until after the roundup. But the roundup had been over for a week and she hadn't seen him or heard anyone speak of him. It was as if they'd banded together to not mention his name, which, considering everything, they probably had.

Everyone seemed to know that she and Morgan had some unfinished business. And that Morgan was part of the reason she'd come apart the month before. That, and discovering she was a Parker.

Christine fingered the dress she was going to wear at the wedding. It was soft and pale blue and fitted her like it had been made for her. Erin's dress, also hanging out in readiness, was bright and pretty and had just the right amount of ruffles to please but not overwhelm her.

Christine had finally come to terms with being a Parker. Really, there was nothing else she could do. She'd looked at all the legal documents Ira had sent Mae and come to the same conclusion as the others. Still, it felt very odd to her, since she was so accustomed to being on the outside.

The Parkers, her kin, had been quicker to accept her. Jodie had thought it a kick to find that Christine was a long-lost relative, Gib had quietly welcomed her to the family, LeRoy had gone along with Harriet and seen the humor in the situation, Shannon and Rafe had received her with compassion and kindness. Everyone had let her take her time. No one had rushed her in any way. Except Mae.

One morning Mae had shown up at her bedroom door requesting a signature on a piece of paper. "It's something our lawyer's drawn up. Makes you an official Parker heir. Gives you voting rights and your piece of the profit."

"Mae, I..." Christine had hesitated.

"Ira would've been better off just coming out with it, I think, but I suppose he did his best. He might not have been thinking too clearly when he hatched the idea, being sick and all." Mae had paused, then said levelly, "It's a fact. You didn't know a thing."

Christine had looked at the old deceptively strong-looking woman, who underneath was as fragile and prey to the same fears as everyone else. "No," she'd murmured, then signed the paper and Mae had been on her way.

Erin had taken the news matter-of-factly when Christine worked up the nerve to tell her. "Ira was my granddad?" she'd repeated. "And your—"

"Father," Christine had supplied.

"So we're Parkers, too?" she'd said with a dawning smile. "Oh! I have to tell the others!" And she'd run off at top speed to spread the news.

Christine let her fingers fall from the beautiful blue dress. Where was Morgan? Why hadn't he come here as he'd said? She would see him at the wedding—he was best man. But that was no guarantee that he'd... She still didn't know what she felt for him, but some of her anger had dissipated. Maybe there'd been no deception. Maybe it all had been perfectly innocent. Maybe he truly...did have feelings for her. Or had.

A couple of hours later she was dressed and outside, sitting in one of the many folding chairs lined up, row after row, to face a flower-bedecked altar. Festoons of blossoms curved and looped from one tent pole to the next. Potted greenery abounded, softening the places where flowers were absent. A band had started to play unobtrusively in a back corner. Christine was amused to learn the band could play both drawing-room music, as they were now, and some of the hottest country-western going, as they would do later for the dancing. Candles were lit, and soon other guests, also in their best, began to take their places.

Christine looked around for Erin. Her daughter had begged to be allowed to see Gwen and Wesley in their finery, but she should have been back by now. Christine strained to see past a cluster of people near the main aisle—and then she saw 'him. He returned her look unwaveringly.

Christine's heart sped up. Morgan was dressed in a perfectly fitting black tuxedo with a string tie, looking the best she'd ever seen him. His hair was brushed carefully into place, shining golden and lightly curling to his collar. His wonderfully carved features were bronzed by the sun. His sky blue eyes, still seemed to see into her soul.

He started toward her and Christine's heart beat even faster. He slipped into the chair she was saving for Erin.

"Christine," he said in greeting.

She sat forward primly, hoping that by not looking at him she could contain her reaction. "I wasn't sure you were coming back," she said, keeping her voice low.

"I had some business to see to."

"I was looking for Erin," she said evasively, glancing over her shoulder.

"She'll be along in a minute. I saw her just now with Gwen. The ceremony's about to start, so I don't have much—"

"Maybe I should go get her, then." Christine tried to stand, but her legs wouldn't obey.

"I think it's time we have our little talk, don't you?" Morgan said. "It's been put off long enough."

Her eyes slid to his and she saw him smile. "Atta girl," he said softly, as if her look had told him most everything he wanted to know. "After the ceremony," he said. Then, as if unable to help himself, he kissed her. Lightly, gently, but with a promise of more to come.

Erin hurried up just as Morgan was leaving. She squeaked when she saw him and threw her arms around his neck as he bent to hug her. "Morgan!" she cried. "I missed you! You said a month, but it seemed so long!"

He grinned. "*Two* beautiful ladies."

"Are you back? Are you back to stay?" Erin demanded.

"You bet I am," he replied, then glancing at Christine, he gave Erin her chair and repeated, "You bet I am," before moving away.

"Morgan's back!" Erin said gleefully as she sat down. "Aren't you glad, Mommy? I really missed him. Didn't you?"

The soft background music changed to something more noticeable. And as the last of the chairs were taken by the guests, it changed again. Soon the first bridesmaid started down the aisle, and at the front of the tent, Rafe, Morgan, LeRoy and the two remaining groomsmen stepped into place.

Two more bridesmaids came down the aisle, followed by Harriet, not looking particularly pregnant,

Wesley in his custom-made suit, then Gwen, dressed in a scaled-down frillier version of the bridesmaids' dresses, strewing flower petals from an open basket she carried. And finally came Shannon, holding nervously on to Gib's arm. Shannon had no close male relatives, she'd told Christine, so she'd asked Gib to do the honor. He was taking the job seriously and walked proudly at the bride's side. Shannon's dress was particularly beautiful. White silk under silk gauze, with thousands of tiny beads hand-sewn in a delicate pattern. Her veil was short, diaphanous. Beneath it, she seemed to glow.

Christine's gaze followed Shannon to the altar, then switched to Morgan and Rafe. The groom looked amazingly handsome in his black tuxedo, with his dark hair and eyes and strong chiseled features. Morgan was a perfect foil, with his blond good looks. Night and day, the best of friends.

Christine couldn't take her eyes off of Morgan. Throughout the ceremony, she watched his every move. She watched as he supplied the wedding band and patted Rafe on the back. She watched as he broke into a wide smile as Rafe kissed Shannon soundly. As he followed the happy couple back up the aisle to the rear of the tent, accompanying one of the bridesmaids since LeRoy had claimed Harriet.

Everyone broke into shouts of congratulations and laughter as Rafe swept Shannon up into his arms, and one of the cowboys—they were all in attendance and dressed in their finest regalia—made a ribald remark.

Christine lost track of Morgan as the crowd broke up, everyone transferring to the other tent, where champagne was to be served, along with dinner and cake.

Erin dragged her to the other tent, as well, after spotting Jessica with her brother and sister and Dub and Delores. A tall solidly built man, somewhat older than Morgan, stood with them.

Delores did the introductions as the children ran off to inspect the multitiered cake. "Christine, this is Russell, our oldest son. Russell, Christine Grant. Or should I add Parker?"

Before Christine could answer Dub spoke up. "Who wouldn't be proud to be a Parker?" He seemed far more comfortable now that he no longer wore a full cast or the restricting brace on his arm, only an elastic wrist support.

Russell Hughes took her hand. "Nice to meet you, Christine," he said with a friendly smile. Looking closely, Christine could see a family resemblance. Russell had the same nose and cheekbones as Morgan, and the blond hair, but there the similarities stopped.

"Russell's come to get his kids," Delores said. "I'm gonna miss 'em so much!"

"Probably like a case of chicken pox." Russell chuckled. "I'll be glad to get them back, though. It's been a long time."

Champagne corks popped and laughter surged. Dub and Delores and Russell were called away by someone, and Christine edged around the revelers.

Jodie rushed up to her. Dressed fashionably, with her hair caught up in loose curls and her face carefully made up, Jodie turned heads. She looked like a magazine model. "Isn't Shannon beautiful?" She sighed.

"Some day I'm going to have a wedding like this. At one time, with Rio, I didn't care. But today has been so much fun I'm converted! I'll have to break the news gently to my daddy. The bigger, the better now, as far as I'm concerned!" She looked at Christine's empty hands. "Have you had a glass of champagne yet?"

"I don't really want one. I'll wait for the cake."

Jodie looked at her closely. "Are you all right? With all these Parkers around, we're not overwhelming you or anything, are we? I mean, we can sometimes be a bit too much of a good thing."

"I'd just rather wait. I don't drink much alcohol."

Jodie nodded, her copper-colored curls bouncing. Then she spotted someone. "Look, there's Tate. Over there talking to LeRoy. You remember I told you about him? How he used to drive my school bus and how I—" She stopped. "He does look good all cleaned up and out of uniform, doesn't he?"

"I know him," Christine said, her brow furrowing at first and then clearing. "The night Erin and I...the night the rustlers... He was with Morgan, helping to catch them. Then he came by the next day and took our statements."

"He's a deputy sheriff now." Jodie frowned. "Everyone says he's a good one."

Christine saw three people seated at a corner table who were causing a bit of a stir as people stopped by to greet them. "Who are they?" she asked.

Jodie followed her gaze. "Oh, that's Darlene and Thomas and their son, Richard. The house next to Harriet's? We weren't sure they were going to make it back in time. They've been in Amarillo, where Richard lives. Our great family scandal—the divorce." She waved when Darlene looked round and saw her. "I'm going over to talk to them. You want to come? I'll introduce you…but I won't say anything else. They'll hear about it soon enough, anyway."

Christine shook her head. "Maybe later," she murmured, and Jodie smiled.

"They're really sweet," she said.

"Still…"

"I'll introduce her later," Morgan said, having come up behind them unnoticed.

Christine turned and saw he was carrying two flutes of champagne.

"Wow, Morgan!" Jodie teased. "You should wear a tux more often. I had to look twice to make sure it was you."

He grinned. "An' I thought for sure you were Julia Roberts come to visit. I almost called the paparazzi."

"I think there're enough photographers here already," Jodie said, laughing. "What did Aunt Mae do? Tell them to take pictures of everything?"

"Probably, knowing her."

"Where is she?" Christine asked.

"Where else?" Jodie tipped her head. "Up front in the limelight."

Christine peered around a group of people and saw Mae at the head table with Shannon and Rafe. They were drinking toasts and posing for the photographer.

"I hope she's happy," Morgan said.

The way he said it, so seriously, made Christine look at him. He offered her a glass, smiling. "I think

I spilled some on the way." Then to Jodie, "You want some, Jodie? You can have this and I'll go get more."

Jodie shook her head. "No. I'm off to see Richard, to surprise him. I think the last time he saw me, I was twelve."

"He won't recognize you."

"I'll see how long it takes." Then with a wink at Christine and a pointed look at the glass of champagne Christine had automatically accepted from Morgan, Jodie bounced off.

For something to do, Christine sipped the champagne. Morgan did likewise, and then they started to stroll around, the pavilion's open sides allowing the guests to see all that was going on inside and out, as well as letting a breeze pass through.

"Look at Axel and Marie," Christine said, spotting the couple seated together at a nearby table. It had taken a lot of convincing, Christine knew, to get them to agree to be regular guests and to let someone else be responsible for the meal. "They don't look comfortable not being busy."

"I know. Maybe they'll relax after the newness wears off."

"Maybe."

Christine was growing more nervous with each second that passed. What was he waiting for? When was he going to demand their talk?

Suddenly he took the flute from her unresisting fingers and placed it alongside his on a table. Then he clasped her hand and pulled her from the tent, taking her out into the dwindling twilight, away from the people and the music.

"Where are we going?" she asked breathlessly.

"Somewhere private."

"And where is that?"

"You'll see."

He drew her into the compound and up the drive toward Mae's house. When she saw where he was headed, she tried to hold back. "Morgan, I don't think Mae would like it if we... It's her house and we—"

He stopped to face her. "Right now, I don't give a—" He cut off what he was about to say and after taking a short breath, continued, "Most of our problem is Mae's fault. So she'll just have to excuse us if we straighten it out on her territory."

He pulled Christine up the pathway and onto the porch, where he paused to say a soft word to Shep, who was on "guard" duty. In reality, the dog was trying to stay out of the way of the crowd so that he could sleep. He wagged his tail from his prone position and Christine would swear that he smiled at them.

"Did you see that?" she asked, surprised.

"That's one of Shep's special tricks."

Morgan opened the door and ushered her inside, then he headed straight for the stairs.

"Morgan, really, this is crazy," Christine protested.

He didn't listen. He towed her up the stairs and down the hall and closed them both in her bedroom. Then, following up on what he'd started earlier, he dragged her against him and, like a man starved for sustenance, kissed her with such ferocity Christine grew dizzy. She began to kiss him back as his hands made a bold and very thorough exploration of her body.

Untangling her mouth from his, she murmured, "Erin. What if Erin...?"

"Harriet's watching her. She won't come back."

Christine shivered as his lips moved over the curves of her breasts that the pale blue dress—adjusted a bit—exposed. Her fingers threaded in his hair. His warm breath fanned her skin. His body, straining against hers, stirred feelings that, until meeting him, she'd thought were dead.

His hunger was consuming her, and she was fast losing the ability to think rationally. But before they took the next step, they had to talk.

"Morgan." She said his name quietly at first, then she repeated it with more intent. "Morgan, I can't...I won't...not until... We have to talk."

When he drew away, Christine's breath caught at the look in his eyes. She wanted so badly to be a part of him. To have the same heartbeat, the same breath, the same desires and needs.

Breaking contact, he seemed to battle for control. Finally, running a hand through his hair, he said, "Okay, we talk. You first."

"They won't miss us out there?" she asked.

"Who cares? But I doubt they will. Everyone's attention is on Rafe and Shannon."

Christine readjusted her dress and perched on the nearest bed. She knew that might not be a good idea, but she couldn't continue standing. Her knees were too trembly.

"I..." she began, then had to start over because her voice cracked. "I thought everything over, like you said, and...I believe you."

"You *think* you believe me. I can hear the hesitation."

"Morgan, this is very hard for me."

"And it's not hard for me?"

She looked down at her clasped fingers, then back at him. "So much...last time so much had hit me so suddenly. Do you know what it's like to think you don't have any family left and then find out that you do, because you aren't who you think you are? I *thought* I knew who my father was. I looked at his picture every night while I was growing up. He had the same color eyes as me and the same color hair, and I even imagined that I looked like him. Then to find out..."

"Your mother told you this man was your father?" he asked quietly.

She shook her head. "No. She wouldn't tell me anything. I went by the development date on the photograph. He was the man I thought she was dating nine months before I was born." She gave a short laugh. "I'd question the blood tests Ira sent Mae, only I remember that just a few weeks before my mother died, she did something strange. It was around the time Ira said she'd told him the truth. She asked me to go to a specific laboratory and have my blood tested. It was supposed to be for some kind of experimental treatment if I proved to be a proper match for her. Now I see the lab was the same lab Ira used for his own blood test. My mother sent me there to prove to him that I was his daughter. So now do you see why I was so devastated? I thought my mother had hurt me all she could, but I was wrong. Then Ira didn't tell me who he was—and I wanted a father so badly. Then you—you acted for Mae against me.''

"I was never against you!''

Her eyes filled with tears. "It felt like it.''

Morgan knelt on the floor in front of her. "It wasn't like that. I told you the truth. She wanted to know what you were like as a person. I told her what little you let me find out—that I thought you were honest and you put Erin's welfare before your own. She wanted to know who Erin's father was of course. But I couldn't ask you that. For one, I knew you wouldn't tell me. For the other, I knew it would scare you off. And I didn't want you scared off. Not from me. I didn't feel right even with the little I did tell her.''

"You're an investigator. You investigate.''

"Not anymore.''

Christine's eyes met his. "I don't understand.''

"That's what I was doin' this last week. My dad's not going to be able to handle the ranch work like he used to. Not for some time, if ever. He's sixty-four and a bad break like that, especially to his wrist, is tough even for a young man. He's started physical therapy, but that takes him away from the ranch for hours, since the hospital's not exactly next door. So I went to Fort Worth and kinda resigned.''

"What do you mean, kinda?''

"My bosses told me to come back any time I want. They said they'd find a place for me if I ever get tired of wranglin' cows for a livin' again.''

For the first time, Christine reached out to him without prompting. She smoothed the hair that curled above his ear. "But it's what you like to do, isn't it?''

"When I was young. I'm thirty-six now, Christine. I'm ready to settle down." He chuckled. "Rafe would laugh me out of town if he heard me say that. I swore, just a month or so ago, that no woman would ever—"

"What woman?" Christine whispered.

"You."

She closed her eyes. She had seen the sincerity in his gaze. He meant it.

"My mother's been after me to settle down for years. She doesn't like me gettin' shot."

"You've been shot?" Christine asked, startled.

He made light of it. "Winged. Some rustlers are more dangerous than others. Those the other night... My, God, Christine, when I saw you and Erin..."

"You always seem to be there to rescue us," she murmured.

He must have seen the warmth and caring she could no longer hide, even from herself. He said something, it might have been her name, but Christine was too distracted by his shift onto the bed and into her arms to notice.

EPILOGUE

THE CEREMONY WAS SHORT and sweet, no more than five minutes. Christine was wearing a pretty summer dress, and Morgan was in a suit. Erin, in her frilly dress from Shannon and Rafe's wedding, scattered flower petals, just as, she confided, she'd secretly dreamed. The five minutes were momentous, though, because at their end, they were a family.

They stepped out of the tiny church and walked across the plaza. In a few minutes they were strolling along the Paseo del Rio, San Antonio's renowned River Walk. Huge cypress trees and low palms lined the meandering waterway, which was spanned periodically by graceful stone bridges. In places, sidewalk restaurants and cafés vied with art galleries and gift shops, but all in all, there was a tranquillity about the River Walk that allowed a visitor a romantic respite from everyday life.

"Can we ride in a riverboat?" Erin asked excitedly. Her eyes were huge, her expression expectant. She was going to have a great time on their three-day honeymoon.

Morgan's arm tightened around Christine's waist. "Sure," he said, smiling.

The "riverboats" were just flat barges with bench

seats, but they moved smoothly and relatively quietly along the placid narrow river.

After purchasing tickets, they hopped on board a waiting boat. Erin hurried to get them places near the front.

As the boat started off, Morgan settled Christine against him again. It was going to be like this, he knew. Erin would always have to be considered. But he didn't mind. Christine and Erin came as a unit. The little girl was a part of her, and now a part of him. He smiled at Erin when she looked around to see if they were just as excited about the water trip as she was.

Christine's arm had curved around his waist, and her cheek was resting against his shoulder. It was a comfortable yet intimate positioning of body to body, and he still couldn't get over the thrill of having her next to him.

When Rafe had learned how it was between Morgan and Christine, he'd laughed, then welcomed him into the family. But Morgan's parents had been surprised. Well, his father had been. Over the past two months, though, Dub had come around. Particularly when he got to know Erin better. As Christine had seen the relationship developing between them, she'd relaxed, and when she relaxed, Dub relaxed—to the point of encouraging the marriage.

"When ya gonna make an honest woman of her, son?" he'd demanded. What he didn't understand was that it wasn't Morgan who was holding back, it was Christine.

Then, at last, she'd agreed.

"You won't regret this, will you, Morgan?" she'd asked just after they'd set the date.

"I'd regret *not* doing it," he'd said, then teasingly, "I'd also regret having a wingding like Rafe and Shannon had. It was nice, but—"

"I meant giving up your freedom, giving up your job," she'd cut in. "That's a lot to ask of anyone."

He'd gazed down into her sometimes too-astute eyes, and he'd smiled. "I *have* a job. And when we're married, I'll have three. Providing the brawn for dad, until he's ready to retire, then taking over the post myself. Being a husband to you, and being a father to Erin. That should keep me busy. Who needs freedom?"

"I just don't want you to regret anything," she'd persisted.

"No. Never. Not for a second," he'd replied.

"Penny for them." Her soft voice called him back to the present.

The cool air from the river washed over them as the boat moved slowly along. People at the cafés lingered over their meals, people on the sidewalks strolled.

"I was just thinking," he said, "about how much I owe Ira and your mother."

She looked at him, frowning slightly. "Why?"

"For giving me you."

Her smile grew. "Then I owe the same to your parents." She paused. "Do you think they'll mind us eloping? We could have told them and had them come along."

He grinned. "Three's enough on a honeymoon." Then, unable to resist, he kissed her as they went under a bridge and was still kissing her as they came out into the light. Reluctantly they pulled apart.

All too soon for Erin, the boat ride ended. She was chattering on about what she'd seen and they were smiling indulgently back when an elderly woman who'd been sitting on a bench somewhere behind them approached, cane in hand, to say loudly enough for everyone to hear, "I was watching you earlier. You make an absolutely *lovely* family!" And she beamed all kinds of goodwill at them.

"Yes, we do, don't we?" Morgan replied, smiling proudly.

And everyone on the landing had to smile with him.

Heartbreak RANCH

Four generations of independent women...
Four heartwarming, romantic stories of the West...
Four incredible authors...

Fern Michaels
Jill Marie Landis
Dorsey Kelley
Chelley Kitzmiller

Saddle up with Heartbreak Ranch, an outstanding
Western collection that will take you on a whirlwind
trip through four generations and the exciting,
romantic adventures of four strong women who
have inherited the ranch from Bella Duprey,
famed Barbary Coast madam.

Available in March,
wherever Harlequin books are sold.

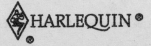

HARLEQUIN ®

Look us up on-line at: http://www.romance.net

HTBK

LOVE *or* MONEY?
Why not Love *and* Money!
After all, millionaires
need love, too!

How to Marry a
MILLIONAIRE

**Suzanne Forster,
Muriel Jensen
and
Judith Arnold**

bring you three original stories
about finding that one-in-a million man!

Harlequin also brings you
a million-dollar sweepstakes—enter
for your chance to win a fortune!

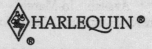

HARLEQUIN ®

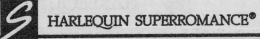

HARLEQUIN®

Don't miss these Harlequin favorites by some of our most distinguished authors!
And now, you can receive a discount by ordering two or more titles!

HT#25645	THREE GROOMS AND A WIFE by JoAnn Ross	$3.25 U.S.	☐
		$3.75 CAN.	☐
HT#25647	NOT THIS GUY by Glenda Sanders	$3.25 U.S.	☐
		$3.75 CAN.	☐
HP#11725	THE WRONG KIND OF WIFE by Roberta Leigh	$3.25 U.S.	☐
		$3.75 CAN.	☐
HP#11755	TIGER EYES by Robyn Donald	$3.25 U.S.	☐
		$3.75 CAN.	☐
HR#03416	A WIFE IN WAITING by Jessica Steele	$3.25 U.S.	☐
		$3.75 CAN.	☐
HR#03419	KIT AND THE COWBOY by Rebecca Winters	$3.25 U.S.	☐
		$3.75 CAN.	☐
HS#70622	KIM & THE COWBOY by Margot Dalton	$3.50 U.S.	☐
		$3.99 CAN.	☐
HS#70642	MONDAY'S CHILD by Janice Kaiser	$3.75 U.S.	☐
		$4.25 CAN.	☐
HI#22342	BABY VS. THE BAR by M.J. Rodgers	$3.50 U.S.	☐
		$3.99 CAN.	☐
HI#22382	SEE ME IN YOUR DREAMS by Patricia Rosemoor	$3.75 U.S.	☐
		$4.25 CAN.	☐
HAR#16538	KISSED BY THE SEA by Rebecca Flanders	$3.50 U.S.	☐
		$3.99 CAN.	☐
HAR#16603	MOMMY ON BOARD by Muriel Jensen	$3.50 U.S.	☐
		$3.99 CAN.	☐
HH#28885	DESERT ROGUE by Erine Yorke	$4.50 U.S.	☐
		$4.99 CAN.	☐
HH#28911	THE NORMAN'S HEART by Margaret Moore	$4.50 U.S.	☐
		$4.99 CAN.	☐

(limited quantities available on certain titles)

	AMOUNT	$
DEDUCT:	**10% DISCOUNT FOR 2+ BOOKS**	$
ADD:	**POSTAGE & HANDLING**	$
	($1.00 for one book, 50¢ for each additional)	
	APPLICABLE TAXES*	$_____
	TOTAL PAYABLE	$_____
	(check or money order—please do not send cash)	

To order, complete this form and send it, along with a check or money order for the total above, payable to Harlequin Books, to: **In the U.S.:** 3010 Walden Avenue, P.O. Box 9047, Buffalo, NY 14269-9047; **In Canada:** P.O. Box 613, Fort Erie, Ontario, L2A 5X3.

Name:_____

Address:_____ City:_____

State/Prov.:_____ Zip/Postal Code:_____

*New York residents remit applicable sales taxes.
 Canadian residents remit applicable GST and provincial taxes.
Look us up on-line at: http://www.romance.net

HBACK-JM4

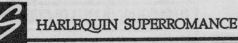

HARLEQUIN SUPERROMANCE®

THE MIRACLE BABY
by
Janice Kay Johnson

If having a baby with a stranger is what it'll take to save her eleven-year-old daughter's life...Beth McCabe is willing to have one.

Is the stranger?

Nate McCabe hasn't seen or spoken to his identical twin brother, Rob, for fifteen years. Now Rob is dead and Nate learns that Rob's widow, Beth, and her young daughter, Mandy, need him—but only because he's Rob's twin. Only because they need a miracle.

Mandy will die without a bone marrow transplant. When Nate's tissue fails to match, Beth persuades him to step into his brother's shoes and father a baby—Beth's baby, a child who has a one-in-four chance of saving Mandy's life.

Watch for *The Miracle Baby* by Janice Kay Johnson.

Available in April 1997,
wherever Harlequin books are sold.

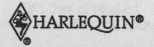